'Geechee

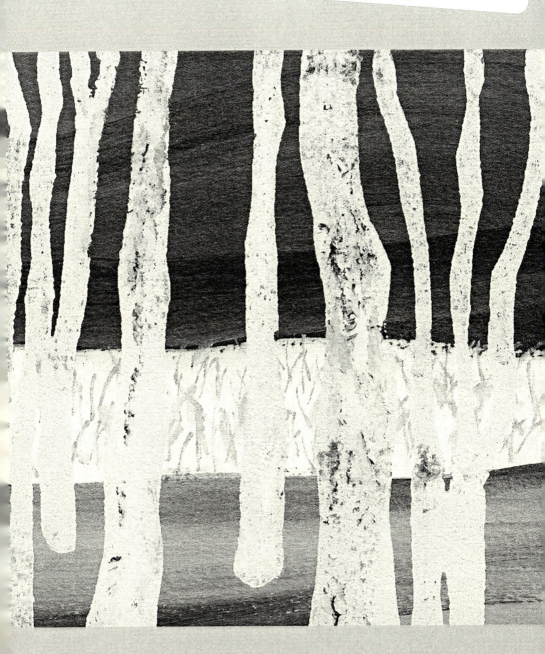

a novel by *Lisa Harris*

The cover: "Copper Swamp" by Carol Spence, used with permission.

Excerpts from the novel have been published in the following venues: *Feminism 3*, Westview/HarperCollins, Boulder, CO; Bright Hill Fiction Award, chapbook winner, Treadwell, NY; *The Habersham Review*, Piedmont College, GA; *Phoebe*, SUNY, Oneonta, NY; *Cantaraville*, New York, NY; *Zone 3,* Austin Peay University, Clarksville, TN; *ginosko*, online literary journal, San Francisco, CA.

Support for the writing of this novel came from the following: Landsman Fellowships from Milton Avery Graduate School of the Arts, Annandale-on-Hudson, NY; Constance Saltonstall Residencies, Ithaca, NY; Hambidge Colony Residencies for the Creative Arts and Sciences, Rabun Gap, GA; Ithaca College Provost Grants, Ithaca NY; an appointment through Ithaca College to the A.D. White House at Cornell University, Ithaca, NY, New York Council on the Arts; and ongoing support from friends, readers and others who gave encouragement....

This is a work of fiction. Its characters, settings and scenes are fictional and not meant to represent actual people, places or events.

Copyright © 2013 by Lisa Harris

ISBN: 978-0-9851520-9-3
LCCN: 2013936658

Published by
Ravenna Press
Spokane, Washington
USA

FIRST EDITION

*for Jeffrey Spence
and
Sarah Kitchner
with love and gratitude*

*For Becky —
With love ♡
Jim
Happy Birthday.*

'GEECHEE GIRLS

Consider rivers.
They are always en route to
their own nothingness. From the first moment
they are going home.

> *from "Anna Liffey"*
> *by Eavan Boland (1944-)*

Prologue

In Coastal Georgia the rivers rise up to meet the rain almost daily, touching the sore, red land. Fresh-water rivers, brackish water and salt, snake around islands and mainland, rise up against root-weary banks and trees; ebb and flow. What of the land covered with kudzu and long tired vipers—lazy from the heat? Tree roots break through the dirt; live oaks hold mistletoe and dangle Spanish moss. To get from island to mainland and back, people travel over drawbridges, waiting for shrimp boats and yachts to go through below, waiting for the bridge to drop and form a road to carry them past oleander in the direction of their need.

Rain falls twice a day most days on Broad Street and Victory Drive, on Highway 17 and Isle of Hope, in Pooler and Thunderbolt, on the rich and poor people, white and black and every shade in between. It is almost guaranteed in the summer—close to 2:00 P.M. and then again before sunrise. And this rain has its own smell, made of gardenias and rot and sweat. It falls in pieces of wavy glass, distorting vision. In offices and banks, beauty salons and garages, fields and bars, workers stop what they are doing in anticipation of the short-lived cooling air that will follow. People—anxious to have the hot dust driven from their cars, their gardens, their houses, and their throats—sigh when the rain comes.

When the afternoon rain pulls open the sky, many pour themselves a cool, sweetened tea and receive the gift. Some idly imagine the rain as medicine cooling their southern fever. Some feel they are receiving forgiveness for wrongs committed but never confessed. Some imagine they *are* the rain with its power to cleanse the world.

Once the shower is over, sun turns the rain into a humid mist, and people return to their work—filing reports, crediting deposits, brushing out perms, draining oil, weeding the field, and drinking boiler-makers as they let go of the shift. They turn their gaze away from windows, and look again upon the task at hand—the file poised over the manicure; the unsigned contract for Brazilian lumber at rest on the desk; the men at the watchdog station staring into vats where pulp juices simmer.

Before dawn when the clouds gather again, the peepers sing—croaking and squeaking from under magnolia leaves, from beneath mimosa branches, and from their perches on exposed roots. Stars are driven back from the sky, and the rain comes from the satiny blackness.

Stench from the papermill, thick and invisible, fills the air in and around Savannah. Those who live in the mansions on Victory Drive or on Wilmington Island smell it as surely as those in trailer parks and the suburbs. The mill's cement block building is surrounded by every size, shape, and color of pickup truck. It could be a warehouse or a tool and die shop if it were not for the stench, heavy as magnolia, but bitter and wretched. Men file in and out on the three swing shifts—7–3, 3–11, 11–7: all colors and ages of reckless, careful, fat and thin men. Some carry a bag lunch, some a black bucket. Bologna sandwiches and cheese, a thermos of coffee, a bottle of Royal Crown Cola, a pack of Little Debbies wait for them. In the mid-1950s, only executives go out to lunch.

Employees of Union Bag and their families are guaranteed a life of regular meals and health insurance and money to pay the mortgage. Each has a few vacation days in the summer to go out on the river to fish and shrimp. Most who work there are born and bred in or near Savannah. The river is their bloodline, their heritage, their memory, and their hope. They choose to work the hard job at the mill and the hard job on the boat rather than give up the smell of salt, the ocean spray on their faces and the sound of the heavy nets hitting the deck.

A fence surrounds the cane and bamboo experimental station located on Highway 17 South. Managed by the U.S. Department of Agriculture, it is funded to determine which types of cane can withstand extreme weather conditions and continue to produce lots of syrup. A large royal blue sign with yellow lettering announces: Ogeechee Canebrake and Bamboo, Established 1933. A white stucco gatehouse with faded blue shutters guards the entrance.

About two miles past this, tucked away on the right side of the highway, is Little Bit of Paradise Park. If you drive by fast, you'll miss it because of the oleander, gardenia, azaleas, bamboo, and palm trees. Only single trailers park here, there are no slabs for double-wides. Whoever started the park had the right intentions. Attempting to lure quality people, they planted flowers for beauty and trees for shade. And they didn't buy the pink neon flamingo sign with the blinding white letters, which said "Little Bit" that some Yankee tried to sell them. Instead, they drove into Savannah and hired a bricklayer to build a gigantic square inside of which they placed an artistically hand-painted sign. Around that they seeded tiny 4 O'Clock flowers. True to their name, the magenta flowers open at 4 p.m. every afternoon to let loose an odor so sweet that people in the park call the later afternoon funeral time.

Ray, Laura Jean, and Tessie Harnish; Josephine and Annie Osaha and her grandfather, Thomas Osaha; Henry, Emily and Fred Simmons; and Jenny and Earle Conroy all live on Highway 17, the Ogeechee Road, on the outskirts of Savannah, near the papermill.

-1-
Fire

Everything pointed Laura Jean toward heat the spring of her seventeenth year. The sun rose faithfully for 40 days straight; the relentless humidity turned the air thick, making it hard to breathe or think. Each day Laura Jean rose from her bed, her skin sticky and her mind full of Ray: how he smelled, how he talked, how his jeans fit, and how he watched her as if she were the last food on earth and he was starving.

On a bright, scalding May morning, she looked at herself in the hall mirror before she left the house, admiring her dark hair and bright blue eyes. She reached into her purse for her lipstick. While she was looking down, her mother sneaked up behind her and grabbed her by her hair. She wrenched her head back and spit in her ear, "You play with fire, Laura Jean, you gonna get burned."

"I know what you think, Mama, but I know what I'm doing, and Ray and I don't play with matches and we aren't going to get burned. Now let go of my hair. I said, let go!" Laura Jean panted and hissed.

Laura Jean's mother gave her ponytail another tug that broke the rubber band. Laura Jean's hair flew around her head and cascaded down her back.

"Well, I'll just wear it down, Mama. Does that suit you? Now people won't just imagine I'm a wild thing, they will know it." She turned on her heel and stomped out the door.

At school, Ray was waiting at her locker.

"Laura Jean, you are my beauty girl," Ray whispered. He kept his face about four inches from hers. She knew he was going to kiss her, and she wanted him to and she wanted him not to. She wanted to taste him, but not here in the hallway in the school. If any of the adults saw them kiss, they would both be suspended. His closeness, his insistence, and the possibility of being caught set Laura Jean on fire. So she ducked under his arm and slipped down the hallway to her next class.

She didn't see Ray again until the end of the day. He waited for her in his truck, right in front of the gym door so she couldn't miss him. The Chevy was a deep blue and he added shiny chrome pieces to it whenever he had any extra money. Ray loved shine and he loved the shine of her hair and the shine in her eyes.

He had bought the truck with money he earned shrimping. It didn't matter that the truck was used; it was his, and he kept it polished and perfect so he could drive around with Laura Jean beside him.

"Get in here, darlin'," Ray said.

Laura Jean opened the door and jumped in. He drove them to the pecan groves, threw the truck in park and they kissed until they made themselves sick. The heat and humidity pressed in on Laura Jean until she put both her hands on Ray's chest and pushed him away from her right in the middle of a kiss so deep, Laura Jean had stopped breathing.

"What, darlin'? What's the matter?" Ray asked.

"I can't breathe, Ray. I feel as if my chest is going to open up, right here in the pecan grove, and my heart is going to pop out of my chest. Its big, messy redness is gonna land right in your lap. I'll be dead and you won't even know what happened."

"What are you talking about, girl?"

"I'm on fire. I got a fever because of you, Ray. I can't keep kissing like this day after day and then stopping and going home to my mother and daddy who keep saying, 'You play with fire, you gonna get burned.' We have to stop seeing each other or we have to go all the way."

"Are you daring me, Laura Jean? Because you know I'm never leaving you. We ain't gonna stop seeing each other. Are you crazy? Come here, girl." Ray jumped out of the truck and lifted Laura Jean down beside him so that he stood her on the ground before him. "Are you sure you want to do this?"

"Yes."

Ray undid his pants, unbuttoned his shirt, and slid out of his underwear. He stood naked before Laura Jean. She stared at his chest and his shoulder muscles. She couldn't look down and she couldn't look at his face either.

"You do the same, Laura Jean," Ray said.

She obeyed as if he was God.

She took off one piece of clothing at a time, undressing as if she were performing a sacrament. She laid her clothes on top of Ray's, and then he lifted her up, and she wrapped her legs around him and sat across him. He kissed her and kissed her and kissed her. She was his wine and his host. She kissed him back, searing his lips with hers. He burned his way into her. The weight of her body against his made him fall backwards onto the red Georgia clay.

* * * * *

"Don't go out with him anymore, Laura Jean. He hangs with all those bad boys down at the gas station. And you know what they say, 'Birds of a feather flock together.' He ain't gonna come to no good, and he's gonna take you down with him. Just like your daddy did to me. You hear me, Laura Jean?" Laura Jean's mother yelled at her as she was leaving the house.

"Yes, Mama, I hear you, but you're wrong. Ray ain't bad. He's just not been loved enough. I can love him right—turn him around, turn him good," Laura Jean said.

"He doesn't see you, Laura Jean. You just a feather in his cap, a trophy in his case, a notch in his belt. You'll be loving him right and he'll be doing you wrong. Somewhere in the wrong and right of that loving, you gonna find yourself with a baby, and you gonna have to be the one to feed her and protect her, teach her and love her," Laura Jean's mother said. "Having him with you will be harder than doing it alone. Having him there will be worse because he ain't gonna be no help. He's gonna want all your love and he's not gonna give one good damn about that baby. You gonna find yourself with two children, a baby and a grown man with less sense than a child. And he's gonna make you pay—gonna try all different kind of ways to prove to himself that you love him best. He'll be fighting with his own child for your love, Laura Jean. Mark my words. I've seen men like him all my life, up and down the 'Geechee Road. They are the rule, not the exception. Mark me. He's mean. I can tell it. I can tell when he's been drinking, too. Don't go out with him anymore, Laura Jean. You hear? 'Cause if you do, don't expect to come home to me and your daddy. You make your bed, you gonna be lying in it alone or with the likes of him!"

"How do you know, Mama? Huh? Answer me that! How do you think you know my life? That I'm gonna have a baby? How come you think you so smart? I can handle myself, Mama. Yes, I can," Laura Jean yelled back as she ran out the door to meet Ray.

* * * * *

South Georgia winters are mild and the sky is full of stars so close that you can grab them. Laura Jean and Ray made love over and over again in the bed of his blue Chevy under a blanket on a brisk January night. The heat from their bodies kept them warm and they made a baby.

They got married in March and Ray, who was crazy in love with Laura Jean, tried to please her. He knew she was mad at him for getting her pregnant, but he figured she'd get over it once the baby arrived. He knew she was beyond angry with him for causing her to drop out of school.

They moved into a trailer in Little Bit of Paradise Park. Ray worked at the paper mill and shrimped on other men's boats when he could.

One Saturday when he drove into Savannah to get groceries, he stopped at the pet store and bought Laura Jean a Siamese cat to cheer her. It wasn't her birthday or a holiday, but he knew she loved cats. Next he went to the Piggly Wiggly and picked up some tuna-flavored wet cat food. He could have fed the cat some fish from the boat, but he thought spending extra money on canned food would please Laura Jean, and he was right.

She was pleased! She loved that kitty and named her Baby. She opened the canned food and the smell knocked her over. Her morning sickness made her throw up. Then she hugged Ray's neck. "I love you, Ray. I do. I swear."

Next, Baby wanted fresh shrimp and fish or raw, red meat. To give Baby what she wanted, Laura Jean walked half a mile to the butcher's shop and bought sliced filet mignon for Baby. She took the money for Baby's food from the money for her and Ray.

"Where's my beer money, darlin' heart?" Ray called out from the kitchen.

"I've been using it to buy Baby filet mignon," Laura Jean said.

Laura Jean expected him to be angry, but he wasn't. Instead he sat on the couch in the living room watching her feed the cat one slice of meat at a time. It was the first time he had seen Laura Jean happy since they had gotten married. He ate his salami and mustard sandwiches, drank a glass of milk, and smiled with her.

* * * * *

During the time Laura Jean was pregnant, she often found birds with broken necks outside her trailer. She heard them hit the picture window, and she went outside and brought their still warm bodies in. She plucked their feathers and put them in a shoebox under her and Ray's bed. She needed the feathers to fill the baby's pillow and to make the baby's mattress. She believed the feathers would fill her baby's mind with possibility. She used blue ones, lime ones, red ones and brown ones, short ones and long ones, and the downy feathers that lay close to the birds' bodies. She loved browns, sad shimmering grays, vermilions and the dark iridescent feathers. They created a memory of caves and caverns, of a time when the connection between birds and reptiles was immediate.

On the day she went into labor, Laura Jean salvaged a painted bunting. She carried the bird's body into the trailer, removed as many feathers as she could, and then wrapped it in fabric remnants. She buried the bird in the soft clay where it eventually merged with the mud of the swamp. She filled the little mattress and a tiny flat pillow with bunting feathers.

*****

Laura Jean birthed her baby October 25th, when the best expression of a Georgia autumn appeared—green leaves spotted with gold, a red leaf or an orange one every so often, a few big brown magnolia leaves, and still blooming Black-eyed Susans along the roadside, in the fields, and along the banks of the Ogeechee River. The baby arrived at high noon. Laura Jean named her Elizabeth Opal. The fiery gold from the trees shone outside the hospital in the full Savannah sun. Elizabeth's sapphire blue eyes made Laura Jean dream of fire opals with all their sparkle. The drug they gave Laura Jean knocked her out. She shouted, "Give me my baby!" when she awoke in the recovery room.

"You have a beautiful baby girl, 21 inches long, 8 pounds and 10 ounces. This baby's full of fire, Mrs. Harnish. You've got yourself a handful."

"I know I do. Bow your head," Laura Jean said. The nurse looked down and Laura Jean began to pray, "Rejoice, oh ye flocks, for unto you a child is born, unto you a daughter is given, and her name shall be unspoken and her flights unmapped and unrecorded. Her pink-skinned wings will carry her. All glory shines around, and the wise follow stars in her eyes."

The recovery room nurse called for a sedative and gave Laura Jean the shot herself. What the patient said sounded as if it was from the New Testament, but the nurse didn't think it was. While Mrs. Harnish slept, the nurse checked to see if she was married to a minister or had any previous record of mental illness. Neither. She was married to a man who worked at the paper mill. The nurse didn't know how to interpret any of it. Nothing about mental instability on Mrs. Harnish's chart. So next she checked to see what drug had been administered during delivery. When she saw it was morphine, she wasn't quite as taken aback. She believed a good night's sleep would bring Mrs. Harnish back to normal.

* * * * *

"What do you mean you want her middle name to be Opal?" Ray said when he returned to visit his wife and baby girl. "That's a stone. You wouldn't want to call this girl Diamond or Ruby. Anyways, opals bring bad luck because they crack easy. And you already a little cracked, Laura Jean."

Laura Jean began to cry.

"I'm just fooling with you, honey pie. Please stop balling," Ray said.

"Shut up, Ray," Laura Jean said. "My grandmother's name was Pearl and I had a great-aunt, Ruby. I don't see what you are getting so het up—"

"No, by God. She's my child, too, and we ain't having part of her name sound like she belongs in a jewelry store."

Ray's face puffed out and got red. Laurie Jean, who was pale from labor and had a light around her head like a halo, looked at Ray differently, as if he were a stranger, and she didn't like him.

The floor nurse rushed into the room to see what the yelling was about. "This has to stop, Mr. and Mrs. Harnish. We have sick people here. We have mothers waiting to give birth. On the ward above us, we have people dying."

Both Ray and Laura Jean shut their mouths.

* * * * *

Rain fell hard on the day Laura Jean and Ray brought Elizabeth Opal Harnish home from the hospital. Laura Jean pulled out her deepest dresser drawer and made it into a crib for her baby with the magical mattress and pillow. She took extra feathers she had not used and stuffed them into her own pillow. She wanted both of them to be able to dream in color about flight. "I'm gonna call you Tessie, baby girl," Laura Jean said as she kissed the baby's forehead and laid her on a blanket on the floor.

Next she cut out six circles to make faces for the drawer crib. She didn't want Tessie to feel lonely. She drew big eyes and a huge smile on each face and taped them around the drawer. She placed the drawer on the floor beside her bed so she could feed and quiet Tessie easily and without disturbing Ray.

For the first six months, Ray was patient with Tessie getting all of Laura Jean's attention, but after that, he wouldn't have it anymore—the baby in the room in the drawer crib, the baby nursing in the same bed he slept in.

"This trailer has another bedroom in it. You got your choice—put her in it or I'm moving there myself," Ray said.

He was certain that Laura Jean would say, "Oh Ray, honey, of course, I'll move the baby out," because he could remember her hunger for him when they were wildly in love and 17.

Silence, thick as swamp mud, seeped into their bedroom while Ray waited for her answer.

Laura Jean knew if she didn't speak soon, Ray would explode, so she spoke in her winning voice. "Why Ray, this little girl of yours is the sleepingest baby in the whole wide world. She is so quiet, you don't even know she's here."

"Of course I know she's here. I hear her sucking and burping and farting—feels like I'm in the room with a baby pig," Ray said.

Laura Jean looked at Ray. She wanted to scream at him, "Who are you? What kind of man are you?"

Instead she joked. "That ought to suit you just fine Ray, seeing as how fond you are of baby backs and Boston butt."

Ray didn't laugh.

"Who you gonna choose? Her or me?" Ray barked the words at her.

"Well, Ray, maybe for the next couple months, you'd be better to sleep in the spare room—just until I get her to sleep through the night. Then we'll move her into the other room. 'Sides I'm still healing from the birthing. I'm not much good to you right now anyway," Laura Jean said.

"You got that right! You smell like sour milk and blood. Here I am sleeping in a room with a sow and her piglet. I'm glad to be moving down the hall, and I may come back when you beg me hard enough!" Ray said.

Laura Jean could hear the liquor in his voice, so she tried to forgive him for being selfish and mean; but her heart hardened.

"Now, Ray…" Laura Jean began.

"Now Ray nothing. Healing, hell! My mama never said no to my daddy. She wanted him even when it hurt. That's all a part of loving someone, Laura Jean. You're lucky I don't like blood or I'd go ahead, no or yes from you. You hear me, Laura Jean? You're my wife. You agreed to honor and obey. So when I'm ready, willing and able, you gonna be ready to obey," Ray said.

He lurched toward the dresser, emptied his drawers into a box, and lifted the box. Then he put the box down and grabbed the drawer where Tessie lay sleeping. He reached into it and ripped out the laughing faces, balled them up and threw them at Laura Jean. He picked up the drawer, put it into the dresser and closed it, shutting his daughter into the dark. The baby woke up crying.

Laura Jean didn't move or yell while he was in the room.

She heard Tessie whimpering but willed herself to stay put.

When Ray slammed the door behind him, Laura Jean flew to the drawer and freed Tessie. She pulled the drawer so hard that she fell backwards and Tessie fell out. Laura Jean gathered her up and held her, cooing, "It's all right, darlin' heart. It's all right."

* * * * *

Ray went to work, came home, ate dinner, and watched T.V. He did it all in silence. He came close enough to Laura Jean to smell her. Laura Jean had anticipated that he would do just that. She knew that as long as he smelled blood he wouldn't try to seduce her or force himself on her.

Laura Jean called Josie Osaha on the phone. "Can you get word to Fuddah that I need a jar of chicken blood?" Laura Jean asked.

"What do you want that for, Laura Jean?" Josie asked.

Laura Jean explained the deception, and Josie understood. She walked deep into the swamp to her father's place and returned with a glass jar filled with chicken blood. She took it to Laura Jean while Ray was at work, and Laura Jean put it under her bed. Several times a day she went into her room and poured a little onto a sanitary napkin that she wore underneath two pairs of underwear so she could keep the blood away from her body. She kept the blood scent strong enough to ward Ray off.

"Why are you sniffing around me like an old bloodhound, Ray? I told you I can't yet," Laura Jean said.

"I don't trust you worth a whit," Ray said. "I'll get me some sugar another way, Laura Jean. I don't need you, y'hear?"

Laura Jean knew he could, and she also knew he wouldn't. He loved her and she knew it. She didn't know if she loved him anymore. Tessie took all she had, day and night. Laura Jean was beginning to forget herself. She was hearing things and seeing things that scared her. She heard the sound of sirens when there were none. Little worms hung from the kitchen ceiling and she found bugs in the crevices of her body. She didn't tell anyone what she heard and what she saw. When Ray found her sweeping the ceiling or nit picking herself, he laughed.

"What's got into you, girl?" Ray said.

She didn't feel moony toward him anymore when she looked into his eyes. She didn't get goose bumps when he walked around with his shirt off, showing his hard muscles. She felt a twinge of desire now and then when she saw him sleeping on the couch. That's when she could see how Ray was beautiful just like Tessie.

* * * * *

Jenny Conroy dropped over to see Laura Jean about twice a week, cigarette in one hand and coffee mug in the other. She was worried about Laura Jean, but she had her own worries, too. She let herself in the trailer and found Laura Jean sitting at the counter without the baby.

"She's sleeping!" Laura Jean announced in a high-pitched voice.

"Well, then, Laura Jean, you best go get some sleep yourself," Jenny said.

"I can't. I'm not tired," Laura Jean said.

"Great God Almighty! How can you say that? You look like you haven't slept in six months," Jenny said.

"That sounds about right," Laura Jean replied.

"How's Ray?" Jenny asked.

"Don't ask," Laura Jean said.

"He's not going to believe you are bleeding forever," Jenny said. "When are you going to remember what it's like to be his wife and not just Tessie's mother?"

Jenny's jealousy twisted her face. The one baby she had carried had died the day it was born. The doctor's had barely saved Jenny's life. There were never going to be any babies for Jenny Conroy.

"He's like a hound dog, Jenny. He doesn't use his brain; he uses his nose. With the magic Fuddah gave me, I don't think Ray is going to figure things out for a while," Laura Jean said. "I got my last jar two weeks ago. Soon as this one is gone, I'll go back to my duty. But I got to tell you, Jenny, I'm not interested."

"Oh, you'll be all right, Laura Jean. It's like riding a bicycle," Jenny said.

Laura Jean didn't tell her that her body was infested by bugs because she was certain that Tessie and Ray could see them, and if they could, then Jenny could, too.

She tried to right herself. She read books every chance she could and read to Tessie. By the time Tessie was three, the age when she put everything into her mouth, Laura Jean encouraged her to tear the pages from her storybooks and, piece by piece, eat them.

"What the hell, Laura Jean," Ray yelled when he walked in from work and Tessie was stuffing her mouth with the silky pages of a children's book.

"Oh, Ray, it can't be any worse than that old paste we ate in grade school. Besides it might make her smarter," Laura Jean said.

"Well, then, you better eat a whole heaping bunch of them yourself, Laura Jean, because I swear you get stupider by the minute," Ray said as he threw himself onto the couch and ripped open a pack of Camels.

-2-
The Rain

Ray grew up on the Ogeechee River where the water runs black and the tree limbs hang low from the weight of cottonmouths, sunning. He knew he couldn't count on the shrimp to run, and he knew that if the shrimp were running, he couldn't count on their landing in his net. There wasn't much Ray could count on, and he and his family knew it. Laura Jean and Tessie loved Ray, but they didn't think they could count on him, either. Ray and Laura Jean counted on their neighbors, the Conroys, and Henry Simmons to help them out with their baby girl.

Ray would have always chosen Henry Simmons, a bachelor, to watch his daughter, but Laura Jean didn't agree with him. She didn't really think a man could take care of a child, not even Henry who was kind and gentle. Henry lived by a gentleman's code: look out for yourself, take care of women and children, and no matter what, never lie. His mother had been half Seminole, and Henry had her looks. His black hair and rich brown skin made some white people think he must be mixed. Laura Jean liked how he looked. "Something exotic about Henry, don't you think, Jenny?" Laura Jean said to her friend.

The day Ray and Laura Jean brought Tessie home from the hospital, Henry was waiting on their couch when they walked in, he had a casserole in the oven and a bouquet of Four O'clocks on the table. He rose and walked toward his friends and their new baby as soon as they entered their trailer. He hugged them both, and then said, "I've always wanted a little girl of my own," Henry said. "May I hold her?"

Ray handed Tessie to him, and Henry's heart opened.

Henry babysat Tessie every time he could from the time she could walk until she was 5. He retrieved her pacifier for her from the dirt road when she was learning to take her first steps. He played bronco with her on his knee, and he held her hand when they walked near the river. He showed her how to skip rocks on the water, how to catch a frog, and how to sit still while a hummingbird hovered and fed on the trumpet vine on the live oak outside his trailer.

"I swear I will always look out for this girl child of yours, Laura Jean. As long as I am around, this child will be safe," Henry promised.

At first, Laura Jean didn't believe him. She said, "Ray, I don't want her staying alone with a single man. It just don't make sense." Laura Jean raised her eyebrows and stared at Ray until he turned away from her.

Eventually, Laura Jean believed Henry, and she relented. "Ray and I need a sitter this Friday night so we can go out dancing," Laura Jean said to Henry on the phone.

Henry dropped what he was doing and arrived at the Harnishes' trailer.

* * * * *

Right before Tessie's sixth birthday, Henry phoned Laura Jean and practically yelled into the phone. "I got news," he said. "I got me a job offer. I need to talk with all three of you. Can I come over for dinner?"

"Sure, Hen, sure 'nuf. Come on over. I'll put on the coffee. Where's the job, Hen?" Laura Jean asked. "Doing what?"

"I'll tell you when I get there," Henry said.

"Well, hurry up, then."

As soon as Henry arrived he began talking. "The job is in and around Columbia. I'll be doing construction," Henry said.

Tessie started to cry. "That mean you gonna be leaving me, Uncle Hen?"

"Yes, darlin', it does, but I'll come back to visit. You can count on that," but even as he said it, he and Tessie had their doubts. They could see it in each other's eyes.

Tessie cried herself to sleep for the first two weeks after Henry left. She sat on the stoop waiting for him to come visit on Friday nights, but he didn't come. "He ain't coming, Tessie," Ray said. "He's gone, at least for now. I reckon he'll come back to us once he finds what he is looking for."

"What's he looking for, Daddy?" Tessie asked.

"He's looking for a woman to call his own," Ray said.

"He's got me, Daddy," Tessie said.

"Ain't the same thing, Tessie," Laura Jean said.

* * * * *

One evening when Tessie was 6, Ray left Tessie with Earle to go in search of Laura Jean. He couldn't remember why Laura Jean had run off this time. He just knew she was gone and it was late and he was scared.

"Look a here, Earle. Can you keep an eye on Tessie while I try to find her mama?" In the same breath, he directed, "Tessie, you just lay yourself down here on the couch and get some sleep. You can watch a little TV with Mr. Earle while I go looking for your mama." In the next breath, he called over his shoulder, "I won't be long, Earle."

"I want Uncle Henry, Daddy," Tessie whispered to her father.

"Well, look around. You see him? He ain't an option," Ray said. "You gonna have to get used to it, Tessie."

Earle nodded in agreement with Ray.

"Jenny ain't here right now, so I'm just gonna lay down with Tessie until you get back, Ray. Maybe Laura Jean and Jenny are out together," Earle said.

"I don't think so, Earle. Now you mind Mr. Earle, Tessie, 'hear?" Ray said.

"Yes, Daddy. Find Mama and hurry back for me, please," Tessie pleaded.

"Yes, ma'am," Ray said and pecked her cheek.

Tessie listened to the radio and a song came on from "Paint Your Wagon," a movie that her daddy and Earle had taken her to see a couple times. She heard the lonesome cowboy wailing, *Away out here they got a name for rain and wind and fire. The rain is Tess, the fire's Jo and they call the wind Mariah.* Her daddy sang the song to her sometimes when he put her to bed at night. Hearing it on the radio made her feel safe, and she fell asleep on the couch with Mr. Earle.

She woke up confused. It was very late and the radio was off. Earle was lying beside her holding something in his hands and rubbing it furiously. "Oooh, aunh," he moaned through clenched teeth.

"What's the matter? What are you doing?" Tessie's voice startled him. He got up from the couch, trying to run away from her while he also pulled at his pants. He tripped himself. Just as he fell on the floor, Ray arrived to take Tessie home.

"What the hell are you doing, Earle?" Ray bellowed.

Tessie ran toward the door, but Ray caught her before she ran out. He picked her up and carried her to the trailer where Laura Jean was sitting waiting for both of them. Her mother had a sour, sweet smell.

"I'm going back to Earle's to see what was going on, Laura Jean," Ray yelled. "You see to the girl. Check her to make sure he didn't do nothing to her."

Tessie didn't want to stay with her mother and she didn't want to go back to Earle's trailer either. She tried to go to her bedroom, but her mother had caught her by the arm. "You come here, you little vixen. What did you do to get Earle going? Let me see you. Come here."

Laura Jean lifted Tessie's dress and pulled down her underpants. "I don't see any blood nor smell man smell. Are you okay? Come on up here and give your mama a little sugar."

Against her will, Tessie curled up close to her mother. Hot tears fell down Tessie's cheeks. Laura Jean put her arm around Tessie and lit a cigarette while she waited for Ray. He arrived with a bloody nose and a hurt hand.

"He says he didn't touch her, Laura Jean, says she was sleeping and he decided to jack off. Is the girl all right?"

"I don't think he touched her, but she isn't all right. What in God's name were you thinking leaving Tessie with him without Jenny being home? I just can't trust you with our girl, Ray," Laura Jean said.

"You can't trust me? You can't trust me? You stupid cow! You left without telling anyone where you were going. I find you drinking in some bar on 17 with a bunch of rednecks I got to work with at the mill. Both Tessie and me was worried sick. I wasn't gonna drag her bar to bar looking for you, so I left her with the neighbor, like you do all the time."

"Well, ain't you the perfect husband and father all of a sudden?" Laura Jean stubbed out her cigarette and tried to pick Tessie up, but she was off balance, and she fell.

Ray set Tessie on the couch. He turned away from her and slapped Laura Jean hard. Her nose bled and she screamed. "You think you're all that, Ray. Well, you ain't! You touch me again and I'm calling the police."

"Oh, shut up and go to bed, Laura Jean. I'll put Tessie down. Go on, leave me with the girl," Ray said.

He lifted Tessie carefully and took her to her room where he tucked her in. When he kissed her goodnight he said, "I am sorry, baby. Nothing like that will ever happen again. I swear."

"Sing my song, Daddy, please," Tessie said. She couldn't think of anything else but the music when he sang.

"All right, darlin'." Ray started with the last verse.

> *"Out here they have a name for rain and wind and fire only.*
> *When you're lost and all alone, there ain't no name for lonely.*
> *And I'm a lost and lonely man without a star to guide me.*
> *Mariah blow my love to me. I need my Tess beside me."*

The next morning, Tessie did all she could not to look at her mother's swollen nose and her purple eyelids, and she looked away from her father's sulking face and bandaged hand.

* * * * *

Eight year-old Tessie carried five blonde dolls down the narrow corridor of the trailer from the living room to her bedroom holding them by their hair. When she reached her room, she dropped them on her bed. Next she went toward the bathroom and, without knocking, entered the mint green space where her father stood with one foot resting on the toilet, clipping his toenails. She had seen the dark hair peeking out from under his shirt at the supper table. Now she knew it grew all over his body, and hanging between his legs was something—a bird's nest?

"Oh no! No Daddy! You have one, too? Like Mr. Earle?" Tessie screamed and then she flew away from him, down the hallway and out the door.

Ray put his pants on and chased after Tessie. She ran straight for the creek and the swamp. She was no longer thinking about dolls, and she wasn't thinking about copperheads, cottonmouths, or canebrake rattlers either. Her stomach had knotted. She saw and smelled and heard Earle Conroy, and tasted bile in the back of her throat.

She splashed into the creek and ran in its shallow waters, ran until she was chest deep in the river, and there she stood until Ray came wading in to her. Ray lifted her and held her close.

"I'm sorry I scared you, kitten. Maybe next time you'll knock," Ray said.

But Tessie didn't answer him, wouldn't look at him either. She turned her face away from him.

"Mr. Earle," Tessie whispered. "You didn't tell me you had one too, Daddy." She held so tight to his neck that she pinched him.

"Let loose, Tessie. I said, let loose." He grabbed her hand and pulled it off his neck. Tessie flailed like a bird caught in the house. "You got to calm down, Tessie girl."

"I do not. I do not. I do not!" Tessie took a deep breath and growled out, "You can't make me be calm." She collapsed against him.

On the way back to the trailer, Ray held her close to him, mad at himself, mad at her, but mostly mad at Earle Conroy. He didn't want a scene with Laura Jean—yelling and weeping and hollering. She always made bad things worse, and anything that went wrong between Tessie and him, she blamed him for it.

Laura Jean was waiting for them on the porch.

"Where in the hell have you two been? What's wrong? Did he hurt your, Tessie? Ray, did you hurt her? I swear to God, Ray, if you hurt my baby, I'm gonna get a gun!" Laura Jean's hair flew around her face like serpents. Ray and Tessie feared that any minute Laura Jean would rush into the trailer and grab Pap's rifle.

"Hush, now, Laura Jean. Hush now," Ray chanted. He whispered into Tessie's ear, "You run up there to your mama, Tessie, and put your arms around her legs. You remember, girl? We don't want no cops coming out here. We have to stop her before she shoots that gun."

"Don't tell me to hush, you sorry assed…." And there Laura Jean stopped. She couldn't think of a word bad enough to curse Ray with and good enough that she could also say it in front of her girl.

Tessie jumped out of Ray's arms and ran to her mother. She wrapped herself around Laura Jean's legs and chattered, "He didn't hurt me, Mama. Honest. Daddy didn't do nothing to me, Mama. Mr. Earle neither. I swear. Please don't go after that gun. Okay, Mama? You stay right here with your Tessie girl."

"What is it, baby? What on earth? You all wet, you got a chill? Look at her, Ray, your own flesh and blood, shaking and trembling!" Ray didn't look at Tessie. He looked straight into Laura Jean's black eyes, her pupils so big he couldn't see the blue. No matter how mad Laura Jean got, she remained beautiful. Even when he hated her, he was drawn to her.

"What are you looking at?" Laura Jean said.

"I'm looking at you, Laura Jean. Let's get inside before the whole park is out here with us. Come on, darlin'. I can explain." Ray lifted Tessie by her arm, wrapped his arm around Laura Jean's waist and headed toward the door.

By now, Jenny and Earle Conroy pulled their blinds so they could ignore the fight. The neighbors on the other side had come out on their stoop to watch it.

Laura Jean jerked herself away from Ray. She grabbed Tessie. "Give me my girl, Ray."

"You already have her," he said. "She's clinging to your legs. Please go inside."

"All right, I'll go in, Ray, but don't be calling this a house. It's a trailer, just like all these other metal boxes. If I'd known it was gonna be a trailer and that you'd be doing whatever you been doing to upset our girl, I never would have married you!"

Once inside the trailer, Laura Jean kept hold of Tessie with one hand and scratched Ray across the face with her other, drawing blood. Ray struck her again, and Tessie ran down the hall to her room. She heard a glass break against the wall. She heard the gun shot. She threw herself under her bed. From there, she heard the front door slam, heard her father's truck peeling out, and then minutes passed before she heard the sheriff's car coming with the siren wailing.

Tessie wondered who had called the police.

Next she heard the sheriff's siren going away from the trailer following after Ray. She whispered over and over, "Let Daddy come home. Let Daddy come home."

Her mother pounded down the hallway and rapped on her door. "Tessie, let me in. Tessie, you hear me? Open the door!"

"Go away, you big bad wolf. Go away, Mama," Tessie yelled.

Tessie stayed in her room until she heard the car wheels on the gravel outside the trailer. She peeked through the Venetian blind in her room and saw Ray get out of his truck. Bubba Jones pulled up behind him in his squad car. After they spoke and shook hands, Bubba got back in his car and drove away. When Ray came back in the trailer, Tessie unlocked her bedroom door and met him. Laura Jean didn't come out of her and Ray's bedroom, even though Tessie was sure she had heard him come back in.

* * * * *

Three days later, Tessie sat at the dock waiting for her father's boat, the *Laura Jean*, to return. While she sat, she listened to the poor white and black women as they headed shrimp and picked crabmeat from the crimson and cream shells. Tessie's favorite storyteller was Josie Osaha, her mother's friend and a mixed woman of 'Geechee, French and West African descent. She was also Annie Osaha's mother. Green eyed, chocolate skinned Annie was Tessie's best friend.

Tessie was part 'Geechee and part Irish—black haired, blue eyed and with honey colored skin. She and Annie played together on the docks whenever they could. They played in the swamp, too, where they watched the snakes and the alligators, the turtles and the frogs. Josie taught them how to sew A-line skirts and placemats. She made them chop the onions for the Brunswick stew. She read to them from the Bible. She sang to them in a language neither girl understood. Josie also made dolls from rags.

The women who worked on the dock wrapped their heads in faded cloth. Josie wrapped her head in shiny red and green satin scarves. Three days after her parents' fight, while Tessie waited for Ray at the docks, Tessie listened to Josie brag to the other women, "I got me a ches' full of velvet and sateen—all colors."

"Uh-huh."

"Sure ya do, Josie."

"Keep talkin' it up, Josie. Go on."

Josie ignored them.

"Ever' night when I get home, firs' thing I do is scrub myself with lemon and lye to kill this fish smell. Then I go into my cabin and I open up my trunk. Piece by piece I take out the cloth and lays it on my cheek. Velvet and sateen—fabrics for a queen, I think. And I think myself into magic. I take out the needle and thread and I sew—dresses and capes, headwraps, and pinafores, but I'm thrifty, like my mama taught me. So I make the clothes to fit these little people." Josie told her story, and the women who pretended not to listen heard every word. Tessie listened, too, and waited.

She watched as Josie wiped her hands on the cleanest cloth, before she reached inside her big blouse. She pulled out five miniature dolls, carved from wood, dressed in royal red and purple and green. Josie had painted the dolls' faces black with round white eyes and full red lips. Tessie sat on her hands so she wouldn't grab the dolls from Josie. That's how bad she wanted one.

Josie whispered, "Come here, Tessiedoll, and hold these lady queens for me. If I hold onto them they soon be smelling of the sea.

Ain't no lady wanna smell like fish. Humf—sure you know I don't wanna be smellin' that way." Josie's laughter filled the air. The women laughed with her because everything at the docks smelled of fish and the sea and the paper mill. There was no escaping it.

Tessie rushed to Josie's side and gathered up the five black faced queens in their regal clothes.

"Fact is, Tessiedoll, you might should take those ladies home and put them on a shelf. What am I gonna do with five fancy ladies in my house? Sides, I can always make me some mo'. You take 'em. Go on, girl," Josie said.

"Oh, Miss Josie, thank you, thank you! Such beautiful ladies. I'll take good care of them, ma'am, I promise you that. And when I play with them, I'll think of you and your trunk of fancy cloth. My mama keeps a trunk of fabric, too, and she makes pillows and curtains, but she never has made me a doll, let alone five of them! Will you tell my daddy that I went on home? I got to get these ladies in bed before it gets dark. You will tell him that I went home so I don't get in trouble when he brings the boat in and I'm gone?" Tessie said.

"Will do, sugar. You go on now. I'll talk to Mr. Ray." Josie looked Tessie straight in the eyes, and Tessie began to feel uncomfortable, as if Miss Josie was getting inside her. "You go straight home, you hear?" Josie ordered.

"Yes, ma'am," Tessie said.

Tessie put the dollies in her pockets and walked down the sand road, making her way through the trailer park. She tiptoed into the trailer, past where her mother slept on the scratchy couch, and into her bedroom. She lined the new dolls up on her windowsill, and she made a little sign that she hung with tape, "Five Lady Queens by Miss Josie."

The first night the dolls slept in Tessie's room, she kept waking to the smell of burnt wood, but there was no fire. The second night, she woke to rustling fabric, and when she opened her eyes, she saw the dolls grown large as pine trees dancing around the room. The third night, Tessie awoke to singing and rustling and the smell of burnt wood. And before her the five dolls danced, singing strange words in Josie's unknown language. Smoke came from their wooden mouths and little blue flames danced around their heads in the shape of halos. From then on, Tessie began to understand that all things had power.

* * * * *

At school the next day, Annie passed a note to Tessie. "Meet me after school at the creek bed. I have something I want us to do."

Tessie didn't write back. She didn't want to get caught passing notes, so she dropped her pencil and when she picked it up, Annie could see her mouthing, "Okay."

At the end of the school day, both girls hurried home, dumped their books and did their chores. Ray yelled to Tessie as she headed down the path, "You stay away from that black injun, Tess. You hear me? I'll get the switch out if you don't listen."

Tessie didn't care what he threatened her with. Annie's friendship was worth whatever he might do. Besides Laura Jean and Josie were friends, and Ray knew better than to mess with them. The girls met each other at the ancient magnolia tree that guarded the entrance to the swamp.

"Come with me, Tessie. We're going to carve a heart into the trunk of a tree I found," Annie said. "It's really two trees that have grown together."

Annie had brought two knives. When they arrived at the tree, she cut E.H. in one half of the heart she carved. She gave Tessie the other knife to cut A.O. in the other half. Neither of them talked while they carved.

Tessie forgot about the dolls, her mother and her father. She was happy to be with Annie. "Best friends can hold silence like a river bed holds water," Annie said.

Tessie nodded. "I like that idea, Annie. That's us!" After they finished carving, Annie wrapped the knives back up in a piece of gray felt. The girls hugged, sealing their pact to be friends forever. They held hands as they walked out of the swamp. Ten years old and free.

* * * * *

Tessie woke up the following day to her parents talking about the rising creek beds near their trailer park. She got out of bed, put on her robe and walked to the kitchen.

"I ain't seen the river this high since last spring," Ray said,

"Me neither," Laura Jean said. She poured more coffee for Ray where he sat at the kitchen counter.

Laura Jean reached for Ray's hand. "I like it when we can just talk, Ray. You know, just be here at our place and not be mad at each other and the world all the time."

Ray nodded. He held fast to Laura Jean's hand. "It don't happen enough, does it, Laura Jean?" There was no accusation in his question.

"No, baby, it doesn't," Laura Jean said.

"Maybe we can turn that around," Ray whispered.

"Hi, Mama and Daddy," Tessie said.

"Hi, sugar," Ray said and let go of Laura Jean so he could help Tessie climb up the stool to sit in his lap.

Tessie ate a small bowl of cereal, then put on her rubber boots and an old jacket and hurried down to see the rising, swirling water. The water ran red with Georgia clay. Tessie sat in the pouring rain and watched. She hoped Annie would join her to tell stories about the dead rising from their graves or maybe about God, but Annie didn't come.

While Tessie waited, she collected bits and pieces of objects, and she collected whole things. She thought about her doll collection: the soft rubber ones from Newberry's; the hard rubber ones that she sent for through the mail; the handmade corncob dolls crafted by the black men who worked on her father's shrimp boat; the ones Miss Josie gave her.

She gathered bird bones, feathers, squirrel skulls, snake vertebrae, and small pieces of colored glass that washed up on the banks of the 'Geechee River: pieces of brown, pale green, clear glass, and some pieces of cobalt blue. She found bleached animal bones and fossils, Indian arrowheads and old clay beads that the Ogeechee had used for trading. She carried the pieces home and put them on the shelf where she kept Josie's dolls.

Later that night she put all the broken pieces of things on her bed. She saw herself laid out in pieces—her brittle heart, her throbbing bones, and the glittering blue glass of her eyes. Her skin was lying right next to it all, resting for tomorrow when she would have to put it back on to keep herself alive. Her black hair turned into raven feathers, her eyes into cobalt glass. Her last thought as she fell to sleep was of the dolls Josie had made for her. She was afraid to tell Annie about them because she didn't want Annie to be angry or jealous. She knew that's how she would feel if her mama had made the dolls and given them to Annie instead of her.

Before she left for school, she packed the dolls in her book bag to show to Annie. After all, how could she keep a secret from her best friend? Before the teacher called the class to order, Tessie said to Annie, "I brought my new dolls to show you. We can play with them at recess. Not those sorry old ones from Newberry's neither, Annie. These are different. Better."

Annie clasped her hands together in anticipation. Neither of the girls could concentrate in reading class. Finally, the teacher sent everyone out into the sunshine.

Tessie unpacked the dolls with pride and fear.

"My mama gave you those?" Annie asked.

Tessie couldn't read her voice or her face.

Before she could answer, Annie spoke again. "I can't believe you still playing with dolls. Tittie baby! I quit playing with dolls. Only reason my mama gave them to you is because I don't want them."

"I ain't no tittie baby! Besides, these aren't regular dolls, Annie. They come alive at night. They can talk and dance. Miss Josie gave them to me three nights ago at the dock and already they are doing magic."

"Those dolls cannot come alive at night, Tessie. Have you lost your mind? You act like you in some kind of fairy tale. My mama makes magic, but her dolls don't. So please, I don't want to hear anymore about it. Go on now. Put those dolls away. I'm going to play kickball."

"I don't care that you can't believe in magic, Annie. I'm not going to put the dolls away. Go ahead and play ball. I'm staying here. You believe what you want, but I know what these dolls can do," Tessie said.

She sat for a while on the bench in the playground and watched Annie on the kick ball field. Then she packed up the dolls and went over to join the game. She played on the opposite team from Annie and didn't talk to her for the rest of the day.

-3-
Wind

The silence of one day led to the silence of another. The girls didn't speak to each other for a week. Each time Annie came near Tessie's desk, Tessie looked down at her paper. On the playground, Tessie went to the swings to avoid Annie on the kickball field.

Annie didn't speak Tessie's name in front of Josie, and Tessie, who still went to the dock after school to wait for her dad, spoke to Josie but not about Annie.

Finally on Saturday morning Josie broke the silence. She waited at the old white and red chipped table for Annie to join her. Seven, seven-thirty, eight, eight-thirty. At 8:45 a.m., Annie zigzagged her way from her bedroom to the table. Josie tapped her spoon on the table surface as if she were telegraphing a message.

"All right, Anne Osaha, I've put up with your quiet all week, with your sour puss and your 'No ma'am--yes ma'am' answers, and I have not said nary a word. But enough is enough, child. It's high time you tell me what happened 'tween you and Tessie. Or if you gonna stay silent with me, then figure it out between the two of you. No way I'm sitting through an entire weekend with your lumpy old sad self. You hear me?" Josie's voice cut the air like lightning.

Annie scowled at her grits and eggs. Then she looked up and frowned at her mother.

"Are you giving me a deadline, too, Mama? Just like the teachers and the bus driver and any other adult? I got to tell you what happened or make up with Tessie—one or the other—by 2 o'clock today or you're going to lock me in my room?"

"Child, child, child." Josie clicked her tongue. "Look at your miserable self, so miserable you willing to sass your mama who made you grits and eggs and let you sleep in! What has come over you?" Josie didn't give Annie any time to respond. She picked up her chipped coffee cup, plucked a cookie that had been left out overnight on the green Depression glass dessert plate, and went out on her front porch where she sat in her rocker.

Annie heard the creak of the porch boards in response to her mother's rocking. She pushed her breakfast plate away and went back to her room where she threw herself across her bed. She was past crying, past being angry. She had a hole in her heart from missing Tessie. She wanted to jump rope or play jacks with Tessie. She wanted to hear Tessie's stories about the dolls and have a closer look at them. When the dolls had been in her house, she hadn't been interested in them even though Josie had tried to teach her how to craft them and had showed her how to use the dolls for props when she told stories.

Annie stood up, brushed out her hair, then braided it. She put on her pants and a shirt, her socks and her shoes. She strode out to the porch where she knew Josie was waiting for her.

"Mama, I am so sorry. You are right. I have been all sour pussy. I'm going to walk over to Tessie's and apologize for calling her names. If she forgives me, can I bring her back here for lunch, please, ma'am?"

Josie kept rocking, sipping her coffee and smoking. "Come over her, Annie." Josie's voice was all tight invitation. Annie's heart raced. "Come on over here, now, girl, and get your hard love," Josie growled.

Annie walked over to her mother and stood in front of her. "Bend. Bend before you break," Josie said "You know what I have to do, don't you, girl? You don't leave me with no other choice. I can't let you sass me. You understand?" The tightness left, the growling had ended, and in its place was Josie's velvet voice.

"Yes, ma'am." Annie bent down to her mother, as if she were going to give and receive a kiss.

Josie slapped Annie on one side of her face. "Now turn," Josie commanded in a whisper. She slapped Annie on the other side. "Kiss your mother, Annie, and thank me for doing the hard thing," Josie said.

"Yes, Mama. Thank you." Annie's face burned from where she'd been hit. Tears only made it worse, but she kissed her mother's forehead like Judas did and walked down the steps, past the collard greens and the mustard greens, past the blooming okra. Then she ran toward the short cut that led through the swamp to Tessie's trailer.

*****

Tessie sat on the narrow stoop of her trailer tearing fat crab grass into thinner strips and laying them beside her on the narrow boards. Maybe Annie will come and save me, Tessie thought. Neither Ray nor Laura Jean had come out of their bedroom yet even though it was almost 10 a.m. Tessie tiptoed into the kitchen to check the time and to see if she could find anything to eat for breakfast. Empty potato chip bags, long necked beer bottles, and ashtrays filled with sour cigarette butts littered the kitchen counters.

9:45—She knew the rule: no TV until one of her parents was out of bed. She went back to the stoop.

She missed Annie. If they had not been fighting, she would've spent the night at Annie's and had grits and eggs for breakfast. Struck by hunger and self-pity, Tessie began to weep. She knew better than to wake her parents who would be hung over and mean.

Out of the corner of her eye, Tessie saw a flash of red and blue and heard the sound of rustling sugar cane. "Annie?" Tessie jumped up and ran toward Annie. As soon as Annie saw her, she sped up.

The two girls collided in a hug, crying and laughing.

"I'm sorry. I'm sorry." It was hard to tell who spoke first, and it didn't matter.

"Shhh, now, Annie. Hush! Please don't wake them!" Tessie begged.

"We're too far from the trailer for them to hear us, Tessie. Go get your dolls and write a note to your parents that you're at my house. Hurry up now. It's Saturday and mama said she'd make us something to eat if you came over. She figured Ray and Laura Jean are still abed and you didn't get breakfast!" Annie said.

Tessie gave Annie one more hug and a kiss, and then she pulled back when her lips felt the welt on Annie's cheek.

"Oh, Annie, what did you say? What did you say to her?" Tessie whispered.

Tessie traced the welt with her fingers.

Annie pulled her shoulders back and looked toward the sky. "Never mind, Tessie. Just never mind. Go get your things."

"All right. I'll go. You wait here." Tessie turned toward the trailer, taking giant strides to reach it, then tiptoed up the steps and went inside.

Annie watched her friend disappear. She waited, tapping her foot and humming. Why does it always take that girl so long to do things? she wondered.

Tessie reappeared with a boot box. She must have the dolls Mama made in there, Annie thought. The girls hurried back through the swamp to Josie who was waiting for them on the porch in her rocking chair. The girls stomped up the path to her house. "Don't you two look happy?" Josie said. She stood up and called, "I'm hurrying to the kitchen to cook up more grits and eggs, Tessie. We gonna start this day all over again."

Annie smiled. If her mother was cooking for her, she knew she was forgiven.

After the girls had breakfast with Josie, they played outside on the tire swing, weeded the garden, picked a mess of lady peas, and ate watermelon. They competed for who could spit their seed the farthest. Night fell. "You go ahead to bed, Tessie, me and Annie will do the dishes," Josie said. "You are looking faded as my jeans!"

"All right, Miss Josie, if you say so. I surely am tired," Tessie said. "Did my parents call?"

"No, no Tessie, they didn't. I called them. They know you're safe, here, with us," Josie said.

Annie helped her mother do the dishes. Tessie went into the bedroom and laid the dolls out one by one on Annie's dresser. She lit a candle on the nightstand, put on one of Josie's old work shirts, and climbed into bed. "Please let the dolls come alive for Annie and me tonight," she prayed. Then she fell asleep.

Annie didn't bother to change into pajamas or a nightshirt. She tiptoed into the room, blew out the candle, and got in beside Tessie.

Tessie woke to the smell of soot. Damp air descended around her like fog. She had forgotten where she was so when she felt another body in the bed beside her, she flinched. Her sudden jerk woke Annie who knew where she was and that Tessie was with her, but the fog in the room confused her.

"What's going on, Tessie?" Annie said.

"Hush. Do you hear the rustling? It's their wings brushing against their clothes. Keep as quiet as you can," Tessie hissed.

A single haunting melody hung in the air. The girls held hands and listened. The music got louder and then Annie's bedroom door opened and Josie thundered in.

"What's going on in here? Why's this room damp? Is this smoke? You girls smoking something?" Before Josie could say more, one of her dolls fell off the dresser at her feet.

"Oh, uh-huh. I see what's happening here. I guess I don't know the power of my own magic!" Josie bent down and picked up the doll. She gathered the other four in her arms and took them with her. Annie and Tessie followed her to the kitchen.

"Set yourselves down, girls. I'll be making us some tea. Don't touch the dolls! I have to do a little more work on them to keep you and them safe," Josie said.

"What are you going to do, Miss Josie?" Tessie asked.

"I'm going to soak them overnight in vinegar water until those doll babies are just that—dolls. They got a little too much of me wrapped around in them in those fancy outfits I made—it's like I sewed my moods right into those seams and those dolls can't help but act like I been feeling," Josie said. She shrugged and then she chuckled. The three of them waited for the kettle to whistle, and when it did, Josie poured hot water on the chamomile flowers to brew tea and sat back down with the girls.

"Things are going to be all right, babies," Josie said. The girls weren't sure if she was talking to them or the dolls. They raised their eyebrows at each other. "I'm gonna put those dolls right in the sink and pickle the Devil out of them. Now drink your tea."

The girls didn't move. "Something else troubling you?" Josie asked.

"No, ma'am," said Tessie.

"No, Mama," Annie echoed.

"Good. That's good. I don't want y'all to be troubled," Josie said and took a sip of tea. She set her cup down, and then Josie gathered the girls into her, one under each arm. She had wanted two children, and now she felt she had them. Maybe I can save these 'Geechee girls, Josie thought as she pressed their noses into her soft, warm skin. I've scared myself this time with those dolls. If Fuddah finds out that I don't know my own power, he's going to be beyond angry with me. He loves me because he promised Mama he would, and he's been trying to make me in his own image. Maybe he's right about me and my moods, that I don't know my own power."

"Let go, Mama, please. You holding us too tight," Annie said.

"All right, Annie. You and Tessie go back to bed. Go on, now," Josie said

"No, Miss Josie, if you please, we want to hear about the 'Geechee," Tessie said.

"All right. I will tell you all what I can remember about the 'Geechee even if it is in the middle of the night," Josie said. "My father taught me about the Ogeechee when I was a little girl, Tessie, so if you got the patience to listen, I'll tell you what I know."

"Yes, please," the girls spoke at the same time and then giggled and linked pinkies.

"Jinx," Annie said.

"The 'Geechee are as old as the red clay this house stands on, and you are part of that clay and them. Both you girls. And don't be silly about this, either, or I won't tell you the rest of what I know," Josie said, and knit her brows to make her point.

"It don't matter a'tall that you don't look like Indians or each other, because you got the strength of the 'Geechee and the patience of God," Josie said.

"The 'Geechee began with the name Yuchi'i, and Fuddah say they lived in and near Ebenezer Creek in Screven and Effingham Counties, in the old towns of Intatchkalgi, Padshilaika, and Tokogalgi —the names the Creek gave to them. The Yuchi'i's names for those places are long lost to us. Fuddah say we did not mix with the Creek until we had a common enemy. We were never a large tribe but we were a strong one. Our people were feared and respected. The Creeks say we were their salafki, their slaves, but we were never slaves. No one enslaved our spirits," Josie said. "You hear me, Annie? Tessie?"

"Yes, ma'am," Annie said, and Tessie nodded.

"We 'Geechee are blessed by the sun, and we obey the heat. All we have comes from the sun—our food, our wood and the warmth of our spirits." Josie stared into the distance while she talked. Her voice dropped low.

"What do you mean, Mama?" Annie asked. "I thought we believed in God."

Josie didn't answer.

"You're looking sad, Mama. Why?" Annie asked.

Josie didn't answer. An owl hooted. Tessie looked at the stars outside the window. Then Josie spoke.

"I believe in God, I believe in the sun, and sometimes, I don't believe in anything," Josie said. "Now go to bed. Both of you."

-4-
Jesus

At 6:30 a.m. the next morning everyone at the Osaha household awoke to a clear blue Savannah morning. The girls lay twisted in their sheets, their clothes clinging to them like cellophane. They locked eyes—each of them trying to figure out what was real from the night before. "Where the dolls?" Tessie asked,

"In the kitchen sink—soaking, remember?" Annie paused. "Mama? Mama?"

"Come out to the porch, young'uns. We need to talk. And don't stop in the kitchen. I don't want y'all at the sink near those babies," Josie said.

The girls scurried out to the porch, past the sink and the dolls, and crouched at Josie's slippered feet. They waited.

"Mama, we here and ready to listen," Annie said.

"Yes, child, I know you are here, and that makes me happy." She reached for Annie who slid by her and sat down. Then she patted Tessie on the head as if she were a cat. "You, too, Tessie. I'm glad you are here, too."

A mockingbird cat-called in the distance. Sleepy mosquitoes circled around Josie's arms and face, so she lit another menthol cigarette to keep them away. She drew deep and long, held the smoke in, and then exhaled as if she were Mosquito Control.

Josie shifted in her chair, leaning back and leaning forward. Her restlessness alerted Annie that she was getting ready to speak. Tessie cleared her throat to speak, and Annie elbowed her sharp in the ribs to silence her. She wanted to hear her mother's thoughts.

"Truth is," Josie began, "that I been messing where I shouldn't have been messing when I made those dolls." She looked Tessie deep in the eyes. "You know that, don't you, Tessie? Those dolls came alive to you, didn't they?"

"Yes, ma'am, they did," she said.

"That's dangerous," Josie said. "I can't let that happen again, so we're going to begin something today that's bound to change our lives."

The pause that followed was heavy as a rock and dark as the 'Geechee River.

"Today we are going to meet Jesus. All three of us. First thing we have to do is get cleaned up, then we're going to stop at Little Bit and tell Tessie's folks we're taking her to Church of the Epiphany." The girls shifted their eyes, a quick cut that Josie didn't see.

Tessie knew the church. An Episcopal Church with red doors and big azaleas all around. Only blacks went there. "I don't think we ought to stop by my folks' place, Miss Josie. They probably aren't awake yet and they get mighty mad if I wake them on a Sunday morning." Josie didn't respond. "I think we ought to just go to church and tell them about it afterwards, when you drop me off." She paused. "Please, ma'am," her request a prayer.

Josie nodded. She could hear fear and truth in Tessie's voice. "I know neither one of you ever been to a church before so I want to prepare you. You best uncrouch yourselves and put your bottoms square on the porch. It's going to take me a while.

"Annie, I brought out the picnic basket. It's over yonder in the shade. Run. Go get it. You girls can have some corn bread and sorghum while I talk."

Once Annie returned with the basket and the girls were sitting flat on the porch, Josie spoke. "You got to get your hair pulled back, Tessie, and Annie, you need to use the hot comb. I want each of you to wear a dress, white socks, and black shoes. Will Annie's fit you, Tessie? You don't think so, well, then, you go ahead and wear your sneakers, but spit shine that swamp mud off the soles, you hear?"

Josie took a big swallow of coffee and inhaled more smoke. "Once we get there, we walk in real quiet and in a single row. We are going to get looks, you can count on it. One thing, I haven't set foot in that church since you were born, Annie. People still trying to figure out who your daddy is." Josie snorted. "And two, we have Ray and Laura Jean Harnish's girl with us and she's white." Annie and

Tessie cut their eyes at each, again. When adults stated talking about race, they felt uneasy and sad.

"Of course she's white, Mama," Annie said, "but she's also 'Geechee!" Annie flung her arm around Tessie's shoulders.

"Well, it ain't so common for white folks and black folks to be friends or for them to go to church together, Little Miss Smart Mouth."

Tessie didn't want Annie getting hit again for sassing, so she prodded Annie with her elbow. Annie took the cue and answered with Tessie. "Yes, ma'am," the girls chorused

"Don't look left and don't look right. Don't look up and don't look down. Keep your eyes straight ahead. Annie, you look at my back, and Tessie, you look at hers. We will sit down and listen to the music. When the music stops and the minister says rise, we will stand up, and when he tells us to pray, we will kneel on the pew. We will sing songs, and then we will approach the rail for communion. Afterward, we will shake hands with the people around us, and then we will go out under the mimosa tree for lemonade and a sugar cookie."

"How can you be so sure that this is the way it will go, Mama?" Annie asked.

"Because I done been there a thousand times before you were born and a couple hundred in my mind since I stopped going. I want you to know how you supposed to be this first time and to get used to it, because we are going to go from now on. Now go get dressed. You girls are about to meet Jesus."

* * * * *

Things went pretty much as Josie said they would. For Tessie, the best part was being with Annie and Josie after the service under the mimosa tree, sipping lemonade and eating her sugar cookie cut in the shape of a cross. There had been music and prayer, singing and communion, but Tessie had not met Jesus. None of the men had long hair. None of them wore sandals or robes. None of them had marks on their hands where the nails had been.

* * * * *

As they drove down Highway 17 and back to Josie's place, Tessie spoke. "Don't take me home dressed up, Miss Josie. Let me come back with y'all so I can put on my regular clothes and walk back through the swamp."

"You always trying to keep the truth from your parents, Tessie? How come?" Josie asked.

Tessie hung her head.

"Look at you, hanging your head like a bad pup. It's all right, Tessie. I am going to have to talk with Mr. Ray and Laura Jean. I won't lie to them. Somehow we will make this all right. Besides, they might not mind at all. Ever occur to you that you are wrong about what they think?"

Silence sat with the three of them in the car. Tessie thought it was the Holy Spirit.

"All right," the girls said in unison. They knew Josie was right, but they were scared of Ray and Laura Jean.

"Mama, what happened to the dolls?" Annie asked.

"Never you mind, Anne Osaha. That's for another time," Josie said.

Josie pulled her old Chevy into her driveway, put the automatic shift in park, and turned off the key. Maybe the girl's right. Maybe it's just best not to tell them about going to find Jesus at the church.

* * * * *

I am like a snake, Tessie thought. I can make my body the same temperature of those things closest to me. I am not afraid to be in the swamp. I am like Jesus, and the swamp is my wilderness and the world is my devil. Jesus should have been much more afraid of Jerusalem than he was of the devil in the wilderness. And then she stopped herself—wherever evil lived, God lived there too—Jesus knew that. And he chose not to be afraid. That's what I have to learn: not to be afraid.

I'll make a ritual for myself from all I know and all Miss Josie's taught me. She got out her notebook and wrote:

Rub your hand against cottonwood bark to keep a cottonmouth away.
Rub your back against a standing rock to gain strength.
Rub your forehead slowly across pine bark to ward off sadness.
Lie down on one side.
Touch your cheek to the night-cooled red clay.
Rest there.
When the snakes begin to night hunt, they will lie against your body as against a log; they will not rattle, hiss or bite but will be as still as your body is, as still and as cool as clay. And they will coil up close to you when the hunt is done.

Tessie made up the rules for sleeping in the swamp with snakes, and then she memorized them.

Cottonwood and cottonmouth. Canebrakes and canebrake rattlers. Copper bracelets and copperheads. Tessie liked to think things in pairs. *Milk and honey, black and white, glory and power, bourbon and water, sun and rain, now and never, life and death, sound and silence, him and her, mother and father, crazy and sane.*

Cottonwoods and cottonmouths, canebrakes and canebrake rattlers were natural and sane, gave the world order because they were predictable and followed a pattern. Trees provided shade and were good for climbing. She loved to break the cane and suck sugar from the end. And snakes, which everyone she knew feared and detested and killed every chance they got, were her friends. Other girls slept with stuffed animals from Newberry's. Tessie slept on the riverbank with snakes curled around her. At first the snakes took her for a log, but eventually they knew her for what she was—human—and for reasons of their own let her pick them up and pet their bellies until they fell asleep.

-5-
Earth

Josie buried the dolls in the garden, under the low hung boughs of the fig tree. Before she buried them, she cut off their button eyes so they wouldn't be able to see and find their way back. She opened the lid on her button jar and dropped their eyes in. Next, she took the silk head wraps that decorated the dolls' heads and wrapped them around the dolls' mouths to silence them. She had no intention of telling either of the girls what had become of the dolls, knowing that soon the girls would forget to ask about them.

Every third Thursday, Annie and Tessie walked together to the bookmobile, cutting through back yards and playing chicken against the cars on the highway.

"People think the bookmobile is safe, Tessie, because they can't see snakes or get bit by mosquitoes in there. But Mama says books are the most dangerous things of all. More powerful than hurricanes, more potent than snake oil, more liberating than the constitution," Annie said.

"What on earth does she mean by that, Annie?" Tessie asked.

"I think she means a lot of things, Tessie—she thinks books can get you a new life. She said to me, 'Annie, books are going to be your ticket out of here,'" Annie said.

"Well, I know books matter, Annie, but I don't think of them like hurricanes or snake oil, and the onliest way they seem like the constitution to me is they are both made out of paper with words on them," Tessie grumbled. She hated feeling dumb, and that was just how she was feeling.

"Stop and think about it, Tessie," Annie said.

Tessie stopped in the middle of the road and thought. Annie broke out laughing.

"You remind me of Winnie the Pooh, Tessie. I swear. You so literal all the time. I don't mean stop in the middle of the road, you fool." Annie grabbed Tessie so the oncoming car didn't hit her. The girls fell on the side of the road and rolled in the dirt. Tessie's braided hair got dirt and small twigs in it. Annie picked the twigs out and dusted the dirt out of Tessie's hair.

"It's all right, Annie, I'm clean enough. Come on, now, quit picking at me. I don't care if I got some dirt on me," Tessie said.

"I care, Tessie. I want you to look your best. You so pretty," Annie said. She reached for Tessie's hand and the girls skipped along.

"What you gonna get today, Annie? More mysteries? Love stories? What?" Tessie asked.

"I don't think I'm getting anymore love stories or mysteries, Tessie, I don't believe them anymore." Annie kept her head down when she spoke and went from skipping to walking.

"Why not?" Tessie asked.

Annie didn't look up or answer, so Tessie let it go.

"I asked Mr. Hanks to get me biographies and autobiographies, Tessie. I want to read about people's lives. I want to find out what they did to succeed. I want to learn how they turned things around when they were failing. Remember Father Jones told us at Sunday School that if we each read 10 biographies or autobiographies, he'd take us into Savannah to the big public library and then let us have lunch on River Street with him paying for it."

Tessie nodded. She remembered. She loved the idea of going into Savannah—especially since she would be going with Annie.

Mr. Hanks was opening the door and putting down the steps when Annie and Tessie walked up to the bookmobile. The girls were his most regular customers. He was happy to see them and he sat outside the bookmobile while they looked at the books.

This week he'd brought a box of real life stories for the tall black girl who had asked for them. He was surprised when the white girl signed out a couple of them, too.

When they left, Annie carried a biography about Eleanor Roosevelt under her left arm. Roosevelt's story didn't have any references to tidal waters, red clay, or copperheads hanging from the riverbank trees, and that was why Annie picked it. She was tired of

Savannah and its Spanish moss and reptiles. Annie's other book was about the dust bowl. The book jacket forced her to think of the windblown plains, dry hot air, and emptiness.

"I'll tell you what, Tessie, you couldn't pay me a million dollars to live in Oklahoma where the air is heavy with dust," Annie said. She began reading the blurb about the eroding land and the cracking earth aloud while they walked. "The central part of North America, known as the plains region, has dust storms daily," Annie read.

As Tessie listened, she became the landscape—her throat the dry plains and her emotions the ceaseless wind. Tessie knew she would never live in Oklahoma either because her soul yearned for the ocean and the salty breeze.

"Damn! Double damn!" Tessie said. "I left my books right there at the check out with Mr. Hanks."

"Here then, Tessie, you take this one." Annie handed her the book on Oklahoma and the dust bowl. "Tell me about it when you are done."

* * * * *

Several months later, true to his work, Father Jones, had arranged the trip into Savannah on a Saturday. Even though the 'Geechee Road was only about 20 minutes from downtown, it may as well have been in another country for as little as Annie and Tessie got to visit it.

As part of the preparation, Annie spent Friday night before the trip at Tessie's. Josie had finally told Laura Jean about going to the Church of the Epiphany and taking the girls with her.

Tessie's fear about her parents' reaction to her going to church had been dead wrong. They were glad she was gone on Sunday mornings and they were hopeful that learning about God and Jesus might save her the way it had never saved them.

The girls woke early to the sound of wind. They cuddled down under the sheets until the alarm went off.

When they went into the kitchen, Laura Jean looked more worried than usual. Finally she spoke.

"Sounds like a hurricane's coming, ladies. I'm not so sure you're going anywhere today." Laura Jean reached across the girls, who were sipping orange juice and eating sticky buns, and turned on the radio.

"A hurricane warning is in effect for Savannah and Route 17, especially around the Ogeechee Road. Some telephone lines have been downed by fallen trees. The Georgia State Police recommends no unnecessary travel," the radio announcer said.

Laura Jean picked up her phone and called Josie. "We're safe. Yes, Josie, now don't you worry. The girls are safe here with me. Soon as the storm warning is over, I'll walk them over to your place to play."

"Oh, Mama," Tessie pleaded, "we only going into Savannah. No wind's bad enough to stop that little tiny trip."

"Yes, it is, Tessie. Don't be giving me a hard time! What do you know about hurricanes anyway?" Laura Jean stood firm in front of her daughter. Tessie opened her mouth to speak, and Laura Jean back-handed her. "Don't you even be thinking about sassing me—you neither, Annie."

Tessie knew plenty about hurricanes, and knew tornadoes came in many shapes and sizes, just like people on the 'Geechee Road. She'd seen a tornado rip up the pavement like peeling an orange. And she knew about hurricanes, not because she'd seen one, but because she'd read about them—and she knew that tornadoes and hurricanes were related storm systems—the way her parents were.

"Well, I've lived through a hurricane or two, Little Miss Know it All! And we ain't going driving about when the police and the weather service say there's one brewing!"

Annie and Tessie ran down the hallway and slammed and locked Tessie's door.

-6-
The Jars

For Tessie's eleventh Christmas, Laura Jean gave her three cobalt blue jars. She had put each one in a separate box, and wrapped each one with the most magical paper Newberry's Five and Dime had—white tissue with tiny red, green, and cobalt blue stars. She tied each one with a different colored ribbon: red, dark blue, and green, and then she placed each of the packages under the Christmas tree. Tessie shook the boxes every day, but the only sound she heard was a thump. On Christmas morning, Tessie untied the bows, unfastened the tape, and folded the tissue paper up to be used another time. She smiled at Laura Jean, but the jars didn't make any sense to Tessie. After breakfast, Tessie asked her mother to help her iron out the wrinkles in the ribbons and the creases in the paper so they could be used again.

"Don't you like the jars, Tessie?" Laura Jean asked.

"I do, Mama. I just don't know what to use them for," Tessie said.

"To put pieces of the things you love in them, honey. That's what they are for. You know, like the feathers and bones, or trinkets and broken glass that you find at the river," Laura Jean coached.

"Maybe, Mama. I just don't like putting beautiful things away. The lids on the jars seal everything in too much, don't they, Mama? I love them, though. I love the blue glass. What color do you call that blue?" Tessie asked.

"Cobalt, Tessie. Aren't they lovely, darlin'? They made me think of the river, the rain, the sky, and your eyes. They are all for you. You can put anything you want in them, fill them with magic potions or gather salamander eggs from still water. Whatever you want. If they were mine, I'd leave them empty with their lids off and hope they'd be filled with my bad dreams while I slept," Laura Jean said.

"Maybe you just ought to keep them for your own, Mama," Tessie said.

"No, Tessie, they for you. Even when I am gone, you can have them and think of me," Laura Jean said.

Tessie didn't know what to say back to that, she wasn't even sure what it meant. "What do you mean, 'when you are gone,' Mama?" Tessie said.

Laura Jean didn't answer her.

Tessie hugged on her mother's neck that Christmas morning. She circled her arms around her, trying to hold her in place. She watched the pulse in her mother's neck and smelled stale "Evening in Paris" perfume and old cigarettes.

Laura Jean sang, *Hush little darlin', don't say a word, Mama's gonna buy you a mockingbird.* Tessie asked her to sing Greensleeves or Silent Night instead, since it was Christmas, but her mother ignored her.

When Tessie got up on New Year's Day, her mother was gone. Ray's truck was gone too, and there was no note from either of them. They must have gone off together, she thought. Then she called out, "Mama, Mama? Where are you?"

No one answered. Tessie went into her parents' room to make sure no one was at home. Her mother might be in her room and not have heard Tessie calling for her since her new best friends were her sleeping pills.

Ray came home later.

"Mama with you?" Tessie asked.

"I don't know where she's done run off to. Leave me alone, Tessie. I wanna be alone. I been up and down Route 17 looking for her and ain't no one seen her," Ray said, his voice tight from too many cigarettes and not enough air.

So Tessie waited for him to go to the back of the trailer, and then she wrote a note on the scrap paper that said, "On the river." She left him on his own. Next she went to the river to take Ray's 16-foot Mitchell out. Being on the river calmed her, and now she had enough skill to navigate it on her own. She skimmed across the top of the water for a couple of hours.

When she got home, she saw that her dad's truck was gone. She took a deep breath and exhaled before she went into the trailer and fixed herself a bowl of cereal with water since there was no milk. She heard scratching coming from her parents' room. She went in expecting to see a critter. She opened the closet and found Laura Jean.

"Mama? Mama? What on earth! Come out of there right now. Please," Tessie said.

Laura Jean didn't move or reply.

Oh my God, Tessie thought. I must have been born into the wrong family, or maybe I am an alien. "Why are you hiding and lying to me and scaring Daddy? What's the matter with you?" Tessie picked up her mother's hand mirror and hurled it through the window. Then she fled out the door.

Tessie ran through the swamp to Annie's house. Josie was already gone and Annie was standing on the porch. "Come with me, Annie—I got the boat and we can be out on the river all day. We can go to the island and camp. Leave a note for Josie, come on," Tessie begged.

"Mama's gonna kill me. I got chores to do," Annie said. Then Annie looked at Tessie's face and she knew there was something very wrong; at home, of course. I don't care if Mama beats me again, she thought. I got to go with this girl to an open space and let the water work its wonder calming Tessie down.

"Oh, never mind about the chores or Mama," Annie said.

The girls ran back into the house and packed some snacks. Annie wrote a note and the girls went to the dock. Tessie started up the old Evinrude on the first try while Annie threw what few provisions they had brought with them into the bow. Tessie steered the boat away from the dock with care. As soon as they cleared it, Tessie opened the outboard as wide as she could until they were flying over the water. She drove them straight to the island.

Once they got there, she and Annie pitched their tent. They built a small fire and roasted corn and toasted marshmallows.

"You know something I do all the time, Annie, night and day, rain and shine, winter and summer?" Tessie asked.

"Pray?" Annie said.

"Well, I do some of that, Annie, but that isn't what I am talking about. I rub myself to sleep. It's the only way I get over being scared, and the only way I can fall asleep. If I don't take care of myself, I can lie in bed all night long and do nothing but worry and stew."

In the firelight, Tessie watched Annie's sober face scrunch up. Annie didn't know what to say to Tessie. She touched herself, too, but for pleasure, and she never talked to anyone, not even Tessie, about it, and she knew better than to ever mention it to Josie.

"You better find some other way to get past being scared, Tessie, or you going to rub yourself out." Annie's laugh wasn't kind. Her dark eyes glittered in the firelight.

"The truth, Annie? I'm lonely. Each morning after I cook my daddy's eggs and grits, I wash the dishes and scrub the counters. Then I take a shower and wash my hair, and scrub my face until I can see myself shine," Tessie said.

"You watch who you let see you when you all shiny-bright, Tessie," Annie said.

Is she warning me or threatening me? Tessie wondered.

"Oh, I don't care, Annie. If I'm too bright for some folks, I don't care. They already talking about me all the time. 'Poor Tessie, you know they're gonna take her mama off. And her daddy is running dope on his shrimp boat.' And I heard one of the neighbors say, 'Ray's gonna be behind bars soon, or the Chatham County Sheriff's Office is dumber than I think they are—and that's dumb!'" She paused. "Annie, I found Mama in the closet this morning. Best I can tell she's been there a day and half 'cause that's the last time either Daddy or me saw her. When I spoke to her, she didn't answer or move. She'd been scratching against the door like a critter, which is how I found her in the first place."

Annie got up, gathered sticks and built a small fire. The girls sat in front of it, arm in arm. Mosquitoes began to bite, so they unpacked their sleeping gear. They tucked themselves in under the faded cotton blankets. Tessie tickled Annie's back until she could hear Annie's shallow breathing like a tired cicada. Then Tessie tickled her own skin the way her mother had when she was a little girl. Finally she rubbed herself harder, the way her mother rubbed her father's shoulders when he had been hauling shrimp nets in all day. But she was still awake, so she rubbed herself in patterns that lead into the darkness reserved for lovers, a darkness that also led her into sleep.

The next morning at the break of dawn, Annie left the tent. She couldn't be with Tessie another minute. She liked how Tessie had tickled her back and she didn't like it. She had listened to Tessie moaning. She didn't want to see her friend, didn't want to look at her sadness and loneliness.

Tessie heard Annie stir, but fell back to sleep. When she awoke, she was confused. She looked out through the open flaps expecting to see Annie sitting at the smoldering campfire. She wasn't there. "Annie? Annie?" She threw back the blanket and went in search of her friend. She wasn't sitting in the low slung oak limb or wading in the creek. She was simply gone. Tessie's stomach clenched and then she began to wail. She ran to make sure the boat was still beached, and it was.

"That dumb-assed Annie!" Tessie kicked the boat. She knew Annie had heard her rubbing herself and moaning. She knew her friend was scared of her and she knew Annie had swum back to Josie's rather than face her.

* * * * *

Tessie packed up camp, threw garbage and goods back into the boat, and steered the boat back toward shore. The whole time she was thinking about loneliness, which she knew like the back of her hand. Laura Jean and Ray had stayed to themselves a lot of the time, more in love with their booze and their craziness than they were with her or each other. If it weren't for Josie and Annie, Tessie knew she'd be adrift as sure as if she were an unmoored boat.

Annie knew loneliness as if it were her sister, and so she loved Tessie as if she were kin. She could recognize loneliness in Tessie's eyes and her silence, in Tessie's voice and in her shoulders, held high up near her ears, as if she were carrying wings beneath her old cotton shirt. Josie watched over them both with a stern eye and a firm hand.

Being with the girls, looking out for the girls, making lunches for the girls, cooking smooth grits for them—all these actions kept Josie from her own loneliness, born of man-hunger, exhaustion, and the endless sewing she did patching clothes for her family and other families on Highway 17.

Whenever Tessie and Annie fought, each felt as if her skin were a seam being ripped open. Tessie remembered the last fight and how Josie had broken it up.

She had demanded their attention. "Listen to me! Anybody who has 'Geechee blood ought to claim it," Josie said. "And you both have it. You both carry the stories of the old ones in your blood. You girls best link arms and claim each other. You are 'Geechee. You both came up on the 'Geechee River and the 'Geechee Road. Just because one of you is black and 'Geechee, and the other'n is white and 'Geechee, doesn't matter. You got way more in common than you have different," Josie said.

Maybe she's right, Tessie thought as she tied the boat off at the pier, and because we got some of the same blood in our veins, we are going to have to fight it out sometimes.

Once she was out of the boat, she pretended to wait for Ray. What she really wanted was for Josie to come to her. She scanned the docks. No sign of Josie. I'll even put up with the yelling I'm gonna get for leaving the mainland and taking Annie along with me. I need to talk things out with Annie about touching her and telling her how I touch myself. I'm going to promise never to do that when we are with each other—even if I think she is sleeping. She listened as the women at the pier talked and pulled crabmeat from the shell.

"Excuse me, ladies. I'm wondering where Miss Josie is," Tessie said as she approached the women who were heading shrimp.

"Ladies? Who you be callin' ladies, Tessie Harnish? Oh us!" The women broke out laughing. "She's not here, child? You see her? You seeing things, Tessie, like your mama does?"

Tessie pulled away from the women, moving her neck like a goose in retreat.

"Now calm down, girl. We learned a long time ago that if Josie is not here with us, we don't go lookin' for her. You be wise to learn the same," one of the older white women said.

Tessie nodded and walked away. She could not decide where she was going—to her trailer or to Josie's house.

She decided to go home and not take the shortcut. She walked along the 'Geechee Road, and her mother drove right past her. As she got ready to pass by Josie and Annie's house, she heard Josie call to her. "You a long way from home. Didn't you see your mama drive by?"

"What is my mama looking for?" Tessie asked,

"Don't you think she is looking for you?" Josie said.

"No, ma'am, I don't," Tessie said.

Josie furrowed her brows. "Well, I guess you might as well know, honey. Your mama is looking for her mind. She's done lost herself. I think Ray's going to take her to Milledgeville."

Tessie had known it for some time. She ran back to her trailer and sat on the stoop waiting for Ray. When he walked up to the trailer, Tessie said, "Daddy, what is Mama looking for?"

"What are you talking about Tessie?"

"Why does she drive around on the side of the road? Why does she wrap herself in a blanket and hide in the closet in y'all's bedroom? What's the matter with her?"

"Nothing and everything, Tessie. Now go on. I'm tired. Go on in the trailer. Where is your mother anyway?"

"I don't know, Daddy."

"Heat me up some beans, girl," Ray said in a worn out voice.

Tessie opened the canned beans, heated them in a pan, and watched while her father ate them. He was almost done when the door flew open with a bang.

Laura Jean was standing in the doorway in her bra and her jeans. "Hey. I'm home."

"Where are the rest of your clothes, Mama?" Tessie asked.

"How the hell should I know? I couldn't stand having the bugs on me. They were crawling all over my shirt, so I just took it off and threw it out the window. You got a problem with that, girlie?"

Laura Jean snatched Tessie by the arm and rammed her into the refrigerator.

"For Christ's sake, Laura Jean, leave the girl alone," Ray didn't even yell anymore. He said it the way someone might say 'It's raining.' That's how Tessie knew it was hopeless.

Ray grabbed for Laura Jean, but she ducked him and ran back out the door.

"You all right, Tessie? Yes? You sure?" Ray said.

Tessie nodded and picked herself up off the floor. Ray opened the door and then he stopped. "What am I doing chasing after your mother? Shit. Oh shit. I can't live like this no more," he said and slumped down on the couch.

"Go get your mama a shirt and put it on the stoop. I think she'll come back for it. I'm calling Jenny Conroy. It's time we all did something about your mother." Ray picked up the phone and dialed Jenny's number. Tessie couldn't hear what he was saying. Maybe she didn't want to. Then he hung up and dialed again. Fifteen minutes passed. She didn't talk and Ray didn't move.

Tessie heard the siren coming. She thought there was a fire in one of the trailers. Then she saw the ambulance and she knew. It was coming for Laura Jean. They didn't pull right up to the trailer but stopped at the end of the road. Two men in white hospital clothes got out of the ambulance. Ray met them and pointed toward the 'Geechee Road. Tessie could hear him. "Yep, she's out on the road. Yep, I got a picture of her." He took his wallet out and handed the men a picture of his family--from last winter when they had been shopping at K-Mart. The police waited until dark when Laura Jean came stumbling out of the swamp. She was streaked with mud, and when the men came toward her, she got in the back of the squad car without fighting anyone.

"I'm gonna go away for a spell, Tessie. Maybe I can get better," Laura Jean said in a tired voice.

* * * * *

Tessie spent even more time with Josie and Annie.

"Your Mama still up to Milledgeville?" Josie asked.

"Yes'm. She's getting better, Daddy says. She's talking again, but she's still not herself," Tessie told her.

"When is she coming home?" Annie said.

"I don't know. Can we talk about something else? Let's talk about my birthday. Maybe she will be home by my birthday—five weeks and I'll be 12." She searched for joy and hope when she said it. Mostly she felt empty.

Later Ray came by to pick Tessie up. "Well, I think we got us some good news. The doc says Laura Jean can come home, and she's gonna be let out in time so she can be here when you turn 12."

* * * * *

Laura Jean came home again. No sirens announced her return. She rode home with Ray in his pick up.

Tessie ran out to meet them and gave her mother a cautious hug, then went to get Annie.

"Annie? Annie? You here?" Tessie called.

There was no light on and no supper smells coming from the house. Everything around Tessie seemed to swirl: the porch, the leaves, the ground. Disappointment twisted in her stomach. If Annie sees Mama, and Annie thinks she's better, then maybe I can believe it, too, she thought. She found paper and a pencil on the counter and wrote, "Annie, please come home with me on my birthday, October 25th at 5:30. Mama's back and she's going to make all my favorite foods. Love, Tessie."

Tessie turned and ran back through the swamp, back to the trailer park. Even before she broke out of the trees, she could smell turnip greens and bacon mixing in the air with wisteria and rain. She ran up the steps to the front door and flew into the kitchen.

Laura Jean was bent over the stove, pulling out fresh baked cornbread from the oven. "Happy Birthday, honey. Where you been?" she said. "Sit down, sit down."

"It's not my birthday, Mama."

"I know that, baby, I'm just practicing for when Annie comes over next week," Laura Jean said. She sipped her sweet tea and stood by the side of the table.

"Will you sit with me, Mama?" Tessie asked.

"Okay, darlin'." Laura Jean sat down at the end of the table after she spoke. She lit a Pall Mall off the one she had been smoking and poured Tessie a Royal Crown Cola.

"Tessie's home," Laura Jean yelled out, and Ray emerged from the back of the trailer.

"Good. Come give your dad a hug, girl. What's for supper, Laura Jean?" Ray said.

"Tessie's favorites, Ray. Remember? It's her birthday."

"It's not my birthday, Mama. That's next week," Tessie said.

"Oh, I know that, sugar. I'm just practicing, right?" Laura Jean said. "I'm making greens, Ray, one of Tessie's favorite things, right, sugar?"

"Yes, Mama, especially the way you make them," Tessie said, trying to keep the worry out of her voice and the fear out of her eyes.

"It's bad enough I got to eat greens every night when I'm cooking, Laura Jean. I thought we'd go out on your first night home. I can't stand having you sitting down at the other end of this itty-bitty table sucking on your cigarettes and sipping whiskey," Ray said. "The doctor said no whiskey."

"It ain't whiskey, Ray, it's sweet tea. And if you don't believe me, come take a sip," Laura Jean said. "Anyway, it ain't your birthday. It's Tessie's, I mean, it ain't Tessie's either, I'm just trying to make some food she likes, so hush, please."

Tessie picked up her plate to go to her room. "'Scuse me, please."

"Where the hell do you think you are going?" Ray yelled.

"I swear to God, Ray, if you don't learn to be kind to our girl, she's going to turn into..." Laura Jean spat the words at him.

"Into what, Laura Jean? Into you?" Ray asked, his voice breaking.

Tessie stopped. Ray put his head between his hands and wept. Tessie put her plate down on the table, and went to him. She cushioned him in her arms and said, "It's gonna be all right, Daddy. My arms are gonna be like the arms of Jesus for you."

Laura Jean laughed. "Look at the two of you!"

Tessie glared at her mother.

"Get away from us. Get away! Here you are just home, and look—Daddy's crying and I'm too upset to eat the greens you made. I wish you were back in the hospital, you crazy bitch!" Tessie yelled and lashed out at her mother with her free arm.

"Never mind, Ray, never mind, Tessie. You can have this trailer and your weepy, pathetic selves, I'm gonna go drive around," Laura Jean said. She picked up her purse and her cigarettes and left.

After her father calmed down, Tessie tiptoed to her room. She wanted the comfort of Josie's dolls, but she didn't have them anymore. She wanted their smoky scent to cover up the smell of the paper mill. Tessie fell asleep on top of her comforter. She woke once to dolls' voices, and then she realized it was peepers and the croakers. She knew she would go to Annie and Josie, wherever they were, tomorrow. She had to find them.

*****

The next morning, Laura Jean was sitting at the end of Tessie's bed. She didn't smell like alcohol and she didn't look wild. Those two facts were reassuring.

"I am sorry about last night, honey. When your dad accused me of drinking, it pissed me off. I am going to make it up to you. I drove over to Annie and Josie's while you were sleeping and I invited them to join us for cake and ice cream tonight instead of on your birthday. We'll celebrate a little early this year, okay? Josie can't come, but Annie can. They want you to come there for supper and then you girls can walk over here for dessert and Annie can spend the night. All right, sugar?" Laura Jean said.

"All right, Mama. Can I hug you?" Tessie asked.

"'Course you can," Laura Jean said as she reached out her arms.

Laura Jean expected the girls around 6 for dessert and when the clock showed 7, she went out looking for them in her Ford Galaxy. She saw the girls before they saw her. Tessie was leaning on Annie's shoulder as they walked down the side of the road. She pulled the car right up beside the girls and got out to help Tessie in. She was crying and moaning. Blood ran down her legs and she had a black eye.

"What happened, Tessie? What on earth, Annie?" Laura Jean said.

Before Tessie could answer, Annie spoke, "After we ate dinner, we decided to walk by the old playground before we came over for dessert. We got jumped by a bunch of boys after we beat 'em at marbles." Annie patted Tessie on the back, which made Tessie feel happy and sad at the same time. It was the first time things had seemed normal since Annie had swum back from the camping trip.

"Can I have a sweet tea when we get home, Mama?" Tessie asked.

"'Course you can, Tessie," Laura Jean said. She drove home and helped Tessie inside and onto the couch, then fixed her a great big glass of sweet tea.

Tessie took a big long sip of the tea before she began to talk.

"Well," she started, "Annie gave me crystal marbles for my present, a ruby one, a sapphire one, and an emerald one. John Henry dared me to play a game of marbles, Mama. I met him fair and square on the red clay spot where we shoot. I let John Henry draw the circle. Everybody stood around watching—no one cheering or teasing. I shot my ruby crystal and won John Henry's ball bearing. He snorted and hocked an oyster inside the circle. I laid my crystal and his ball bearing on the red piece of velvet that Miss Josie had stitched into a bag for me to carry the marbles in. When I turned around, there was John Henry staring down at me like an angry bull. Then he picked me up and threw me on the ground, hard as he could. My knees hit first and burst open like watermelons. John Henry pulled out a knife and cut the velvet cloth into shreds, took his ball bearing and my crystal and walked away."

"Left her there to die, I swear, Miss Laura," Annie said in a whisper.

"Oh girls, oh girls. Annie, you go down the hall and bring me my emergency kit and I'll get working on these knees," Laura Jean said.

"Wait until Josie and Ray hear about this. John Henry's sorry-assed self is gonna be even sorrier after Ray and Josie get done with him!"

-7-
Mud

Josie and Ray heard about John Henry from Laura Jean. And both of them wanted to go after him, wanted to walk right up to his metal frame house where he lived with his grandmother, the metal house with the tin roof that leaked, and pull him out of his bed. They wanted to take him out to his front yard and whip him right there in front of everyone who walked by or looked through their smoky windows or stepped out onto their stoop. They wanted him to cry out for mercy; they wanted him to apologize for hurting Tessie.

Tessie and Annie overheard the adults discussing the plan over coffee at Laura Jean's counter. Once Laura Jean had told them what had happened, she stopped talking and waited to see what Josie and Ray would say.

"Mad as you are," Tessie said, as she walked down the hallway from her room to the kitchen, "mad as I am and hurt, beating John Henry in front of his whole street isn't gonna make anything better."

"What's this, Tessie? You gonna stick up now for that great big bully boy?" Josie said. She looked straight behind Tessie at Annie who stood a full head taller. Annie nodded her head with vigor, agreeing with Tessie. "Great God Almighty! You two are something else! Either one of you'd be willing to lie to save the other, and the other one would swear to whatever lie the other one made up. But I guess we don't have anyone lying here. So I'm listening," Josie said. "What do you think, Mr. Ray?"

"Well, I don't know what to think, Josie. Let's hear them out. Go ahead, girls. Why shouldn't we whip this boy silly? Give me some good thinking on that. I dare you. And if'n we don't whip him in front of his people, what you propose we do instead?"

Annie stepped up beside Tessie. The girls looked each other in the eyes, then turned to look at Josie and Ray and Laura Jean, then nodded at each other again.

"Speak up, now. Or hold your peace," Josie said. "This is your chance to be heard."

"Miss Josie, Daddy," Tessie began. Her throat went dry on her. She kept swallowing trying to moisten it, but she had no saliva in her mouth to help.

"Mama, Mr. Ray," Annie began. Then both girls started talking at the same time.

"Hold up. Hold up, I say," Josie shook her finger at the girls while she spoke.

"Slow down, slow down, one at a time," Ray said.

And just as quickly as the girls had begun talking, they stopped.

"You go first, Tessie," Annie said and stepped back behind her.

"All right, Annie. Thank you." Tessie smiled for the first time since she had come into the kitchen. "This is how it shouldn't go. Beating John Henry…"

Ray interrupted. "We ain't going to beat the boy, Tessie. We was talking about whipping him. There's a difference."

"Well maybe, Daddy, but doing either one in front of his street will end up having the same effect. John Henry will end up dead or wish he was," Tessie said.

"That's right, Mama, Mr. Ray," Annie chimed. "All John Henry's got in the whole world is his reputation and those marbles. You whip him in front of folks, Mama, and all the white boys will see him as a candy ass and a fool, getting whipped by a black woman. And if you whip him, Mr. Ray, all the black boys will have just the proof they need that John Henry can't hold his own with the whites."

Josie and Ray stared at the girls. "Of course, you're right," Ray said. "I forgot he's mulatto. Don't belong to neither group and both sides always trying to prove that to him, just as he's always trying to show he's both!"

She remembered how her father used to feel about her playing with Annie, how he didn't want the races the mix. And she felt a measure of pride in how he had changed.

"What do you propose we do instead?" Josie asked. "Because something gotta be done to rein that boy in before he really hurts someone and ends up in jail or dead—one."

"You need to go to Reverend Jones, Daddy," Tessie said. "Let him be the one to go talk with Miss Veda. Between Reverend Jones and John Henry's grandmother, they ought to figure out a way for him to learn his lesson, for John Henry to keep his pride and stay alive, too."

Ray sipped his cola. Josie stared at the window, and Laura Jean lit another cigarette. It felt like hours passed.

"Well?" Annie said.

"You girls sure you all right with this?" Ray asked. "Because I'm more than willing to give that boy a whipping with a long piece of fresh cut cane."

"Uh-huh," Josie said. "I'm with Ray on this one. That boy—whether he be white, black, 'Geechee or mixed can't be going around beating up girls. Nothing good gonna come of that, right, Laura Jean?" Josie said.

"That's right," Laura Jean said. "Only thing someone learns from beatings is how to take one and how to beat on someone else. That's how John Henry turned out like this in the first place."

"All right then," Ray said. "Will you be the one to talk to Reverend Jones, Josie? I'm not too at ease with a man of the cloth."

"Certainly, Mr. Ray, will do," Josie said.

Josie went home and sat on her porch. Mulatto—the very word is a lie. Blacks and whites are not two different species, not horses and donkeys, Josie thought. Her own complexion showed the lie; she was black and white and 'Geechee. She looked at the faces of people, up and down Highway 17, and she saw mixes of all kinds. She also knew people like John Henry couldn't be allowed to beat on anyone. Reverend Jones may be able to work a miracle here. Maybe. Maybe he can save him.

Josie heard her father come in the back door of her shotgun house. She heard him pad down the hallway in his roughened bare feet. "Hey there, Daddy. I'm out on the porch Come on out and sit with me and tell me what you know good."

"I've come to talk," Fuddah said. "I've come to talk about the girls and John Henry—everybody on the 'Geechee Road talking about that. And I've come to talk with you about Annie and Josie being friends."

"About Tessie and Annie being friends? About them becoming women? About me loving both of them?" Josie challenged.

"I come to talk afore things get worse." Fuddah said.

"Things ain't bad, Daddy. Things are good. I take up for both these young 'uns and I look out for Tessie with her folks," Josie said. She pushed against the ladder back of her rocker. "It's gonna change, Daddy. These girls are gonna work their own magic. Mark me. And Mr. Ray and me working something out with Reverend Jones and Miss Veda that's gonna help."

"I suppose it could be true, Josie, girl. The black mud mixes with the red in the 'Geechee. Different things mix. You're mixed. I'm mixed, too. But some white folks don't like it when black folks and white folks mix. All the full blood 'Geechee are dead. All what's left of them is mixed with the whites or the blacks." Fuddah said and then he stopped talking and cleared his throat.

"I know you worried about rape, about lynchings, about dead girls found on the 'Geechee Road. I promise I'll talk to the girls, Daddy, soon as I figure out what to say to them. I promise," Josie said. "Now go on back to your swamp and leave me be. Go on now."

Tessie and Annie arrived home from school to no supper and Josie still seated on the front porch.

"What's wrong, Mama?" Annie asked.

"Sit down, girls. We gotta to have 'The Talk'," Josie said as she used her fingers to make little quotation marks in the air.

The girls exchanged a worried look and rolled their eyes. Their health teacher, Miss Lamphere, had already had the big conversation with the eighth grade girls about sanitary napkins and periods and boys. In another room down the hall, the boys' physical education teacher was having a different conversation about hygiene, condoms and girls.

"We already know, Mama," Annie said.

"You already know what, Miss Annie?" Josie's voice cracked.

"About boys and periods and sanitary napkins," Tessie ventured.

"Uh-huh, I see," Josie almost smiled when she spoke. "That isn't what I am going to be talking about today, but I will check back with you on this to see just what you know." Josie slapped her knee. "I want to talk to you about being mixed and then mixing with someone else who is mixed."

"You mean you don't want me to date black boys and you don't want Annie to date white ones?" Tessie asked.

"No, that is not what I mean!" Josie said. "I want to talk to you about how this city—the rich parts, the poor parts, and the in between parts—don't take kindly to a white girl and a black girl being friends. You right, they aren't going to take kindly to you dating a black boy, Tessie, or you dating a white one, Annie, but before that even starts to rise above the horizon, lots of folks won't trust either of you because you trust each other."

The girls kept their eyes on the porch with its crooked boards and chipped paint. Then Tessie said, "You ain't telling us that we have to stop being friends, are you, Miss Josie? 'Cause I can't pay any mind to that!" Tessie said. "Don't be mad with me. I'm not wanting to be disrespectful, honest. It's just if I can't be with you and Annie, where will I be and who will I be? You are really my family. Daddy and Mama fight so much, and Mama…." Tessie's voice trailed off and she hung her head.

Annie hugged her friend.

"It's all right, Tessie, Mama doesn't mean we have to stop seeing each other, do you Mama?" Annie said. "We the mud puppies, Mama. Don't you see? We all mixed up with different blood and different colors. We are like those nasty ole fish and their muddied up colors," Annie said. She reached over and took hold of her mother's and Tessie's hands. "We will just become the mud sisters, Mama. Don't you worry about us."

"Your Granddaddy Fuddah was here," Josie said. A long silence followed.

"What'd he want?" Annie asked.

"He wants you to be safe. He wants you to stay alive, and he thinks for those two things to happen, you gotta stop spending time with Tessie," Josie said in a cool tone.

"I'm not going to go fishing with him anymore if he won't take Tessie, too, Mama. He can barely see as it is. Talk about safety and staying alive! We are taking our lives in our hands when we ride in that old truck of his to get bait, and his crazy voodoo magic makes me scared," Annie said.

"Last time I had to reach over and grab ahold of the steering wheel to protect the cars coming toward us, Miss Josie. Fuddah's truck was crossing over the line and people were honking their horns," Tessie said.

"I have Fuddah's words stuck in my head, all his talk about the 'Geechee River, the 'Geechee Indians, and his magic. I'm gonna just turn all that around into my own stories, Mama, and I am going to tell those stories to whoever I please," Annie said. She walked away from Tessie and her mother, picked up the old metal bucket and went to the corn barrel. She put three cups of corn in the bucket and began calling, "Here chick-chick-chick. Here chickee!"

Tessie sat with Josie on the porch.

"Tessie, I'll tell you a story about my parents, Fuddah and Dolly. You judge for yourself what parts of it are real and what parts are true," Josie said.

Tessie thought about what Josie said. How could some parts be real and other parts be true? Weren't those ideas the same thing?

Josie took a deep breath as if she was getting ready to dive under water, and then she began talking.

"Once upon a time there was a little girl named Annie, and she lived in a very old house in the 'Geechee Swamp. Her grandfather, Tom, worked in a house on Victory Drive. Great pillars held the roof up and underneath each window a lady pink azalea bloomed. The driveway was marked by a statue of a black man holding a lantern, always waiting for the master's carriage to return. Tom stood beside the statue and sometimes he looked as if he was a statue, too. White folks called him Black Tom, and his wife, Dolly, called him Han'some Man when she was happy with him. He was beautiful when he was all cleaned up. His hard-muscled arms gleamed in the sunlight and held her just like she wanted to be held. Dolly called him

No Good Tom when he was drunk because he had spent his wages on liquor instead of on her and their girl, Josie.

"I call him Mighty Tom in this once-upon-a-time story because of what he overcame having to wear so many masks. It takes a mighty man to be one person's slave and another person's lover.

"Finally Dolly left him because he spent all his time drinking and gambling. He lost his savings. He lost his wife. Then he began borrowing from Staggolee. He couldn't pay him back. So Staggolee cut him—first on his arms and then on his face. So Mighty Tom went back to work at the house on Victory Drive, but pretty soon the white man turned him out.

"'I can't keep you 'round here with a face looking like old meat,' the white man said.

"So Tom went to West Broad Street and lived in one of the empty buildings condemned by the City of Savannah.

"Annie was still a little girl, and she missed Tom. 'I'm going to go look for him,' she told her mother, Josie. She went to the gutted buildings on West Broad, and she found him. He looked bad, ancient. He smelled like dried urine and bad wine. For days she carried food to him and talked to him and listened to him talk.

"'My Dolly is as tall as a sky scraper. Her legs reach halfway to the stars. She one fine woman, my Dolly. She lifts more weight than a man. She's long, tall and strong. She can sing and chant and tell a fine story to help a weary man fall to sleep at night. She wears shiny silk scarves everywhere she goes. At the end of the day, she uses magic to get the fish smell off her hands. When I was with her, I believed for a while that life could be better, that life could be good.'

"'I know, Grampa. I love Dolly, too,' Annie said.

"'Of course you do, Annie. I know you are Josie's girl,' he said, but it was as if he had just remembered it.

"The more Tom heard himself talk about what used to be, who he had been and what his dreams were, the more it seemed as if Tom might find his way back to life.

"'Can you take me to Josie?' he asked.

"'Not right now, Grampa. First we have to clean you up,' Annie said.

"Annie sneaked a towel and water and food to Tom. She stole a razor and shaving cream for Tom. She remembered when Tom had fixed her broken dolls and had let her stay with him while he gardened or polished or scrubbed. For three days, Annie kept the secret of finding Tom from Josie, and she kept the secret that Dolly was dead from Tom.

"On the third day, Annie arrived with her mother. Her mother didn't believe Annie had found Tom, but when she saw him, she could not deny him. She brought him home and tended to him.

"'Don't call me father no more,' he said. 'Call me Fuddah. It's the name my mother gave me, and it's the name I intend to keep.'

"As soon as his strength returned, he moved to the swamp. He built a one-room cabin there at the other end of this property. He paid attention to the plants and the roots and the snakes. He watched the clouds, learned about tides, and lived on the fish he caught. He learned to respect his cousin snake, especially the snake, because he had seen it shed its old self and begin again, just like him."

Tears were running down Tessie's face. She knew Annie had found Fuddah, but she had never heard the story.

"You know what folks say about Fuddah now, don't you, Tessie?" Josie said.

"Some," Tessie spoke softly. "I know people say he can help a person change, that he knows how to get people to shed who they been so they can become someone better. I know the Sevillas at the docks think he is eternal."

Josie howled with laughter. "Listen here, Annie," she called. "The Sevillas think Fuddah is eternal."

"Tell me more, Tessie," Josie begged.

"They say that he brought himself back from the dead, just like Lazarus, just like serpents do, just like Jesus. They whisper averepiu anni d'un serpente when he passes and they cross to the other side of the street. They believe he has more years to live than the great sky serpent."

Josie's laughter sounded more like crying to Annie, so she put the bucket down and came back to the porch.

"Oh, Lord," Josie said, "the Italians think because he's black that he has black magic and because he has strength, that he has control of the evil eye. They can't tell the difference between Sicily and here!"

-8-
Patterns

"I'm going to join Annie in the garden, Miss Josie. Thank you for the story. I need some quiet now," Tessie said. She waited. She counted to 1000. Then she stood up. Finally Josie looked at her.

"It's all right, child. I understand. You run along now," Josie said.

Tessie escaped to the big garden where Annie had begun weeding. "I'm done with feeding the chickens, " Annie said.

Tessie knelt down beside Annie among the okra plants and lady peas, lima beans and watermelons, butter beans and collards. Neither of them wanted to think about Josie's story or talk about Fuddah. Annie had heard everything her mother told Tessie.

"I want everything to be quiet and easy. I want us to live on an island alone away from all these crazy adults," Annie said.

"I understand. I don't think *your* mama is crazy. I wish I lived here with you and Josie, all the time."

"Remember that at least at Little Bit you got a toilet and running water, Tessie," Annie drawled, her voice sticky as mimosa flowers. "And you got a roof that doesn't leak and the comfort of neighbors all around you. If you want to, you can get a game of Tin Can Annie started or find someone to shoot marbles with."

Tessie flinched when Annie mentioned marbles.

"Sorry, Tessie. I wasn't thinking about John Henry hurting you," Annie said.

"It's okay. I'll get past being scared before too long," Tessie said.

"All I got here is chores, and of course, Mama. She's almost as good as a whole neighborhood when she's home," Annie said. Both girls smiled.

"Miss Josie is the best mama in the whole world. I don't know how you ever got so lucky!" Tessie said. "I envy you, having a frame house instead of being cooped up in a trailer. I envy you for having Josie, but I love you for sharing her with me, Annie."

The girls watched a hummingbird feed on the flowers. They ducked when two painted buntings swooped into the garden.

"Let's go back and see if Mama needs us," Annie said. She helped pull Tessie up and they headed back to the house.

Josie was at the sink shelling lady peas when the girls entered. "Hey, girls. You hungry?"

"Yes, ma'am, we are," Annie said, and they ran to Josie and put their arms around her.

"Stop that now. It's too hot for hugging," Josie said, but she loved having the girls wrapped around her like apron strings.

After lunch, the girls walked back over to Little Bit to Tessie's trailer.

"Listen," Tessie said.

Annie stopped.

"That's Jeb Fisher peeing, and yep, he's flushing. Hear? And you hear that swearing? That's Otis James. He's probably cut himself shaving again. Sometimes his wife yells at him, 'Otis, you keep your hands to yourself. I already took my bath. You hear me, Otis James? I said, keep your hands to yourself. Leave me alone.' But I can tell he don't listen to her at all because the next thing you know, their trailer's rocking."

"Oh, hush, girl. That trailer's too big and heavy to rock!" Annie said.

"You know what I mean, Annie. You know," Tessie said.

Next the girls walked past Miss Bowser's trailer. Annie could see layers of fat hanging off Miss Bowser when she looked through her screen door. On a hot day like this one, Miss Bowser walked around naked. Tessie caught Annie looking, saw what she saw, and both girls began laughing so hard they fell on to the sandy ground.

Tessie stood up first, then she pulled Annie to her feet. Tessie was thinking about a space where Miss Bowser and Otis didn't exist. In that place, there was no trouble, no arguments, and all the flowers bloomed all day long. In that space, she lived with Annie as her sister and with Josie as her mother.

"Annie," Tessie said, "I tell you what. It's time we became sisters, real ones, blood sisters."

"Oh no. I done told you before, I am not doing that," Annie said. She pulled her shoulders up to her ears and cringed.

"Yes you are. I do all kind of fool things you ask me to do. This is the one thing I need you to do for me." Tessie dragged Annie into her parents' trailer and planted her feet firmly on the kitchen floor. She crossed her arms in resolution. Next she picked up a knife off the kitchen counter and sliced through the tip of her ring finger.

"Put out your hand. Do it! I said, reach out your hand. Now!" Tessie said.

Annie raised up her hand. Tessie cut into the tip of her ring finger. Soon as the blood broke through, she pressed her finger onto Annie's, merging their blood.

"If you get blood on my countertop or on your clothes, Elizabeth Harnish, I am going to whoop your ass," Laura Jean said from the sofa.

* * * * *

Laura Jean expected people to use both of her names, and if they didn't, she wouldn't answer them. People called her crazy. She'd stop in the middle of cutting up okra, sewing a button on a shirt, or singing a song, and stare into space without blinking.

Ray ignored the quiet spells until they began lasting for longer and longer periods of time. "I think your mama is leaving us again, Tessie," Ray said over breakfast. "I'm a thinking I need to pack her up in the truck and take her over to see Doc Maines. I want you to go to school, girl. I'll be home by supper time, either with your mama or without her."

"What do you mean, Daddy? With or without her? Where else would she be if she didn't come home with you?" Tessie asked. "You aren't going to let them take her away again, are you?"

"No, I'm a'gonna take her. You remember the last time, baby. She stayed at the hospital. If she needs help again, they'll send her up to the state hospital. Now, you go on to school," Ray said, patting her shoulder.

Tessie watched as her father got Laura Jean wrapped up in her bathrobe. She watched as he led her out the door, down the steps, and pushed her into the truck. Tessie waved goodbye, but neither of her parents waved back.

* * * * *

Ray drove the truck to Doc Maines' house where his office was, got Laura Jean out of the truck and into the office. Once there, he seated her on a hard pine bench.

"He can see you now, Mr. Harnish," the receptionist said.

Ray got Laura Jean up and herded her into Doc Maines' office.

Laura Jean did not look at anyone or speak.

"Well, Ray, what can I do you for?" Doc Maines asked.

"You can help my wife. She's setting right in front of you like a dummy in a dress shop, for God's sake! She's been sent up to Milledgeville a couple times and comes back kind of fixed. You've known us both since we were young 'uns. Can't you do something to bring her back to the way she was?" Ray asked.

"Is there anything wrong with her physically? I'm just an old country doctor, son. Not a head doctor. I can't heal a mind. Never have done, never will," Doc said and shook his head.

"So what am I supposed to do with her when she gets like this?" Ray asked. He gestured at the statue that Laura Jean had become.

"You take her home and wait for her to come back, wake up, get with it—whatever normal looks like, that's what you look for," Doc said. "The only other option is to send her back to Milledgeville, son, and I know you don't want to do that, now do you?"

"I might, Doc, 'cause if this is as good as it gets with Laura Jean and me, it ain't good enough," Ray spoke slowly, as if he was weighing each word.

Doc didn't like Ray's answer. "You said for better or for worse didn't you? Well then, you best take her home and help her when its worse. No real man wants to send his wife to that loony bin."

Ray nodded.

"If she stays like this for another week, well, we will have to think on this again," Doc said. "You ever seen someone after they have had 'lectric shock treatments?"

"'Course I have, Doc," Ray said, "you're looking at her."

"Oh, she's already had 'em? Well then, we're looking at what comes of 'em. You've seen lightning strike a tree, haven't you, boy? Well, there you go then. Splits the tree right down the middle and the tree ain't never the same again. We're looking at the picture!" Doc held his hands out like they were an ax, and made the motion like he was getting ready to chop down the tree.

Ray looked like Laura Jean in that moment—shocked and vacant. Doc rose from his chair to cue Ray that it was time for him to leave with Laura Jean. He put his hand on Ray's shoulder and led him to the door. He patted Laura Jean on the top of her head.

"No charge, Ray. She's gonna be all right. Give her some time," Doc said.

Ray walked Laura Jean back to the truck, got her in, got in on the other side, and went home where Tessie was waiting.

"I thought I told you to go to school, Tessie. You gone deaf?" Ray said.

"I couldn't go, Daddy. What is it? What's wrong with Mama?" Tessie asked. "Did she have a stroke?"

"Doc says she's gonna be all right. We just have to wait for her to come back to us. She's gone off somewhere in her mind."

"But Daddy…"

"Leave it be, Tessie, I'm tired and you need to go on to school. Last thing this family needs is the truant officer coming around," Ray said. He turned to shut the front door and realized he had left Laura Jean in the truck. "You best help me fetch her into the house. Wait. Better still, you come along with me. We'll get your mama in the middle and you set yourself on the outside of the seat so she can't go throwing herself out the door. I'll take you to school and then I'll bring her home and wait. That's all Doc Maines thinks I can do at a time like this."

It took Laura Jean sixteen hours to come back, and when she did, she didn't believe she had been anywhere. She was confused because she had missed some of her soap operas. "What do you mean I've been somewhere else?" She snapped at Tessie the next day.

"You went to see Doc Maines with Daddy. You were like a house with nobody home," Tessie said.

The next spell came on like a runaway train a few days later. Ray didn't take her back to Doc Maines. He waited three days, and then he decided he had only one choice.

"I'm taking her to Milledgeville, Tessie. This ain't natural. I want you to stay with Miss Jenny and Mr. Earle. I don't want you staying alone with Earle. If Jenny leaves the trailer, you go along with her. You understand?" Ray said.

"I don't want Mama to go away again, Daddy. Please don't take her. Or if you have to, take me too!" Tessie cried out.

"You want her to stay here and be like this forever?" Ray asked. He pointed to Laura Jean's blank stare.

"I'll come with y'all, Daddy. It'll take me just a minute to get ready. I want to come along." Tessie continued to plead.

"No, Tessie, this is something I got to do alone. You go on and get ready to go to Miss Jenny and Mr. Earle's," Ray said.

"Can I at least go to Annie's and Josie's?" Tessie asked.

"Not this time," Ray said. "I don't want to talk about it anymore. Do as you're told."

Tessie gave up, went to her room, packed her bag and went to the Conroys' on Lot 74.

-9-
Return

Ray drove Laura Jean to Milledgeville with the truck doors locked, and when he got there, filled out the forms to commit her.

Within a week's time they began shock treatments again. Laura Jean came out of the depression, but arrived in each present moment empty. She felt as if she was in a trance all the time. They noted entomophobia/severe, delusory parasistosis/acute on her chart. She was afraid of bugs and worms to the point of psychological paralysis. The entomophobia had kept her in her chair in the trailer and it was why she had the Orkin man come weekly instead of once every four months—she preferred the sticky poison to the possibility of bugs. Her other disease was more complicated.

One day the hospital phoned Ray and asked him to bring Tessie to visit so that the doctors could observe her with her daughter. Both of them wanted Laura Jean home, so they drove there together.

Laura Jean seemed calm and rational when they arrived.

"Why it's Tessie, my little girl. You sure are growing up."

Tessie smiled at her mother.

"Come sit with me," Laura Jean said.

As soon as Tessie was beside her mother, Laura Jean began picking at her clothes.

"Stop it, Mama! What's happened to my mother? You aren't my mother!" Tessie yelled. She turned her sapphire eyes on her father.

"Why it's Tessie, my little girl. You sure have grown," Laura Jean recited again. "I am your mother. Have you forgotten me already?"

Laura Jean held onto Tessie and picked invisible lint from her clothes. She tried to go through Tessie's hair, too.

"Doesn't anyone see them? Don't you see them? Can't you feel them, Tessie?" Laura Jean pleaded.

"What is she talking about, Daddy? What is she doing?" Tessie cried.

The doctor came into the room, touched Ray on the shoulder and said, "You can take your daughter now, Mr. Harnish."

After they left the room, the doctor met them in his office to explain. "She sees bugs everywhere. She believes they live in her hair, in her pores, under her nails, in the crevices of her body, between her teeth, under her tongue, in her nose, and along the borders of her eyes. We want to continue with the electric shock for one more month, and then we believe she will be able to return home. She will be subdued, but she ought to be able to do household chores and raise her daughter."

Tessie fainted when she heard this. She didn't wake up even when Ray carried her to the truck. He kept her wrapped in his jacket. The heater in the truck was broken and he was cold, too, but he put Tessie ahead of himself.

One month later, Ray went to Milledgeville to collect Laura Jean.

"Where you been all this time when I needed you, Ray?" Laura Jean confronted him.

And Ray wondered who Laura Jean was now. They stopped twice for coffee on the way back south and east. They didn't talk much, and when they talked it was about the weather.

Tessie was waiting for them on the stoop when they pulled in.

Laura Jean stepped out of the truck, and the first thing she did was hug Tessie. She sobbed and Tessie cried, too. When she was able to speak, Tessie said, "Mama, Mama, it's your Tessie-bird. I'm so glad you are home."

*****

Tessie had done her best to make a life without Laura Jean. She found the good in life where she could. She tried to practice magic, tried to turn broken glass, bits of bone, feathers and fossils back into life. If she could do that kind of magic, she believed she could turn her mother back into herself.

She used Ray's boat on weekends to run the river with Annie. On the water they scared themselves with stories about Snake-man who they only half believed in because neither one of them had ever seen him. They took a cooked chicken for Snake-man just in case he was real. Fuddah said Snake-man liked chicken and he liked to smoke, so they took ten of Ray's cigarettes and threw them in the river, too. After their day on the 'Geechee, Tessie and Annie camped out on the bank near Fuddah's shack under the willow trees. They watched the endless stars and the stars watched them. On the river, Annie and Tessie were at peace.

One night, shortly after Laura Jean's return to Savannah when the girls were camping out, Tessie said, "Tell me a story, Annie, please."

"All right." Annie loved to tell stories, and Tessie loved to hear them.

Annie began.

"The water below this river makes the dwelling place for Snake-man. He the cousin of the Mississippi and brother of the Ohio. When he was first born, he was human, just like me and you. Well, at least like me." Annie sucked air in through her teeth to emphasize her joke. "He ate his breakfast and his lunch, and he ate a great big dinner. One day this boy went on a journey with his best friend, but they forgot to pack their food to take along, and sure 'nuf, before too long those two boys were hongry." Annie reached for Tessie's hand. "We are best friends, too." She squeezed Tessie's hand and kept holding it.

"They rested in the tall grass, and when they began their walkin' again, the one boy almos' stepped on two big eggs. And he said, 'Why, look a here friend, two eggs for us to eat. Don't make a face. You'll eat 'em coz you as hongry as me.' So the boy who found the eggs built a fire and roasted the eggs. He popped the shell and began sucking on the egg, and then he offered it to his friend. But his friend refused.

Tessie stopped her. "You gonna use that accent the whole way through, Annie?"

"Yes, I am. If'n you interrupt again, I gonna stop altogether and you'll never know the truth about Snake-man."

"Well, go on, then, Annie."

"'No, no, no egg for me.' So the other boy ate the bof' of them down.

"Before too long the egg eater couldn't hardly walk no more, and he got sick to his stomach. 'My legs so heavy, I cain't walk.'

"When his friend went to him, he took off his shoes and his buckskin pants. And you know what he saw when he looked down? Scales 'stead of skin—glistenin', shell scales.

"His friend was 'fraid and don't you know you'd be, too. So he took him on his back and carried him to water. He got him a drink, and the two of them rested there, just like you and me are resting here under these stars." Annie patted Tessie's back.

"'I feel better, well enough to swim,' said the boy with the scales. And saying that, he took off the rest of his clothes and flung himself into the water where he swam and swam, and then he swam some mo'.

"'Get out now. Soon you be too tired to get out if you don't get out now,' his friend say.

"And his friend listened to him, like you never do to me, Tessie Harnish."

Tessie screwed up her face like she'd been eating lemons, and Annie laughed.

"He got to the water's edge, but when he went to step out, he found he had no feet. 'Fact, from the waist down he had a snake's body. So he used his arms to haul himself out of the water far enough to stay dry while he slept.

"'Take me home,' the boy who was turning into a snake cried out.

"'All right,' say his friend." Annie threw some more wood on the fire. Tessie curled tighter in her blanket. "The next day, the one boy walked while the other one crawled. By night time the boy who was becoming a snake wanted to get near the water. All night long he swam and splashed, and in the morning his friend didn't recognize him no mo'. When he looked into the water, he saw a large blue serpent who looked nawthing like a man, although he still had his friend's voice, 'cept he hissed mo' and mo' when he s'posed to be talkin'."

At this point, Tessie laughed. Annie flashed her an angry look. "It ain't funny. So hush your mouth and listen or I won't tell the rest." A breeze blew through the live oak trees. The sound of screeching marsh hens and thrumming bullfrogs filled the air.

"It ain't the story that's funny, it's you, Annie. The way you tell it so scary and true at the same time, makes me have to laugh," Tessie said.

Annie raised her eyebrows at Tessie, and then Annie went on ahead with the story. "Snake-man said, 'I've found my home here. I'm gonna turn this piece of water into a great river and name it after our people. Tell our people that they must feed the river—either meat or tobacco. And if they do, I will give them my blessing.'

"The other boy hugged his friend good-bye and went back to the 'Geechee camp to tell the story. And ever since then, people who have any sense have been feeding Snake-man, and you had better do it too, Tessie Harnish," Annie said. She stood up and took a bow.

"We do owe the river, Annie. I don't mind giving it gifts, I just don't understand why a river wants a dead chicken and some cigarettes," Tessie said.

Both girls broke out laughing and then got serious again. It was hard to say what the river heard and didn't hear, what the river felt and didn't feel. In a moment of solemnity, Tessie and Annie said in unison, "God bless us and the river."

Neither girl spoke for several minutes. Tessie assumed Annie was asleep, but Annie was thinking.

"I want a story from you, Tessie. Tell me one, please."

Tessie wasn't very good at making stories up and the only one her mother had told her often enough for her to remember was 'The Boy who Cried Wolf.' Tessie could almost feel her mother's long, polished nails on her back. Then she began her tale.

"Aw right, Annie, but I really only know one," Tessie said.

"On a hill, under the stars, a boy sat alone with his sheep and his staff. He felt lonely and scared, and the stars and the moon were too far away from him to bring him comfort. His father told him, 'Son, if a wolf comes by while you are watching these sheep, just give a holler, and I will come a running.'

"The boy asked, 'Pa, what will the wolf look like?' And the father said, 'You'll know it when you see it.'"

"What on earth does that mean, Tessie?" Annie asked.

"Just listen, Annie. It will all come through in the end," Tessie said.

"So the boy thought he saw something, and he thought it might be a wolf, so he called and called, 'Wolf, wolf, wolf!' And his father came running up the hill, but there wasn't a wolf, only the wind and the stars and the moon.

"The next time the boy was sitting alone on the hillside with his sheep, he heard a sound and he became scared. He tried not to call out, because the last time, when his father had come running and found no wolf, the boy got a talking to. The longer the boy sat and the louder the sound became, the more scared the boy got, until he cried out again, 'Wolf, wolf, wolf!'

"The father arrived. He didn't see a wolf, and he didn't hear a wolf. He heard the bullfrogs and the marsh hens and told the boy, 'You hearing bull frogs and marsh hens. Don't you know what a wolf sounds like?' and he knocked the boy down. 'Don't you call me 'less you sure it's a wolf.'

"The boy stoked up his courage, and turned to his father, 'How will I know if it is a wolf, if I don't know what they look like and I don't know what they sound like?'

"The father said, 'They look like a dog and they sound like a wild thing.'

"A couple more nights passed and the boy, scared and tired and lonely, began to cry like an angry wolf. He began to believe he had a tail, he felt his ears growing longer, and his canines became real canines. He didn't yell for his father. He turned on his sheep and ate them one by one.

"Several days later, when his father came to the hilltop looking for him, he found the wooly white fleece and the bones of his sheep, and no sign of his son. He searched the fields for his son. All he found were his hand bones and his feet bones. The rest of him had disappeared forever."

Annie sat straight up in her sleeping bag, staring at Tessie. "That's not how the story goes, Tessie."

"It's how it goes for me," Tessie said.

"That story is creepy, Tessie. You owe me a back scratch."

So Tessie took her hand and wrote her mother's name across Annie's back, scratching and tickling Annie to sleep. While Annie slept, Tessie cried over the boy who turned into a wolf, choking slightly on the feeling of leftover wool in her own throat.

*****

Laura Jean and Ray heard from Henry Simmons about every two years. He kept silence and freedom as his companions most of the time, but he still liked his old friends at Little Bit. He sent a recent photo of himself in his letter to Laura Jean and Ray. He smiled out of the black and white photo, showing his long crooked teeth.

"Weren't his eyes honey colored, Ray? Sort of like that amber bracelet you got me?" Laura Jean asked.

"Good God, Laura Jean, how would I remember the color of his eyes?" Ray lit another cigarette and went back to reading the almanac.

"You want me to read the letter out loud to you, Ray?" Laura Jean asked.

"OK, Laura Jean. I'm gonna put this book down and listen to you read Henry's letter and then I'm gonna pick this book back up. I best be left alone to read it after that," Ray said.

"Well, ain't you something, with your almanac and all!" Laura Jean said. Then she began to read.

Dear Laura Jean and Ray,

How are y'all doing? How's my Tessie? I'm doing good enough. In fact, only time I was doing better was when I got to see y'all regularly. I've found me a pretty woman in every town I've been to. Each one of them has helped me to keep my loneliness away. I never found one that I wanted to marry me until I met Emily. You remember my old high school sweetheart, Nancy, don't you? The one with the red hair? Well, Emily's nothing like her.

I've got to laugh at how young we used to be. Remember me getting her a pink carnation, a bottle of Jack Daniels and a pearl solitaire ring? Remember that? I told her, 'I got three things to make you mine.' Then I handed her the ring. Her mother told us to behave ourselves. She said something like 'Keep your clothes on Nancy.' But I managed to talk her clothes right off of her, just like you did Laura Jean, Ray. (I hope you're not getting mad, Laura Jean.)

I'm liking Columbia. I had been dating this woman named Jewel, that's how I met Emily. Jewel was another red head. I do have a weakness for a red-headed woman. Her skin was so white I could see her veins through it. She wore her hair in a French twist, all sprayed in place.

Jewel never expected much from me. Maybe because of that I treated her special. I took her out to a good steak house now and again, or sometimes I took her to a movie. I met her at the Neptune, the biggest diner I have ever seen. Every morning I'd go in there for biscuits and gravy. At night I'd go for the special, whatever it was. (I still don't cook worth a damn.)

Then a couple of weeks ago when I went to pick her up after her shift, she told me about her best friend, Emily. You know how some women will talk your ear off? Well, Jewel is one of them women. She told me how her friend had been double timed by a married man who left her pregnant and alone.

Laura Jean stopped reading to drink some of her Royal Crown cola and bourbon.

"God, how long is that letter, Laura Jean? I'm never going to get to read my almanac," Ray said.

"It's only a few pages, Ray. Don't you care about your old friend?" Laura Jean snapped.

"'Course I do, Laura Jean, just settle down. I'm just wondering how much more there is to hear," Ray said.

"Some," Laura Jean said. She wiped her mouth on the back of her hand and resumed.

> *Emily had her a baby boy. She gave him to her mother who lives about an hour from Columbia. She sends money up to them and goes to see them when she can. I think I'm going to ask her to marry me. I'll let you know how it turns out. That little boy's name is Fred, and I guess he ain't so little now—probably about 13 or 14. (Just about Tessie's age, ain't it?)*
>
> *I'm getting tired of traveling around from construction site to construction site, and I'm a'wondering if there's any openings at Union Bag. I put a stamped envelope in here for you to write back to me. Would you send along news of how that girl of yours is doing when you write? Also let me know if there's any work at the paper mill.*

Laura Jean stopped reading.
"You done?" Ray asked.
"Almost. He signed it, *Love, Henry.*"
"Give me that envelope. I'll write him about Tessie and I'll check at the mill," Ray said.

Laura Jean handed the envelope to Ray, and he went back to his almanac. And Ray, good to his word, wrote back to Henry to tell him about Tessie and about the opening for a floor manager at the mill in the pulp vat area.

-10-
Signs

Jenny and Earle, Ray and Laura Jean, and Henry parked their trailers on slabs with the belief that in no time they would have enough money saved to get a ranch house on the other side of town, away from the paper mill's smell and the strip of motels with bars. The parking lots on the 'Geechee Road were filled with local cars as well as with cars heading south and north, to and away from heat. Some cars had tiny rust spots and were from the north. The cars carried tall white people with flat A accents, and short square people who ate too much starch, and lonely people running from families, bleak skies and a deep coldness that twisted around their shoulders and moved right into their hearts.

In the early years, before Laura Jean went crazy, when there were still card games on Saturday nights with the Conroys and Henry, Ray and Henry were offered the same job to help build the interstate in Columbia. They could come with or without their families. Henry didn't have a family so he had taken the job immediately. Ray, who was eventually willing to take the risk of running pot on his boat, and who was drinking half a fifth of bourbon a day, declined the construction job. He wasn't willing to leave Savannah and all he knew. He gave Henry the line: "I can't be dragging Tessie and Laura Jean with me, Henry. It wouldn't be right." Henry didn't believe him.

Henry saw a chance to make a lot of money fast. "Well, you stay if you need to Ray, but I'm going. I want to find me a pretty woman to call my own, and I think I'm gonna find her in Columbia. One of those feelings I got, Ray, just one of those feelings. I'm gonna get me someone I can hold onto for more than just a little bit."

Ray snorted, "Holy Hell, Henry, you using the name of this trailer park in vain?"

Henry pretended he hadn't heard the question. He wanted to pull Laura Jean to him, but wouldn't let himself. She belonged to Ray.

Henry took his ethics with him when he moved north to Columbia. He moved his mobile home from site to site once he left Little Bit. He accepted silence and freedom as his companions. Henry chose to eat with black men on the job sites. His main job was to operate the steamroller to lay the macadam down so more and more cars could travel faster north to south and south to north.

He looked for and found one pretty woman per town to take his loneliness away. Whoever she was, he was kind to her. He took her to the local steak house and let her pick out any cut she wanted. And he paid for her utilities or bought her a stove or refrigerator to make up for her neighbor's comments about her letting a black man love on her.

Henry Simmons liked Columbia. For one thing, he was spending time with a woman named Jewel, a redhead with pale green eyes.

She wore her hair in a French twist. At night when he sat beside her watching TV, he noticed dead flies stuck in the sprayed veneer, so he didn't touch her head when they made love.

He liked the soft white skin behind her ears, and the way she darted her tongue in and out of his mouth. It reminded him of his high school sweetheart, Nancy, who had slipped her chewed teaberry gum into his mouth along with her tongue when they kissed behind the gym. He liked the way Jewel let things be between them, how she didn't pester him about marriage or money. Jewel preferred diners to steak houses, and would rather watch TV than go to the movies.

Henry had met Jewel at the Neptune, a diner in the old part of Columbia, near the warehouses. He went there for breakfast, lunch and supper. Each morning he got the same thing: two over easy with biscuits and sausage gravy. Lunch was almost as predictable—either greens, barbeque and cornbread or grilled cheese and French fries. He got to talk to Jewel anytime business was slow. He studied the menu, and then when she came to the table with his water, he raised his eyes to her, and said, "What are you recommending?"

Jewel, without fail, recommended the special. And Henry, with equal steadfastness, ate it. "No matter what the special is—it's always good, Jewel," Henry said.

"Well, surely you know why, Henry?" Jewel said.

He could see light in her eyes and one of her dimples was showing so he knew there was going to be a punch line. "Why?"

"Because it's the special!" Jewel laughed so hard, she had to sit down with Henry in the red leather booth.

"My name's Henry Simmons, and I think I've fallen in love with you," Henry said.

Jewel walked away laughing. Next time she came by his table again, he grabbed her apron and said, "Hey, sugar, wanna go out for something to eat?"

"You're kidding, aren't you? You just ordered a whole plate full of butter beans, rice and ham with red eye gravy," Jewel said.

"I did. But you haven't had anything. When do you get off?" Henry said.

"At ten."

"Well, I'll be back for you at ten then."

And then she said, "Well, awright."

"Nothing too serious, Jewel. But I won't cheat on you if you don't cheat on me, I promise that, and I'll take precautions," Henry promised.

"Aren't you jumping the gun a little, Mister?" Jewel cocked one eyebrow at him.

Henry hesitated then looked her square in the eye and said, "Am I?"

She didn't answer but walked back to the counter as if he hadn't spoken. Henry finished his dinner, skipped the pie, and went to the register to pay the bill. Jewel took his money. "No, you aren't jumping the gun, and thank you, and see you at ten." She winked then started polishing the counter.

He returned at ten. Jewel was waiting for him out on the sidewalk. "You know, Henry, I almost didn't accept your invitation because of what happened to my best friend, Emily." She waited for him to ask what, and when he didn't, she went on to explain anyway.

"His name was Buford, but everyone called him Buck. He courted my friend Emily with flowers and chocolates. He took her out to fancy restaurants, and I don't mean the Neptune."

"I know the Neptune ain't a fancy restaurant, Jewel," Henry said with a twinge of hurt in his voice.

"She got pregnant after she had been dating him for seven months. That's when he told Emily Hayes that he was married and had two kids at home. He had the balls to say, 'I never lied to you about my life. You just weren't asking the right questions.' Imagine doing that to someone, Henry! Can you?"

"No, I can't imagine doing that, Jewel," Henry said.

"He told her, 'I'll send you money to help pay the hospital bill, but after that you're on your own.' During the two remaining months Buck was in Columbia, he didn't come to see her. Shortly before he left, he had his buddy drop off five fresh one hundred dollar bills. Three days later the baby was born. Buck didn't leave any address with Emily, and he told the people at the field office if she came around, not to tell her anything about him—past, present, or future. I'm a lot smarter than Emily, Henry, and I can tell you aren't a liar."

Henry appreciated that Jewel had a good friend to talk about because it took some of the pressure off him to make conversation. When she tired of her own problems, she talked about Emily's. "Me and Emily have been friends since grade school, I know as much about her as I know about myself." And the more Jewel talked about Emily, the more curious Henry became.

-11-
Take Up Serpents

The Yankees who came through the 76 Truckstop when Tessie worked there often shared the same racist views as their southern cousins. They descended across the Mason-Dixon line, eating their way south on cornbread and fried chicken, on barbecue and collards, pecan pie and shortbread. They rose in the morning and continued south, refueling their cars on cheap gas and tolerating the sticky pile of grits that arrived nestled close to the two over-easies, slathered with grease. Yankees and Crackers alike pierced the egg yolks and went on eating—fork to plate, fork to mouth, no one interested in who among them lived above or below the line.

This long steady stream of Buicks and Chevies, Cadillacs and Ramblers, Studebakers and Fords demanded more and better roads, demanded higher speed limits and more frequent gas stations. Henry was one of the many men who built the roads that let everyone move faster. Tessie imagined her Uncle Henry rolling the macadam. When she thought of him, she felt pride and put her hand to her heart to cover the ache. She wanted Henry to return to Savannah and rescue her.

In his single bed, in his single wide, Henry frequently thought about Tessie and Laura Jean. In his dreams, Laura Jean was his wife and Tessie was his girl. One night, Henry had a dream instead about Jewel's friend, Emily. He hadn't met Emily, but he felt as if he had because she was all Jewel talked about. Henry was a speculative man. That was why he had to remind himself of the idea of enough, because he always wanted more. In the dream, he saw Emily from the back—her tawny hair wrapped into a bun. And he called to her, "Emily, Miss Emily, turn around so I can see your face. Please." She kept walking, and then the wind came up, and carried the smell of ivory soap and bacon grease to him. The smells took him back to his mother's kitchen. He remembered his mother standing at the stove frying up bacon while the dirty dishes sat in soapy water in the sink.

He knew a few things about Emily: she didn't wear makeup and she wore her tawny brown hair up off her neck in a bun. Jewel's voice stayed in Henry's mind, "Henry, honey, Emily, my friend, you know? She'd be real pretty if she'd take some time with herself and quit worrying so much about the next life. She's got enough blonde in her hair that with a good cut and a frosting, she could catch herself a man in no time."

Emily worked swing shifts in a factory sewing piece parts for men's workpants. Her speed guaranteed her better money than some of the other women. She worked Saturdays and evenings to get time and a half for her work. On the weeks when she took no time off, her arms vibrated long after she had stopped sewing from being at the machine for so long. At home, she mended and ironed to help pay her bills, to keep her hands busy, and to have money to send to her mother and her boy, Fred.

The day after the dream about Emily, Henry and Jewel were on their way to the Neptune. Jewel asked, "Can we spin by Emily's first? I need to drop off my mending." She left him in the green Chrysler with the engine running and told him, "Sugar, you wait right here now. I won't be but an itty bitty minute." After ten minutes, Henry shut off the engine and went up to the apartment. The front door was open, and he could hear crying. Henry hesitated at the door for a second, and then he walked in.

Jewel was cleaning up the floor, and Emily was sitting in an old rocking chair, dabbing at her puffy eyes, her left hand wrapped in a bloodstained dishrag. At first Henry thought Emily had cut herself sewing. He had a picture of her in his mind from Jewel's stories: He imagined Emily sitting with a threaded needle and a pair of shears—working, working, working. That night he watched as Jewel sponged up blood, walked to the sink, and rinsed out the pink liquid. Then she walked to the floor, soaked up more blood, walked to the sink, and rinsed. On her third trip he spoke, "Hey, Jewel, get a bucket with soapy water and bring it with you. Otherwise this is going to take all night." The puddle of blood made his stomach swim, made his face twitch, made him want to run. He got control of himself when he looked at Emily. Set against the nausea was the fragile hope that this clean-up might take all night, and he'd get to stay near her.

He looked closer at Emily's bandaged hand and saw the dish towel was a tourniquet around her wrist and, despite it, blood continued to flow through the cloth. "That must be one hell of a pair of shears you were working with, Miss Emily. My name's Henry Simmons. Pleased to know you." He reached with his right hand and then withdrew it. She couldn't let go of the tourniquet to shake hands, so instead he put his hand on her shoulder. When he touched her, he looked into her eyes and felt hot and cold at the same time. He stepped back to the doorway and stood, framed and silent, flat as a photo.

Jewel emptied the bucket of bloody water. "Henry, honey, you wait here with Em until I run down to get Doc Jones. I think he may have to put a stitch in that hand." She spoke from her station at the sink. She picked up her purse, and as she passed him in the doorway, she added in a whisper, "And don't you say a word to him about what she was thinking of doing with this, hear?" She pressed a folded straight edge into his hand.

Henry watched Emily on the couch. Her plain honest face bent like a sunflower heavy with seeds. She had bird wing eyebrows, flat cheekbones, and thin pink lips that didn't quite close over her teeth. He smelled ivory soap. Bacon grease hung in the air. Henry Simmons knew he was home.

Later in the car, Jewel said, "Emily meant to kill herself, but she cut her hand so bad trying to put a new blade in the straightedge that she never got to her wrists. I don't think God is what keeps her here with us; I think it's her hope she'll be able to get Fred back from her mother, and get to love him all over again." Then she said the strangest and most miraculous thing. "It happened, didn't it Henry? You fell for her—clean, honest, country. I knew you would. Ever since I met you I knew you and Emily should be together. I think that's why I talked to you about her so much and to her about you. But I also knew she wouldn't go out with another construction worker. She's the marrying kind, Henry, so be good to her."

"You giving me up so easy, Jewel? How come? And don't give me that innocent look—who'd you meet that looks better to you than me?" Henry felt stung.

"Go on now, Henry. You'll be over me in a heartbeat. Don't you act all hurt with me, man," Jewel said.

"I don't like women letting me go, Jewel. You ain't no exception. It just don't feel…"

"Don't feel what, Henry? Manly? Shoot. I'm a love 'em and leave 'em kind of girl. You got what you wanted from me, and now you found the real thing. I don't want anything that real. I like my life at the Neptune and enjoy a good time with a good-looking man. Don't get all tight with me about this! Now take me home. I'm not interested in another night with you. I got to get my rest so I look my best for the new Mr. Handsome tomorrow." Jewel laughed and patted his hand.

Henry pulled the car over. "Jewel, I'd like to take you to the Hotel Columbia for the best steak money can buy."

"No, Henry, really. What we had was fun, now let me go."

"Well, Jewel, maybe you are right. You take care now, girl," Henry said. He pulled back onto the road and drove her home.

Back at his trailer, Henry phoned his friend, Wally. "You best get yourself to the Neptune Diner soon, Wally, ol' boy. They have the best pies and the best piece of you know what else. Look for the redhead." If she can match make for me, I may as well return the favor, Henry thought.

Henry went back to Emily's every chance he could. If she asked him in for supper, he said yes. He sat silently through the long graces at Emily's. Henry courted her with bouquets of wildflowers just picked from the fields around the construction site, took his hat and boots off when he came into her apartment, and drove her to prayer meetings. He didn't go in with her. Instead, he waited as her chauffeur until she came out. He believed he owed her some kind of explanation, so on the car ride home, he said, "I ain't the church going kind, Emily." Emily looked out her window.

After Henry went home, she prayed, "God, give me the strength to be shed of this man, unless he is the one I am supposed to be with the rest of my life. Let him be a good man, if he's the one. Show me your will. Amen." Emily prayed over and over. When she rose from her prayers, her knees were numb.

*****

Emily had been a sister at The Agape Church of God with Signs Following for six years before she met Henry. After her first date with him, she cross-stitched Mark 12, verses 17 and 18 for a wall sampler:

> *And these signs shall follow them that believe: In my name shall they cast out devils: they shall speak with new tongues; They shall take up serpents; and if they drink any deadly thing, it shall not hurt them; they shall lay hands on the sick, and they shall recover.*

She chose black thread for the words. Next she took out her tablet and practiced drawing until she perfected a snake. She created a border out of snakes that appeared to be chasing each other around the sampler. The snakes were sewn with love and care. While she sewed, she recited: copperheads, canebreaks, cottonmouths. She decorated the snakes with their natural markings in subtle shades of beiges and browns, ochre and mahogany, rust and gold.

The night she finished the sampler was one of the nights that Henry drove her to The Agape Church. The bright yellow moon shone and the crickets hummed. Henry leaned against his Plymouth while he waited. He was mightily surprised when Jewel arrived with Wally. He hardly recognized Jewel with a pink rayon scarf over her flaming red hair, and he had never seen Wally cleaned up, but he knew it was them because they arrived on Wally's Harley with the yellow flames decorating the fenders. Henry called out to them, and they waved, but they didn't walk over to where he was. He watched as they entered the church. I should've known that Jewel went to the same church as Emily, Henry thought. But he was surprised.

Reverend Bobby was the last to arrive. Henry knew he had to be the minister because he carried a white leather bound Bible in one hand and a guitar case in the other. He was dressed completely in white, right down to his white patent leather shoes. Reverend Bobby entered the church. Henry imagined him unpacking his guitar. He heard him strum the chords to "Jesus is Gently Calling us Home." The women hummed the tune while the men sang the words in tenors and basses. Their voices floated out the window. The song ended, and Reverend Bobby began his talk. "Please join hands." Henry imagined all of them in a circle. "You know why we are here tonight, brothers and sisters? Yes, you do! We are here tonight to see who can handle evil and death and continue to live. Sister Hayes has brought us the words of God as given to us in the Book of Mark."

The train whistle screamed and mixed with the voices of people speaking in tongues. Henry imagined them as they handled snakes. Outside, young men leaned against the storefronts of warehouses, smoking cigarettes and telling the sad, funny stories of their lives. For them, the Pentecostals provided a sideshow, and so the young white men waited for the service to get going. Then they entered the church to watch the young women handle four and five foot rattlers.

* * * * *

Emily loved the snakes in the box—the subtle shifting of their bodies. The snakes squirmed all together in the box wanting out into air and space, wanting to go back to the swamp, to the woods, and to the mountains. The snakes wanted life, the way God expected desire to work before the Fall, each of his creatures wanting and receiving what was naturally its own.

Emily loved the snakes in her arms, curling and twining, hissing and undulating, moving in ways she would not let herself move. Before Reverend Bobby opened the lid the congregation became quiet. He picked up, folded, and laid the sampler on his guitar case. Emily removed all her hairpins, shaking her knee-length hair around her amid whispers about Delilah.

"Brothers and sisters—oh my sisters!" Reverend Bobby began in a high-pitched mountain tenor. "Inside this box are the stirrings of our lower selves—death and life are here with us tonight inside this box. 'Are ye able, said the Master, to be crucified with me?' And I ask you the same question, brothers and sisters—Are ye able to take up serpents—as surely a form of death as Our Lord's cross? Can you hold these vipers that worked with our first sister to send us forth from Paradise, can you hold them in your hands and live? Are you pure in spirit? Will you survive?" He paused to wipe his brow.

"Sister Hayes, are you ready to meet your maker if necessary to understand your Lord? Do you have the faith? If you really hold The Light, The Divine Light of Love and Suffering, you can hold these snakes and live. Glory will shine all around you!" Reverend Bobby yelled.

At this point, Reverend Bobby lifted the lid and handed Emily two canebrake rattlers. Entwined and rather sleepy, they cascaded in her arms. She hummed a sad song, a melody no one knew, and cradled the snakes as if they were newborns. The men and women around her rocked and swayed, a few of them screeched while the white men from the street chanted, "Praise the Lord! Praise the Lord."

Emily moaned and whimpered.

"What is it, Sister Hayes? Tell us what you know," Reverend Bobby coached.

Emily dropped the snakes and pulled back her hair on the right side of her neck to reveal the fang marks. A smile lingered on her face after she fainted. People looked to Reverend Bobby for what to do next. "On your knees, brothers and sisters. Let us keep watch over Sister Hayes." He lifted the sampler off his guitar case and draped it over the bite on Emily's neck.

Next, one of the older women in the congregation called out, "Numbers 21, 6-9." The only sound that followed was the turning of very thin paper. The woman began reading, "And the Lord sent fiery serpents among the people, and they bit the people; and much of Israel died. Therefore the people came to Moses and said, we have sinned, for we have spoken against the Lord…"

A man interrupted, "I have sinned, sister. I have lain with women who weren't my wife. Save Sister Hayes, Jesus, don't let her die for my sins." The man speaking prostrated himself by the snake box. Agah mat mah haynah—oh oh jat mide ooo.

"—and against thee, pray unto the Lord, that he take away the serpents from us."

"Not our serpents, Jesus. Take me! Or take Sister Hayes, but don't take away the chance to prove our faith!"

The older woman read tenaciously as if speaking the words let her hold Emily in this world, "And Moses prayed for the people. And the Lord said unto Moses, make thee a fiery serpent, and set it upon a pole; and it shall come to pass, that everyone that is bitten, when he looketh upon it, shall live."

Another member of the congregation passed his cane to Reverend Bobby. "I know she can't see my cane, Reverend, but pretend it is a pole, pretend we got us a fiery serpent, and touch this cane to the bite. Praise the Lord!"

"And Moses made a serpent of brass, and put it upon a pole; and it came to pass, that if a serpent had bitten any man, when he held the serpent of brass, he lived."

People continued praying, and around midnight Sister Hayes opened her eyes and spoke, "What happened?" Some members of the congregation believed that the sampler had cured Emily Hayes; others swore that the reading from Numbers and the man's confession had gained the necessary intercession; while still a few others thought the wooden cane had held holy powers. Regardless, Sister Hayes lived. By the time Emily left the church, Henry was asleep in the back of his car.

Reverend Bobby had the sampler framed—a banner of her victory, a celebration of her faith. He delivered it to Emily who hung it above her single bed.

* * * * *

Certain sections in the city of Columbia knew about the snakebite and salvation of Emily Hayes, except they didn't know her name.

They knew about the full grown woman who shook down her long hair, was bitten by one of two wrestling rattlers, and then saved by her own needlepoint rendition of the guiding Pentecostal scripture—Mark 16, verses 17 and 18. The Columbia Star Gazette tried to track down the woman's name, but no one volunteered anything. People's mouths were as tight as a sealed box of snakes.

Henry was suspicious of snakes and his suspicion extended to those who handled them. So the night that Henry waited outside The Agape Church confirmed Henry's fear that Emily was a snake handler. The service went on for hours and hours. When Emily came out to the car, she had to awaken him.

He turned to her and said, "Were you handling snakes, Emily?" Instead of answering him, she let him kiss her, once, soft, on the lips. She returned a dry, fragile kiss. He held her head, cupping it with his hands as if she were a piece of sculpture. Even as his lips met hers, his hand felt the raised mark, as if two holes had been punched into her neck.

He didn't speak until he drove up in front of her place. "Can I come in? I got something I have to ask you."

"You can come in, Henry."

He barely got in the door before he was down on one knee, "Miss Emily, will you marry me?"

"Yes, I will Henry, but you have to love the Lord as well as me and walk on His path. Can you do it?" Henry nodded. Emily reached for his head and pulled it to her flat stomach, the way the preacher did before he baptized a soul.

Henry rested there a while, then he spoke; he had to know. His insides were a trapped animal, gnawing on its flesh to break free. "Emily, what was all that—the first night I came here with Jewel?"

Emily stiffened. The thick scent of mimosa and magnolia filled the room. "I'll tell you once about this, Henry, and then I don't ever want to hear about it again. That was the last night in my life I thought I had sinned by bringing a baby into this world out of wedlock. It was the first time I believed what I knew all the women at my old church said about me. I believed I was a fallen woman. And I didn't want to live anymore. I gave up my boy. When Jewel came in and saved me, I made a deal with God. I said, 'God, you prove to me you are a forgiving God. You let me hold them snakes and if I live, I'll know you have forgiven me.'

"I am forgiven; that is clear. Now I'm going up to my mother's and bringing my boy back." Emily pressed Henry's hand so hard it hurt.

Henry tried to put behind him the image of Emily Hayes in her second floor apartment with the dishrag tourniquet. He tried not to dwell on the ritual of Jewel's clean up—bucket after bucket of pink water from Emily's spilled blood. He didn't need to ask her about the mark on her neck. Now he knew. He stayed with Emily that night—slept on her couch. "Are we gonna get married at The Agape?" Henry asked.

"My church seldom marries people because it has more important things to do," Emily explained, then paused. "We aren't getting married there, so where would you like to have the ceremony, Henry?"

Henry's surprise silenced him. His palms got sweaty and then cold. Why couldn't they get married at her church? "I don't understand, Emily, I thought that church was something special to you?"

"It is, but not for marrying." She paused. "We could get married at the Justice of the Peace—keep it real simple. After all, the marriage is between our hearts and in the eyes of God—getting a license is of this world. I've fished for years without a license. I am sure God and the fish understand."

Henry laughed. "All right, Emily. Who's gonna stand up for you?"

"Jewel is, who else?"

"Well, then, I'll have Wally stand up for me," Henry said.

Seven days before the wedding, during a lunch break, Henry overheard four of the young men talking about a snake handling service they'd seen at one of the local Pentecostal churches. "Oh Lordy, you should of saw them young women writhin' and wigglin' with those critters. They go in there all proper—you know, wearing those pale pink or blue or green housedresses like they sell down to Newberry's. They got their hair rolled up tight in a bun, and they won't, not for a minute, look into our eyes. Pure as cotton. But let 'em git in there with Reverend Bobby and 'fore you know it, they in rapture."

"I hear ya, Tommy. I seen it myself up in North Carolina. Do you think they go all wild, pantin' and gaspin', when you get 'em in bed?"

Henry seldom spoke to the young white bucks, but the story and Reverend Bobby's name made him move closer and join in.

"You boys talkin' about snake handling?" Henry asked.

"Yes, sir, down to The Agape."

"You mean the small white framed building?" Henry prodded.

"Hey, Mister—no other church around here has a name anything like The Agape Church of God With Signs Following—only is one." The young man laughed and his friends brayed with him.

Henry nodded. He loved Emily. Now he knew for certain how she had gotten the scar on her heart, the scar on her hand, and the new scar on her neck.

Henry and Emily's wedding took place at the Justice of the Peace. On their wedding night, Henry lit a candle. After that he went to the pantry to get a broom. He swept down the cobwebs and collected them. "We gonna use them to repair all the hurt," he told her.

Henry cleaned out the corners where the wall met the ceiling, gathered the cobwebs from the bottom of the broom and put them in a small pile on his pillow. Emily sat at the vanity brushing out her hair and watching Henry's reflection as he worked. She tried to gauge when it was time to rise from her seat and stand at the foot of the bed. She waited until Henry went to the fourth corner of the room and then she stood. He met her at the bed and knelt before her. He picked up the spider webs from his pillow. He took her right hand and together they rubbed the webs onto her neck and her wrist. Then Henry held them over her heart.

"What about you, Henry? Where are you hurt?"

He slowly lifted his hands to his head. He rubbed webs on his forehead and his throat and, finally, his heart.

She kissed him on each eye. "Blow out the candle, Henry," she whispered. He spread the wedding ring quilt she had made for them on the floor. They made love in silence. Afterward, Emily spooned with him. "Thank you for the healing," she whispered.

"It was my pleasure, Emily," Henry said. There was a long pause while Henry tried to think of how to say what he needed to say.

"I know you are thinking about something, Henry Simmons, may as well just say it to me," Emily said in a teasing voice.

"All right, Emily, I don't want you getting mad, though?" Then before he lost his courage, Henry said, "You know, I heard about the snake handling down at The Agape. Now I understand that sampler better," and he pointed to where it hung on the wall.

"The ones in my mother's house read, 'The way to a friend's house is never long,' and 'Home is where the heart is.' I want your sampler to say something like that. I don't want you to be a handler ever again," Henry said. He touched the scar on her neck.

"I don't need to handle them, ever again, Henry. God gave me my sign," Emily said.

Emily kissed him hard. Henry felt a chill as if he were a snake that had been lying on the cold ground, and then his heart broke into pieces.

"Let's do it again, Henry. Come back inside of me, " Emily pleaded. Then Emily took her hands and rubbed him. He felt as if she were touching him everywhere at once. She kept her lips on his lips pressing down on his mouth until neither one of them could breathe. Finally, she wrapped her legs around him and rocked until he entered her.

-12-
Proximity

Laura Jean spent her days sitting on the couch in her trailer. Eternity is never far away, she would think. Then a few minutes later, her next thought might be: even with eternity near, I still best make a list for the grocery store. There's no time like the present to write out the lists of all the things I need for Ray to pick up. Let's see: pretzels, coffee, orange juice, spearmint gum, Pall Malls, a picture of Jesus. Then she crossed off the last one, went over and over it with her pen until she tore right through the paper. No grocery store was going to have a picture of Jesus. She had been drawn to Jesus at the state hospital in Milledgeville. He had walked on electric currents to save her. He had walked beside her through the valley of death. The shock treatments had taught her about suffering. Being away from Tessie had put a hole where her mind had once been. Jesus understood suffering, too—with those big nails in his hands and feet and a sword plunged into his side. Laura Jean would sit with the list in her hand and wait for Ray. She felt Jesus sitting beside her.

Ray got home from the paper mill at 3:30 p.m. Laura Jean handed him the list.

"Please pick up these things for us, Ray," Laura Jean said. "I don't ever want to go back to Milledgeville or anywhere like that, Ray, hear? I hated that place."

Ray looked closely at Laura Jean. Her eyes were bright and clear, she was eating meals at regular times and sleeping from 11 to 7, but she wasn't the same. My world won't ever get back in balance at Lot 71, Ray thought.

"Well, Laura Jean, you won't have to go back, Doc Maines says, as long as you take your pills, eat three squares, and keep moving and talking. It's when you get so quiet you don't move or you start yelling and screaming and can't stop that we have to take you back. Please don't get so scared that you crawl up in to yourself and then the only way to bring you back is to plug you in like you a lamp."

"I'm fine," Laura Jean shot back at Ray. Being with Tessie is the best and the hardest of all, she thought.

Ray took the list from her.

"Tessie'll be home soon, and I will be back before you know it," Ray said. He waved to her and was gone.

Ray drove out of the trailer park just as Tessie arrived home. She stacked her books onto the kitchen counter and sat down on a stool.

"Hi, Mama," Tessie said, feeling shy around her.

"I feel ashamed, baby," Laura Jean said. "I feel like I just can't be trusted to take care of you. Who knows how long I will be myself? Who knows what will cause me to go off in my head again? You know what I'm saying, Tessie?"

Tessie knew what she was saying and she didn't want to hear it. She moved away from the counter and sat in front of the TV. She found a NASCAR race and turned the sound way up. Next she opened a book from the bookmobile. Every once in a while, she looked up at the screen. She pretended Laura Jean was gone. She didn't want to talk about Milledgeville or the sounds and silences in her mother's head. Laura Jean continued to talk, but Tessie had blocked her out with the TV and her pounding heart.

When Ray returned he could hear Laura Jean talking to Tessie.

"Turn that damn TV off and put the book down, Tessie. Your mama is talking to you," Ray said.

"Hi, Daddy." She did as she was told.

"How was it for you staying at the Conroys'?" Laura Jean asked. "I need to know how it was for you there while I was away."

"I don't want to talk about it, Mama, please," Tessie said.

"I need to know if you were all right while I was away, Tessie. Please answer me," Laura Jean said. She held out her hand to Tessie. "Come perch on my lap, sweet bird."

Tessie crossed over to the kitchen counter and grabbed her mother's hand.

"The truth, Mama?" Tessie snarled. "Well, Miss Jenny and Mr. Earle were kind to me, but the kids at school were awful. They laughed when I walked down the hall. They called me Laura Jean's loopy girl. The onliest one who was nice to me was Annie Osaha; she's family to me. Josie's my real mom—not you. There's your truth!

"And the rest of the truth? I missed you so much I forgot how to think, I forgot how to eat, and I forgot how to laugh. I thought you were never coming back. Now that you are back, I am not sure who you are or who I am either. Fact is, I'm not sure I want you here. Your return was the very thing I've been praying for. I guess I best pay heed to the reverend—he says careful what you pray for, you just might get it." Hot stinging tears ran down Tessie's and her mother's faces. I'm not sorry for making her feel bad, Tessie thought as she looked at her mother—white faced and trembling.

Laura Jean reached for her.

"Thank you for telling me the truth, baby," Laura Jean hugged Tessie close. Tessie pulled away.

"I am going outside now. I hope you aren't here when I get back. Because you know, Mama? That's the worst of it. I am never sure if you will be here when I come home. It's just easier having you gone!" Tessie watched her mother closely. "I'd rather just not have to think about you at all," Tessie spat the words at her mother. "Between the medicine and the electricity, you have shorted out, like a loose wire!"

Ray waited until he heard the trailer door slam behind Tessie. He nuzzled up to Laura Jean and kissed her behind her ear. "Come on and give me a little sugar," Ray said.

Laura Jean ignored him. The shock treatments had killed her desire, but touching and sex may as well have been one of the commandments for Ray. "Laura Jean, I love you more than I love my truck." His voice was soft and playful. "Laura Jean?"

Laura Jean stood up and took off her clothes. She walked down the hallway to their room as if in a trance.

Ray hurriedly followed her to their bedroom, taking his clothes off along the way.

He arrived in the room naked. Laura Jean stared at him. He jumped on the bed beside her, kissing and petting her.

Laura Jean croaked, barked, and tweeted in response.

"Please stop making those weird noises," Ray said.

"I can't help it. I hear everything so much better than I used to and it seems to me as if the critters are talking to me," Laura Jean said.

"Never mind, Laura Jean, never mind," Ray said. He rose from the bed, his own kind of Lazarus, put on his clothes and went out to the bars.

* * * * *

The next morning, Laura Jean awoke to find Ray sitting on the bed staring at her.

"You still ain't right, Laura Jean. I'm taking you back—no, not to Doc Maines, back to Milledgeville," Ray said.

Tessie heard her mother's feet thudding down the hallway. She got up and walked in on her father who was packing a suitcase. "What are you doing? Where is she? If you are doing what I think you're doing, if you are taking her back, I'm going with you," Tessie said.

"Something wrong with staying at the Conroys'?" Ray sniped. "Earle doing anything funny?"

"No, he's not, but I can't have Mama ride back there without me. I'm going with you. That's that," Tessie said.

Laura Jean fled to Jenny and Earle's place where she clawed her way under the trailer.

Ray and Tessie put the suitcase in the bed of the truck and walked around Little Bit until they found Laura Jean in her hiding place. They pulled a limp and quiet Laura Jean out from under the trailer, then half carried her back to the truck and loaded her in.

Ray got in and pushed the button on his eight-track. Merle Haggard's voice began crooning, *If I'd left it up to you, it'd all be over now. It'd all be over now, except the crying. I'd be used to spending all my time alone.* Ray joined in.

Laura Jean, wedged between Ray and Tessie in the cab, couldn't open the truck door and throw herself out. She had tried that once before. So she sat between them and moaned. The more she moaned the louder Ray sang. Ray kept rewinding the tape and singing until Tessie couldn't stand it anymore.

"Stop, Daddy! Stop!" Tessie yelled.

He downshifted, pulled over and said, "Hurry up." But she had not meant 'Stop the truck I have to pee;' she had meant 'Stop this craziness, stop your loudness, stop my mama from having to go away again' but it was too hard to explain. She ran behind a bush where she cried, then dried her eyes on a leaf.

She got back into the truck and stared straight out the windshield. "If you only loved Mama enough, if I had a baby brother or sister—then everything would be all right."

"That ain't so, Tessie. It ain't any single thing," Ray said

She didn't answer. Will anything make a difference? Maybe Mama is just broken, and isn't it true that daughters turn out like their mothers? If my mother is broken, how long will it be before I'm broken, too?

Ray began singing again. *It'd all be over now, except the crying. I'd be used to spending all my nights alone.*

"Will you please play some other song, Daddy? Don't we have enough sadness without having to listen to Merle sing this same old sad song a hundred times? Jesus, Daddy!" Tessie said.

"Jesus?" asked Laura Jean, "Jesus, where are you?"

Ray reached behind Laura Jean and patted Tessie on the head. "Sure enough, honey." He took out the Haggard tape and punched in a Tanya Tucker. Tessie was glad there wasn't a fight about it. She was never sure what her father would do, so when he did what she asked she thanked her lucky stars. He was as unpredictable in some ways as Laura Jean.

Ninety minutes later, Ray pulled the truck into the parking lot at Milledgeville—red brick hospital, barred windows, some plants outside in the front, an ambulance at the emergency room doors. The orderly had Tessie wait with him while Ray checked Laura Jean in. Tessie thought it was going to take a while, but it didn't. Ray was back in less than 30 minutes. "I phoned ahead, Tessie. I didn't want us to have to wait. She has been here before, so most of the paperwork just has to be initialed again. Let's go."

Tessie rolled the window down and imagined herself dropping little cubes of bread all the long way home so she could find the way back to her Mama again.

*****

Ray didn't bring women home from the bars. That wasn't how he replaced Laura Jean. He slept instead with a bottle of Jim Beam. He sucked harder on his Luckies. The meanness went out of his drunk. He greeted himself in the mirror: red-eyed, yellow skinned; a shrunken man. He missed the old Laura Jean before she got crazy and the old Ray before he broke apart. Tired, sore, needy and hung over—how he began his day.

Tessie heard him coo himself to sleep—part owl and part turtledove. One night he woke her with his sobbing, and she went to his room.

"What is it, Daddy? What's happened?" He turned over and looked at her with a shiny scared look.

"You know what's happened, Tessie. I've lost everything," Ray said.

"You haven't lost everything, Daddy. You still got me," Tessie answered.

Tessie waited for a response, and when none came, she left his room.

The next day, Tessie went to Jenny Conroy's salmon and white trailer before Ray got up. She knocked on the screen door until Jenny came to let her in.

"Hi, Tessie. Gracious, girl, you look so bad even a good haircut can't save you today!" Jenny laughed at her own joke. As owner and operator of The Bee Hive, part of her public relations approach was to bring hair into every conversation.

"Hi, Miss Jenny. I have a favor to ask. I need you to drive me up to Milledgeville to see Mama. I know you can't probably do it today with the shop and all, but I need to go soon. Please, Miss Jenny. I got to talk to Mama and get her to come home." Tessie's words came out of her mouth like the wind.

Jenny looked Tessie up and down.

"Well, let me see, Tessie. I don't know if I can. I have a very busy day today, but I might could take you today, if it's urgent. Just let me see," Jenny offered. "Uh-huh, looks pretty urgent."

Jenny took out her appointment book. She phoned her three regulars. "I got a family emergency, Miss Elma. Can you come in tomorrow?" "Hello, Evangeline. It's Jenny. Can you wait a day for me to do up that beehive? Okay. Thank you so much, sugar." "Hello, Delores? Yes, Jenny here. It's Tessie—she needs to go up to Milledgeville, and it looks as if I might be the last train running. I knew you'd understand. Thanks so much, darlin'."

"Tessie?" Jenny talked as she walked down the hallway. "All clear. Now you go on home and freshen up a bit. You don't want your mama seeing you looking so sad. Wear something red. Your mama loves you in red. I will be ready to go in about 15 minutes."

Tessie went home, brushed out her raven hair, put on her best faded jeans and her red dotted Swiss blouse, and walked back to Jenny's.

Once on their way, Jenny felt the best thing to do was to keep Tessie talking. "Ask me anything, Tessie! Anything, and I will fill you in."

Here we go, Tessie thought. She loved these escapades with Jenny, because when Jenny said "anything" that's what she meant.

"How can you do the same person's hair the same way for twenty years, Miss Jenny? You have so much imagination, I can't see how you can do that," Tessie said.

"I just think of those ladies as my safe girls. They don't take risks, never have, never will. Evangeline wants clean and neat with her page-boy, and that's what I give her. I can't persuade her that she looks like a mannequin at Belks'. And I worry with my own hair, because, shoot, girl, you know I am a risk taker. I like to put these wide platinum streaks in my hair and throw it into a French twist. You know my philosophy: Do what people want if they know what that is, and if not, do what they need!" Jenny tapped the steering wheel while she talked.

Tessie studied Jenny Conroy—her multi-colored hair and her ice blue eyes got people turning their heads. Jenny looked like she had the sun for her heart; that's how much light shone forth from her.

"What's something else you want to know, Tessie? I think you are holding back, girl, and you'll never learn much in life, Tessie, if you don't have the courage to ask," Jenny said.

"When did you meet Emily Simmons, Miss Jenny? She seems so different from you, really from all of us," Tessie began.

"Oh, Emily, she's an odd one, that's for sure. I met her when she moved back with Henry. She needed a bang trim, and because she sees vanity as a sin, she wouldn't go to a beauty parlor, but she dug around till she found out I owned The Bee Hive and then she came knocking at my trailer door to see if I'd trim her bangs at my house. We did that for about a year, and then one day she showed up at my door crying. Emily is a Pentecostal, but I think you know that. Her boy, Fred, isn't Henry's son but I s'pose you know that, too. She had that baby on her own after she gave her heart to a two-timing son of a bitch. When she found out she was pregnant, you know what he done? He left money at the construction site with the overseer and went home to his wife and three kids. That's what turned Emily Simmons to Jesus.

"She was crying because that no good fool was trying to take the boy from her even though he never had visited or helped other than that first little bit of money. All of a sudden that man got a conscience!"

Tessie could not think of what to say. For a while they rode along in the truck, listening to the radio. Tessie reached up and turned the radio down. "What else?" Tessie asked. "What turned Emily to Henry?"

"He helped her get her boy back. You may as well just turn the radio off if it is going to be that low," Jenny said.

"What do you know about my mama and daddy?" Tessie whispered.

"You know we went to school together since we were six?"

"Yes, ma'am," Tessie said.

"And you know we both got married because we had to. Your mama was luckier than me, Tessie. Her baby lived and mine didn't," Jenny said.

Tessie did know that part, although, increasingly, she wasn't sure what was lucky and what was not.

"We've been living in this trailer park for almost twelve years, now. Your mama has always had a tender heart, Tessie. And she and your daddy love each other—that's for sure—but sometimes they burn each other up or freeze each other out. And when you are older, I promise to tell you some other things about them, but not today."

Jenny reached over and turned up the radio.

Tessie fell asleep in the car and dreamed. There had been confusion at the hospital. Laura Jean's baby had died, not Jenny's. But because Jenny was the nicest woman in the world, she had given her baby to Laura Jean. Tessie felt relief—she wouldn't go crazy like Laura Jean. How could she when Jenny was her real mother? In the dream, she helped Jenny Conroy weed her lily beds. She went with Jenny to The Bee Hive where she looked through fashion magazines searching for new hair-dos for Jenny's clients. She woke up, saliva on her chin. If I had been Jenny and Earle's baby, I would never be in this truck going to Milledgeville. She paused. Earle. She got the chills. No, he's worse than Ray.

"You know what, Jenny?"

"What, Tessie?"

"I just want to live with Annie and Josie."

-13-
Visitations

Miss Jenny's car rattled and clanked from too many trips on the gravel roads with their deep potholes. Tessie rubbed her eyes and looked. Still not to Milledgeville.

"How old are you, Tessie?" Jenny asked.

"Almost 13," Tessie said. "Why, Miss Jenny?"

"Well, I've been remembering being 13. Your mama and I used to spend as much time as we could outside, watching the birds and gathering fallen feathers. Your mama and me used to talk about birds—all kinds of birds: caged ones and free ones, big ones and small ones, live ones and dead ones," Jenny said.

"Miss Jenny?" Tessie prodded.

"Hold on, girl, I am trying to think on how to say this to you," Jenny began whistling Old Susannah. "I think it's like this, Tessie. Your mama's probably feeling like a caged bird, right now, baby. You gonna need to approach her slowly when we get there."

"All right, Miss Jenny. I will," Tessie said. What on earth does that mean? Tessie wondered. Walk slower? What?

Jenny stopped talking and Tessie fell asleep. The car went over tar strips. Ka-thunk, ka-thunk, ka-thunk. Tessie dreamed of a bird flying into the windshield. Ka-thunk, ka-thunk, ka-thunk. She heard fluttering bird wings. She woke. Miss Jenny rolled down the window and threw out her cigarette butt.

"We're almost there, Tessie," Jenny said. "Are you all right?" Tessie nodded.

Jenny pulled into the lot at Milledgeville, put the car into park, and then reached across the front seat, resting her hand on Tessie's arm. "Remember, honey, approach your mama slowly." Jenny's tone was serious and confidential. Before she turned Tessie's arm loose, she winked at her, and said, "Let's go see your mama."

At the front desk, Jenny charmed the clerk to let them in when it wasn't visiting hours. An orderly led them to a common room while another orderly collected Laura Jean and brought her to meet them. Laura Jean cried out, "Why it's Tessie, my little girl—how you've grown. Let me take a look!" Laura Jean took a hold of Tessie with both hands, and then she repeated, "Why it's Tessie, my little girl—how you've grown. Let me take a look!"

Tessie could see through her mother, as if she were glass. Her mother held on to the same few words and said them over and over again. Laura Jean picked off little pieces of lint from Tessie's clothes and dropped them on the floor.

"You have 30 minutes to visit," the first orderly said.

"I will be staying here with the patient," the second orderly said.

Tessie thought both orderlies looked like robots or zombies from a black and white film she couldn't remember the title of.

"Is that you, Jenny Conroy? Why bless your heart!" Laura Jean smiled at Jenny.

"Hey, Laura Jean. Good to see you. Did you hear what the people in charge said? We only have 30 minutes to visit, so how about you stop picking lint and visit with us?" Jenny said.

"Mama? How much longer do you have to be here, Mama?" Tessie's voice cracked when she spoke.

Laura Jean looked straight over at Tessie as if she were seeing her for the first time and said, "Why it's Tessie, my little girl—how you have grown! Let me take a look at you."

"Mama, what has become of you?" Tessie's voice tore out of her chest. "What the hell has gone wrong?" Her loud voice startled the orderly who stepped between Tessie and her mother.

"What's the matter with you, Laura Jean Harnish? Have you lost your mind?" Jenny whispered. She shooed the orderly away, but he didn't leave.

Laura Jean grabbed her hair and began pulling it. The orderly tried to rein in Laura Jean's hands behind her but she continued to flap her arms like a turkey buzzard. It was awhile before he secured her.

Other orderlies arrived, descending upon the room like a flock of birds. An RN injected Laura Jean with something to calm her down.

"Okay, Tessie. We'll go home now," Jenny said.

Tessie reached for Jenny's hand.

"Your mama has lost her mind, Tessie bird," Jenny told her. "Why else would she be in Milledgeville?"

* * * * *

Laura Jean received a shock treatment immediately after Tessie and Jenny's visit. Laura Jean felt the electricity enter her. She met it half way, walked right into the bolts, one after the other, her eyes filling with blood tears, her throat filling with salt. Her final thought before she lost all power to think was *This is the last time.*

Her mind became a bowl of milk that has set too long—a skin forming, separating her from herself and the world. Inside the lightning bolt, she held onto as much of her life as she could. She held on by the skin of her teeth. And the skin that covered her body was both too thick and too thin. So thick that nothing and no one reached her. Just the searing jolts of electric current. So thick that they brought the needles and shot her with a cold liquid to calm her. After the treatment, she returned to herself. She saw birds flying, and by the time she opened her eyelids, the birds were outside the windows, waiting for her. One, two, three, four, five, six, seven.

Laura Jean concentrated on the birds. She had watched them before she was taken for shock, and then watched the birds again after they brought her back. She thought about her skin and the bird skin, buried under layers of feathers. Her mind's eye opened before her actual eyes did, and it was with her mind's eye that waited for the birds.

Neither Tessie nor Jenny talked on the ride home. They didn't turn on the radio. They didn't stop for food. Jenny drove. Tessie stared at the tall Georgia pines and the overcast sky.

After hours of silence, Jenny drove Tessie up to her trailer. "I know I am not your mama, and I would never try to take her place, but I am here for when or how you need me, Tessie. You understand?"

Tessie shook her head.

"Miss Jenny, I need a real mother, someone I can come home to. That's where love comes from, from every day. As far as I am concerned, Laura Jean is dead," Tessie said.

Jenny didn't try to talk to Tessie. Not then. She knew better than to try to reason with a shattered heart.

* * * * *

Jenny phoned Tessie.

"Don't call me for a while, Miss Jenny. I got to think on this," Tessie said.

Jenny picked up the receiver several times a day, just to put it down again.

For sixteen days, Tessie refused to talk to anyone. Not Jenny, not Annie, not Josie, not Ray, and not God.

On the sixteenth day, Tessie left Lot 71 and went to Jenny's salmon and white trailer. She knocked on the door. No one answered. She knocked again.

She must be sleeping. Maybe she's showering. Maybe she is lying down with one of her men. If I was a gambling girl, I'd bet on the last one, Tessie thought. Swing shifts make everybody lonely.

Swing shift—the words had made Tessie happy when she was five—they made her feel light and airy. She felt her parents push her on the swing. Her hair rippled in the wind and she flew toward the blue sky. Daddy is so lucky, she remembered thinking. He gets to swing all day.

Tessie raised her hand to knock a third time, and before she could, Jenny opened the door. Jeb Hoover was seated at the breakfast counter, fully dressed, sipping his coffee. Jenny had on her pink robe and looked flushed.

"You been there long, Tessie? I said to Jeb, 'Jeb, I hear someone at the door,' but he said, 'What?' We were just having our coffee, catching up on things at the mill. How you been, girl? You ready to talk?" As Jenny prattled on, she was making a safe place for Tessie to be. Jenny's questions neither wanted or needed a reply.

"Yes, ma'am. I'm ready to talk, but I can come back when you aren't busy."

"Hush, child! Jeb was just leaving. Weren't you, Jeb?" Jenny tapped an imaginary watch on her wrist to signal to Jeb. He picked up his cap and his lunch pail, said, "Tell Earle I dropped in to see how he was doing, won't you, Jenny? I crossed up schedules, I guess. Didn't realize he was on the 11-7."

"Why, sure will, Jeb. Sure will. Sorry you missed him, and I know he'll be sorry to have missed you, " Jenny said. She smiled at Jeb and winked at Tessie.

Tessie stood on the mat inside the door, not sure whether to go in to the kitchen or back outside.

"Come into the kitchenette and set yourself down. What can I do for you today, Tessie? Here's an orange juice," Jenny said.

"Miss Jenny, I need a ride to see Mama. Will you take me again on Sunday? Please? I can pay for the gas, and I'll pack us a lunch. Please?"

Jenny scrutinized Tessie's face. Sixteen days of crying can make a young girl's face look old. "I don't know if this is a good idea, Tessie. I mean, that last trip was mighty hard on both of us, but you, most of all."

"That's the God's truth, Miss Jenny. But I have to go back. I have to figure something out. I got the money to pay for the gas, but it won't buy me a bus ticket. Will you please take me?" Tessie hated begging.

"Sure will, Tessie. Sure will," Jenny said. She poured herself another cup of coffee and lit a Lucky. "You want coffee? A cigarette?"

Tessie nodded. She inhaled the cigarette and sipped the bitter brew.

The next day they rode silently to Milledgeville.

* * * * *

"When you coming home, Mama? When? Soon? I miss you so bad. There's a rumor that Ray's in trouble with the law and soon they gonna lock him up. What if that's true, Mama? Then what? Who's gonna take care of me?" Tessie stared into her mother's eyes.

Jenny had not heard that Ray was in trouble. How come I don't know about this? No one at The Hive has told me nary a thing! Jenny thought.

Tessie saw Jenny's face twist and turn. She shook her head at Jenny, as if to say, 'Hush.'

Laura Jean stared down at her hands.

"I don't need to be here anymore, Tessie, but leaving isn't easy. The doctor has to say, 'All right, Mrs. Harnish, you can go now."

Tessie looked down at the gray linoleum.

"I am not going to cry, Mama, and I am not going to beg. My crying, begging days are over. Without you, nothing feels right. I am all empty inside. I don't have any tears left. The trailer is a mess and the only time I feel all right is when I am in the swamp or on the river," Tessie said.

"You know that swamp is full of ticks and skeeters, snakes and pole cats. Why you choosing to be there?" Laura Jean asked.

"There are no people there!" Tessie yelled.

"Come here and let me hug on you," Laura Jean said.

Tessie didn't move.

"All right, let me say it this way to you then," Laura Jean began. "I've made a vow I'm gonna get out of here and back to you as soon as I can prove 'competence.' That's the word I hear over and over again. Now tell me what you are saying about Ray? What kind of trouble is he in? Jenny, what you know good or bad about this?"

"I don't know anything," Jenny said. "First I heard of it. Tessie?"

"Well, aren't you two innocent! Dope. He's running dope on the *Laura Jean*," Tessie spat the words at them.

"You watch your mouth," Jenny said. "Don't you speak to your mama and me like that, young'un!"

Laura Jean rose from her chair and began to whimper, "Oh Lord, oh Lord. My mama was right. I never should have fallen for that man." Then she stopped herself. "But then I wouldn't have you, Tessie. I love you, girl."

"I'm sorry I yelled at you, and I'm not sorry, Mama. You hear me? I want a regular life. You all suspicious about the swamp and the river. Well, I'm not afraid there. Only real danger there are the snakes, and Josie showed me how to trick the snakes. She told me to go in when the sun is setting. I wear my shrimping boots, but I take 'em off soon as I reach the river. I lie down on my side on the riverbank. Josie said, 'Rub your cheek against the red clay. Your dreams will come.' I dream you coming home, Mama, and I dream Ray not going to jail. The snakes come to me. They curl up beside me, under the arch of my arms,"

Tessie spoke in a tranquil voice.

"Good God Almighty! That's what you are doing in the swamp!" Jenny's surprise mirrored Laura Jean who sat speechless with her mouth in an oval, as if she was going to scream.

"I don't get any dreams on how to get you out of here. All I see is a white cloud, one white cloud full of rain that hasn't begun to fall. What's that mean, Mama? What's a cloud mean in a dream about the future?" The words rushed from Tessie.

Laura Jean did not answer her. At first, Tessie thought she was thinking, and then when her mother stayed silent her stomach sank. "Mama? Mama? Don't you go leaving us now. You stay here and talk! Mama? Mama!" The last words screeched out of Tessie's mouth.

"Laura Jean Harnish—you come back here, right now," Jenny said to her friend's wandering mind. "What in the hell is the matter with you, woman?" Jenny rubbed her swollen thumb joints. All these year of cutting hair taking their toll.

Laura Jean sat forward on her chair. Then she sat back. Then she sat forward again. "Do you hear the hummingbird's wings?"

Neither Jenny nor Tessie heard anything except their own fast beating hearts.

Tessie closed her eyes against the sight of her mother fading away. She banished the ward and its gray green walls.

* * * * *

Rain fell hard and heavy the night Tessie returned from visiting her mother. It filled the creek beds and turned the hard red clay into slick eroding danger zones. Dark purple clouds haunted the sky. Rain fell in thick sheets, blocking Tessie's vision.

Water prevented her from leaving the trailer, and kept other people home from their jobs as it flooded the flat land. Creeks became fresh water rivers that ran into the brackish water and from there into the tide water that merged with the sea. From Little Bit of Paradise Trailer Park's Lot 71, Tessie watched until all the water ran red with the Georgia clay.

Then it stopped. Mosquitoes spilled from the air, rose from the swamps, and swarmed outside her trailer door. Mosquito Control drove through the park spraying white poison. People hated the hissing, buzzing sound of the insects and were relieved to see the little white truck pull up, the man step from the cab, and hold out his naked arm. For one minute, he stayed there, counting the number of mosquitoes landing on his arm. Then he jumped back in his cab. He killed any mosquitoes still on him before he radioed in the number that had perched for that one minute of exposure.

Tessie hated mosquitoes, too, but she hated the confinement of the trailer more. She had not seen Ray since the rain began. Loneliness drove her forth from the trailer toward Josie's. She covered her skin with Avon's Skin So Soft; so much of it that if it didn't repel the mosquitoes, it was deep enough that when they landed they would drown.

Rain brought the snakes out, too. The cottonmouths came down from their tree limbs. Most slid away as soon as they heard the tromp of human footsteps, but not Big Snake who lived near Tessie's trailer. He wound around the willow tree until he was high enough to watch. Ray wanted to kill Big Snake. "Don't you dare, Daddy!" Tessie commanded, and so far he had listened to her.

She ran to Annie's house and entered without knocking, so excited from seeing Big Snake.

"You should see this snake, Annie. It is longer than a pick-up truck," Tessie told her.

"I will keep my eyes out for it, Tessie, and then if I see it, I am going to get mama's gun," Annie said. Tessie froze.

"Don't you be killing my snake, Annie. I've kept Ray away from it all the years, don't you be the one."

* * * * *

On Tessie's fourteenth birthday, Annie was walking to Tessie's when she saw the snake. At first she saw it as a thing of beauty, as if she were a wild life expert or God. The longer she watched it, though, the more afraid she became of its size and its attitude. She had Josie's gun, as she always did when she went through the swamp.

She stood steadily for thirty minutes watching Big Snake.

Tessie waited on her stoop for Annie. When she didn't arrive directly, Tessie went back into the trailer and made herself scrambled eggs and toast. She heard a shot, and then she felt it. She turned the gas off under the eggs and unplugged the toaster. She put her pink flip-flops on and moved swiftly down the path to the creek.

She saw Annie standing knee deep in the creek with Big Snake dead at the base of the willow. The shot to its head had killed it immediately and simultaneously knocked it out of the tree. Annie, frightened and sick to her stomach, had pounded what was left of the snake's head with the butt of the gun.

Tessie's back hurt as she rounded the bend. Her earrings rattled on her neck.

She half expected to see Ray standing over Big Snake when she rounded the corner. Instead, it was Annie who stood before her with the gun. "What have you done, Annie Osaha? What have you done?" Tessie fell to her knees beside Big Snake.

"I didn't want—I mean, I don't want, I mean, snakes are dangerous—it to suffer," Annie said.

"Fool!! You should have damn well left it sleeping in its tree," Tessie said. She looked at Annie as if she didn't know her. Tessie hugged herself to calm down and sparkling pieces of skin began to fall from her. In her mouth, her tongue split.

Annie screamed.

Tessie fell to the ground beside Big Snake and began writhing.

Annie's face went from one of triumph to a face filled with terror. Annie's thoughts raced. Is Tessie dying because I killed Big Snake?

She lay the gun down and grasped at Tessie, but could not hold her. Then she picked her up and carried her back to Josie's.

Every inch of Annie felt guilty as sin, and she looked it.

"What have you done, daughter, and where is my gun?" Josie wrapped Tessie in wool blankets to soothe and warm her.

Later that day, Tessie got her period for the first time. Josie saw the blood on the blankets when she unwrapped her.

"Do you know what this means?" Josie pointed to the blood. Tessie nodded.

"I'm going to get even with Annie for killing Big Snake, Miss Josie. I have no choice. I would've expected this of Ray, but not Annie. How could she kill something wild and beautiful?" Tessie asked.

"Hush, child. We'll talk this over when you have your strength back," Josie said.

Tessie followed her old ritual to get over her rage. She rubbed her hand against cottonwood bark to keep people who might kill the snakes away from the swamp. She rubbed her back against a standing rock to gain strength. She rubbed her forehead slowly across pine bark to ward off sadness. At night she went to the swamp to sleep. She laid down on the left side of her body and rubbed her cheek against the cool red clay. When the snakes needed to sleep, they mistook Tessie's leg for a log. They lay with her—no hissing or rattling or biting. They coiled close to her and slept. In the swamp she knew peace.

Annie called Tessie on the phone, but Tessie didn't answer. When she went to the trailer, Tessie was not there. Tessie avoided Annie at school by arriving late and leaving early. For the first time, Tessie hated Annie.

Annie felt broken by Tessie shunning her. *What made me want to kill Big Snake? Why'd I go against my friend like that and hurt her?* Annie couldn't answer her own questions. Her heart became hollow and the pounding became louder when she breathed.

Ray noticed that Tessie wasn't sleeping at home, but he figured she was off with some boy, not down in the swamp sleeping with snakes.

Tessie stopped talking except when people demanded an answer from her.

Fuddah had been watching Tessie in the swamp. He saw her mourning Big Snake and practicing her magic. Her grief was doubled: no mother and no Big Snake.

He witnessed Annie killing the snake, and knew there was a mean streak in his granddaughter—just as wide and deep as her kindness. He had been watching for it to emerge.

He went to Josie's porch and waited for her to come home. He didn't waste time with a greeting.

"That girl's gonna break apart 'less you do something, Josie," Fuddah said.

"I know, Fuddah, I know. But she hasn't come 'round here for me to talk to or hug or fix a mess a greens for her," Josie said.

"Go to her, Josie! Go now before she's lost forever," Fuddah said.

The next day Annie awoke to her mother's sweet alto singing the "Our Father." She smelled bacon cooking. She looked at the photo beside her bed of her standing beside her mom at Little Tybee Beach the summer before. In it, she held onto her mother with one hand and held up a four-pronged starfish with the other.

Annie reached under her pillow to make sure that the ball bearing, two of her baby teeth and the snakeskin from Big Snake were there. The ball bearing was her oldest possession. She had found it at the school playground. Twice she had beat the big boys in marbles using it, but after she saw how bad Tessie got hurt from winning against John Henry, she had quit playing. The two baby teeth were the last two she lost, but the tooth fairy had failed to collect.

The snakeskin was powerful magic and killing Big Snake to get it cost her Tessie. Oh yes, the stakes were high, Annie thought. I love the patterns on the skin. I love Big Snake different than Tessie did—I love Big Snake dead, and Tessie loved Big Snake alive.

Annie kept the skin under her pillow, hoping it would give her sweet dreams and tell her the future.

* * * * *

Josie screamed when she changed Annie's bed.

"Annie Osaha! What's this doing in your bed? What have you done? Did that snake bite you? Did it? Get the cane, Annie, and meet me out back," Josie ordered.

"I'm too old for a caning, Mama," Annie had said back.

"No, child, you are not. Bring me that cane now. You'll feel better once it's over. Then you can begin thinking on how you gonna make this up to Tessie. That snake showed Tessie how to survive, and now you done killed it and skinned it and are lying in your bed with it! Shame on you!"

Annie couldn't sit for several days after the caning. She phoned Tessie, and Tessie answered. "Hello, Tessie, it's me," Annie said into the receiver.

Tessie stayed silent and then blurted out. "I'm still mad with you, Annie, but I love you, too. I know you wanted the power of Big Snake. I know that's why you killed him. You got to promise me you won't kill for power again," Tessie said. "Promise me now."

"I promise, Tessie," Annie whispered into the phone.

"Why you whispering, Annie?" Tessie asked.

"I'm in pain so bad from Mama," Annie said.

"Meet me at the river at sunrise tomorrow, Annie," Tessie said and hung up the phone.

The next morning Annie hurried through her breakfast so she'd be on time meeting Tessie. She wrapped her bacon in a napkin, kissed her mother goodbye and ran all the way to the river.

Tess was passing time swinging out over the water on an old tire. "Morning, Annie, I been swinging here, watching the sunrise. Want to take a turn?"

Annie put the last piece of bacon in her mouth and joined her. They got the swing going very high and when they were out over the water, Tessie pushed Annie off.

"Goddamn you, Tessie Harnish!" Annie bellowed as she came up out of the water.

"That's from Big Snake and me—for what you done," Tessie yelled at her.

Tessie jumped from the tire swing onto the riverbank and ran.

Annie swam out of the river, dripping water and anger all the way home.

At school, the girls passed in the hallway without speaking. But by the next morning, a Saturday, dawn found them back at the river, waiting for each other again. They lay on the packed mud of the 'Geechee's bank. Tessie began humming River Jordan, and Annie sang, *River Jordan is muddy and wide, hallelujah. River Jordan is muddy and wide, deep and long. River Jordan is muddy and wide, hallelujah. Cross it to the other side, hallelujah.*

Tessie scooched over to rest her head on the left side of Annie's chest and listened to Annie's heart say over and over again, "I'm your friend. You're safe here."

Annie lay very still. Best friends again. One black girl, one white girl, both 'Geechee.

After the girls spent the day at the river, they went their separate ways.

At the supper table, over a bowl of white rice and red beans, Josie said, "What did you do today, Annie?"

"I played at the river with Tessie," Annie said.

"Did she push you in again?" Josie asked.

"No, Mama. We all over that now. We done with that," Annie said.

"That's good—if it's true," Josie said, nodding her head wisely. "You best get a good night's sleep. Go on to bed early."

In her room, Annie carefully removed the snakeskin, pressed it to her lips for a silent angel kiss, then she wrapped it in tissue paper and put it on the top shelf of her closet. She had changed her mind about having it under her pillow to feed her dreams. She didn't want to know the future.

* * * * *

Josie waited for Annie to go to bed. When she was sure that Annie was sleeping, Josie drove to the mill to find Ray and waited outside for the shift to end. She hollered to him from the parking lot, "Ray, we got to talk. About the girls."

Ray got in Josie's old car and listened to the story of Big Snake. He shook his head. "We got to get these girls away from here, Josie."

"Let's take them to Hungry Mother Mountain to the rattlesnake roundup," Josie said.

Ray pondered the idea and chuckled.

"Yeah, that ought to teach 'em something," he said.

-14-
Hungry Mother Mountain

Ray and Josie loaded the back of the truck with two suitcases, a tent, a cooler, fishing poles, and tackle box. "Tessie! Annie! Tessie! Annie! Tessie! Annie!" Ray yelled.

Once, twice, three times before the girls came running from the swamp. Ray had quit thinking about the color of Annie's skin, and had quit worrying about what other people thought. After all, with Laura Jean gone, Josie Osaha and Jenny Conroy were helping him raise Tessie, and when no one else could find shrimp, Fuddah knew where they were running. Color don't matter to me, no more, Ray thought. I know real friends when I see them. Josie's face, Jenny's, Henry's, Fuddah's all flashed across his mind.

Annie and Tessie are going to be friends forever, Ray thought. Yeah, they fight sometimes as if they are sisters—to the bitter, and not so bitter, end, like over Big Snake, but then they make up. This trip is gonna be a healing for them. He lit up a cigarette.

Ray and Josie sat in the cab while the girls sat in the bed of the truck. Ray could see them in his rearview—talking, talking, talking. Ray often traveled alone, and he only stopped for gas, Yoo-Hoo, and moon pies. He stopped twice as much on this trip with three women aboard.

"You gotta stop, Ray, when you traveling with women and girls. We just have different plumbing," Josie prompted him. At the stops, Ray bought everybody a Yoo-Hoo and gave each person a sandwich out of the cooler.

By the time the truck pulled in at the lake, everyone's stomach was full of white bread, bologna, and chocolate soda. Ray and Josie set up camp—tent and strings, hammers, ropes and poles, spikes and knots, sleeping bags and pillows. Josie built a campfire and spread out quilts for sitting on. Ray sat down, pinched off the filter of his Marlboro and leaned back against a pine tree to enjoy his smoke.

Josie pulled out her book and read under the spreading boughs of a sycamore. Annie and Tessie went walking and returned on a run. "Daddy, Daddy, look a here," Tessie cried out.

Tessie thrust a frog at her father's face.

Be damned if these girls ain't just like little boys in some ways, Ray thought. They ain't so foreign after all. As Ray leaned in to see, the burning tip of his cigarette singed the frog's throat and filled the air with the stench of burning skin.

"Oh, Mr. Ray, you burned it," Annie said, softly—more a statement of fact than a criticism. Around most adults, especially white ones, she didn't speak unless someone asked her a direct question, and then she'd yes ma'am or no sir them into silence. Tessie was surprised to hear her friend talk, and for a split second, forgot about the frog.

"Put it back in the water, Tessie!" Ray yelled.

"Is it gonna die, Daddy?" Tessie asked.

"Who the hell knows! Next time watch where you're putting the frog. You put its neck right on the coal. You stupid or something, Tessie?" Ray looked at her like she was.

Neither girl ate much of the camp beans Ray made. Their thoughts were full of singed frog's neck and anticipation of the next day. Ray planned to go fishing. Josie wanted to go hiking with the girls. "We'll meet back at the truck around noon and go from here to the Rattlesnake Roundup before we head back to Savannah," Josie said.

"I can't wait to see them snakes in a pit, hissing and swarming in that great big old hole," Tessie said to everybody.

Josie slept in the tent, Ray slept in the truck bed, and the girls camped outside by the fire and under the stars where they could talk.

Ray's snores blended in with the bullfrog's thrumming.

"I wonder if the frogs aren't just a little bit quieter tonight," Annie said.

"I doubt it, Annie, but I know what you mean. If that one Daddy burned is still alive, I'm sure he ain't singing, and somehow I don't think he made it. His neck looked so nasty," Tessie shuddered.

The girls stared into the night.

"Tessie, you know what Josie told me?" Annie said.

"Well, Annie, I know she's told you many things. Is this something new?" Tessie inched closer.

"Yes, it is. It's the ritual for gaining courage. And I know how to go about it. Do you want to do it with me? We don't have all the ingredients, but we can improvise if need be," Annie said.

"Gosh, Annie, what do you need courage for? What are you afraid of? You don't seem scared of anything!" Tessie paused. "I know I need courage. What do we need for doing the ritual?" Tessie asked.

"Let me tell you what I'm afraid of first, Tessie. I'm afraid of white people when they're in groups. And I'm afraid of your daddy most of the time. Who knows what crazy things white folk are thinking when they're around black folk! Even you," Annie said, and she poked Tessie in her ribs with a short stick.

Tessie couldn't think of anything to say back to that.

"What I need is a glass, some paper and red water. Mama told me to write COURAGE on the paper and keep chanting, 'I build my house on the heads of my enemies.' She said to say it over and over until I feel strong, then drop the word into the glass of water, drink down all the liquid and then chew up the paper and swallow it." Annie fidgeted with her hair while she spoke.

"We can do something like that, Annie," Tessie said. "Easy enough. Come on." Tessie and Annie took their flashlight and searched until they found a feather, to use as their pen just like Thomas Jefferson. They caught a fish, to use its blood for ink. They took an empty Yoo-Hoo bottle out of the truck bed to hold the blood. Last, they found a piece of birch bark to use for paper.

"We'll write on the bark, drop it in the Yoo-Hoo bottle, add water and fish blood and swallow it down. I'm afraid of so many things. I'd love to have my courage back," Tessie said. They stuck the tip of the feather in the fish blood and scrawled COURAGE in capital letters on the bark, dropped the bark in the bottle and took turns drinking. Annie didn't press Tessie for what she was afraid of. She pretty much knew: everything. After the girls performed the ritual, they fell asleep.

Josie stared at the girls when she came out of her tent. They were spooned together and as close to the fire as they could get without being in it. She added kindling to the coals, lit a cigarette and watched them while the fire grew again. The heat woke them up quickly.

"Hey, Mama. Hey, Miss Josie," the girls called over their shoulders as they rushed to the edge of the lake to escape the heat and wash up.

Josie made the coffee. Ray used an old tin can hung on a piece of wire over the fire to cook bacon. Next he wrapped the bacon in white bread to make sandwiches. Then they broke camp, and the four of them took off for Hungry Mother Mountain and the Roundup. For a long time they sat in a line of cars and trucks as it slowly snaked up the mountain.

Ray slid the back window open. "Tessie and Annie, listen here. Anybody gives you a hard time about anything, little or big, you come and tell me right off, 'hear?"

Tessie nodded. Annie couldn't speak. She was surprised by Ray's kind voice. Tessie nudged Annie, and whispered, "You got to answer him."

"Yes, sir, Mr. Ray. I most certainly will, sir," Annie said.

Finally, they parked the truck and got out.

"Meet me at the truck at twelve o'clock, 'hear?" Ray said.

"Yes, Daddy," Tessie said.

"I'm going fishing with Ray," Josie announced. "You two go on now and have some fun."

"Yes, Mama," Annie answered.

First the girls went to the snake pit. Next, they went in search of a place to swim. They found a small pond on the western side of Hungry Mother. Dragonflies skimmed the pond, buzzing and whirring, feeding on insects and small fry. Tessie watched the hummingbirds hovering around the perimeter of the pond, diving deep into the trumpet vine's orange and yellow flower.

"Annie, oh my God!" Tessie screeched. She could not tell if the dragonfly wanted to eat the hummingbird or mate with it.

"They just playing, Tessie," Annie said. "What you so afraid of?"

"I'm afraid the hummingbird's gonna die," Tessie cried. "Annie, what am I going to do about how boys and men are around me? They think just 'cause I'm pretty, I'm being pretty for them. I can't tell if they want to mate with me or eat me alive."

"Both, probably." Annie felt a lump in her throat. She wanted to protect her friend, but she didn't know how. "I can't lock you up in a tower, Tessie," Annie said. The dragonfly skimmed the pond. The hummingbird was gone.

Tessie and Annie left the pond and walked back to where the truck was parked. They couldn't find Ray and Josie at first.

"Annie, Tessie! We are over here," Josie called. "The truck's over here."

Josie sat on the edge of the tailgate, and Ray lay in the bed where some men had carried him. "Is he hurt, Mama?" Annie asked.

"No, he ain't hurt," Tessie said. "He's drunk. I don't want to sit here with him while he sleeps it off. You want to come with me and have another adventure?" Tessie said.

"Like what, Tessie?" Annie asked.

"Well, we could go watch them snakes in the pit, and we could watch those people outside the pit. I never get tired of people-watching." Tessie kicked a stone as she talked. "Or snake-watching, for that matter!"

"All right, let's go." Annie started walking off.

"I'll stay with him," Josie said. Both girls remembered her story about Fuddah when he was Tom and a drunk and wanted to go back and hug her.

They walked around the snake pit, smelling the putrid odor of too many snakes in a small space. They watched the white people with their big teeth and straw colored hair. They looked closely at the black people with their shiny eyes and tight curls talking and laughing with the white folks, sharing their picnic lunches, swapping out fried chicken and lemon bar cookies for cold boiled shrimp and pecan pie. Neither girl felt any fear at all. Josie's magic courage recipe was working already.

Every so often they circled back to the truck to see if Ray was still passed out. Josie gave them the thumbs up on their seventh trip back. "Where the hell have you two been? I been waiting on you for over two hours," Ray said.

"That's a lie, Daddy," Tessie said. "You haven't been waiting, you've been drunk."

"We're right here, Mr. Ray, sir," Annie said, all brave and strong.

"Well, get in the damn truck. We got a six or seven hour drive back. I'm not feeling so well," Ray said.

"Don't you even want to go to the pit, Daddy?" Tessie asked. "We drove all the way here and now you're not even gonna see the snakes."

"No use being ugly with us because you been drinking yourself stupid," Josie said.

"Well, uh well, I mean," Ray sputtered.

"Don't get attitude with me, Ray Harnish! The girls are riding up front with me. I'm the driver, and you can keep your nasty old self in the back. Mount up," Josie commanded.

She drove hard and fast down the winding road, raging at Ray just as sure as if they were lovers who had been fighting each other all day with words as sharp as knives. Sam Cooke's voice came smoothly over the radio wave. *If you ever change your mind, about leaving, leaving me behind, oh oh oh bring it to me, bring your sweet loving...*

The truck swerved. That's what Tessie and Annie remembered. That and breaking glass. That and metal on metal and then metal on flesh. That and Josie's scream. Darkness tightened around them where their truck, flipped on its cab, and rolled down Hungry Mother Mountain.

A road crew found Ray, thrown clear of the truck and safe, still in a drunken stupor. Volunteer firemen pulled Tessie and Annie from the cab, but Josie was pinned between the steering wheel and part of the door where the semi that hit them had tried to climb right into

Ray's truck. Static hissed from the radio, and Josie hung by a thread between the living and the dead.

"Mama, Mama," Annie prayed, her voice a siren, her body an earthquake.

"Listen here, young'un. She cain't hear you and you just wearing yourself out. You got to quiet yourself till the ambulance comes. They might can pry her out of that tuck with the jaws of life. Now settle, hear? Why the four of y'all traveling together? I mean, two white folk and two black folk in a pick-up in North Georgia ain't real common. You been at the round up? I see you got Chatham County plates."

"Hush, Ike. Now ain't the time to be asking either of these young'uns anything."

"She's my mother," Annie said.

"He's my father," Tessie said.

"And we sisters," the girls said in unison. The men looked the girls over and shook their heads. "That don't seem likely," Ike said.

"Take 'em to the hospital. They already took the man in the ambulance to be checked out. We'll bring the girl's mother soon as we can get her out of that truck."

"I smell gas," Annie whispered. The she wailed, "I smell gas! The truck's gonna blow. Oh God!"

"Take 'em now, take 'em in my Malibu."

Annie and Tessie were bundled up in old wool blankets and hustled into the back seat of the Malibu.

"What about Mama, Tessie? She's gonna die?" Annie cried.

"Hold on to me, Annie. I'll be your courage," Tessie said. And she swallowed her own pink liquid of saliva and blood.

-15-
'Geechee Road

Everyone up and down the 'Geechee Road heard about the accident on Hungry Mother Mountain. They heard by phone, they heard after answering a knock on their door, they heard in the bars, at the grocery store, at the dock. Three brave men walked into the swamp together to fortify each other for telling Fuddah about the accident. People prayed and cursed. People screamed and some got quiet as rocks.

Ray returned first to the 'Geechee Road, within just a few days of the accident. Tessie and Annie came back next, with stitches and bandages, bruises and bumps, and with terror and sorrow in their eyes. Josie returned, too, but as a transfer from one ICU to another.

Jenny Conroy went over to stay with Annie and took Tessie along. Henry and Emily called Reverend Bobby who drove from Columbia with his box of snakes to Josie's house and sat with Annie. "You can handle these snakes if you want, Annie. It'll help you see into the future. Sure will. If you don't get bit, then your mama's gonna be fine. If you do get bit and live, your mama's gonna return to you changed. And if you get bit and die, well, it's the Lord's way of keeping you and your mama together—if you know what I mean."

Annie shook her head no each time Reverend Bobby asked her if she was ready for the snake. He kept vigil with her for 26 hours before Annie reached into the box and took hold of one of the sleeping canebreak rattlers.

"I'm not Emily, Reverend Bobby, and I'm not Fuddha." What she didn't say was, and I killed Big Snake to hurt Tessie and now in some great big snake memory this snake knows that and it's gonna get me for sure.

"I'm praying for a miracle. I'm praying for God to give you a sign. " Reverend Bobby began to hum a tune.

"Hold on, Bobby. You sure you know what you're doing here?" Jenny asked.

"He knows, Jenny. He knows," Tessie said.

"I got me a girl here, Holy God, Heavenly Father, and she needs you to send her a sign. She's holding a viper and trusting in you. She's holding a viper—and she's either gonna be bit, or she ain't. She's either gonna make it scott free, or she gonna be bit. If she's bit, she's either gonna live or die. What's it gonna be, God?"

Annie held the snake in her lap—coiled, sleepy, just opening its eyes.

"You want me to take it for you, Annie? You want me to handle that snake for you?" Tessie offered.

"Won't work, Tessie. That snake is her lonesome valley. Can't you, can't no one walk it for her, she got to walk it herself," Bobby said.

"She can't walk a snake!" Tessie hissed at him.

"You know what I mean, Tessie, and…."

Jenny cut him off. "Hush, both of you. Let Annie be."

Annie picked the snake up and abruptly put it over her shoulders like a chain for pulling tractors. The snake startled and bit Annie on her left hand. She threw the snake away from her and Bobby caught it. Tessie grabbed Annie's hand, bit over the bite, sucked and spat the poison on the floor.

"Well, well. 'Guess we got ourselves an answer—Josie's coming home changed," Bobby narrowed his eyes and stared at Jenny. "Just the answer I expected. Everybody on your knees. Now. We got to thank the Lord for this sign."

"No, sir," Tessie said. "We need to take Annie to the doctor's. Come on, Annie, come on, Jenny. Let's go."

"You got the poison out, Tessie, or Annie'd have started being sick right away," Bobby said.

"No disrespect, but I'm taking her anyway, Reverend Bobby. Then I'm taking the girls back with me to have dinner with Ray. He hasn't touched a drop of liquor since the wreck. He's making fish fry, hush puppies, and greens. You may as well go on to Henry's and Emily's," Jenny said, "or head back to Columbia."

"Get your clothes, Annie. You gonna stay with me at Little Bit until your mama comes home."

After supper, Jenny went back to her trailer. Tessie and Annie stayed over at Tessie and Ray's. They had just fallen asleep when they awoke to pounding on the door. Tessie saw the flashing red light outside her bedroom window. Afraid to breathe, Tessie and Annie hid in Tessie's room.

They heard Ray as he opened the door.

"What you want?" Ray said.

"We come for you, Ray. You're under arrest for running dope. Don't even try to tell us you ain't been doing it, neither, Ray," Buddy Jones said.

"I can't come now, Buddy. Who will stay here for Tessie and Annie? You know they just home from the accident and Tessie's mama is still up to Milledgeville talking with the birds," Ray said.

"I hate you, Daddy," Tessie whispered to the pressed plywood door.

"Are you nuts, Ray? This isn't an invitation to a party. You are under arrest! Don't you have no other family to send the girl to?" Buddy looked at his boots as he asked this.

"No, it's just me and the girl and I got Josie's girl here, too."

"Well then, we will just have to take them in with you. The office will find a foster care placement for them," Buddy said.

"Can they stay with Tessie's aunt?" Ray asked.

"I thought you said you didn't have no family," Buddy eyed Ray.

"We do, we do. We have her aunt, Jenny Conroy," Ray lied.

"I didn't think she t'were family to you, Ray," Buddy sucked air through his teeth as he spoke.

"I'm pretty upset about this arrest, boys. You arresting everyone else on the river? You know I ain't the only one running weed," Ray said. "Go on, Tessie." Ray yelled down the hallway. "Pack some clothes for you and Annie. I know you standing on the other side of that door. You gonna stay with Aunt Jenny and Uncle Earle."

"All right, Daddy," Tessie called out. "When will you be back?"

Buddy spoke for Ray. "Not for a good while. Not for a good while. Annie, how's Miss Josie doing?"

"Answer him, Annie," Ray insisted.

"Not good, Sheriff," Annie said.

"I am so sorry to hear that," Buddy said. He walked Ray to the patrol car and pushed him in to the back seat. Tessie and Annie hurried out the door and began their walk as a two-person parade to Jenny's. The whole trailer park was awake and watching from their stoops or their windows.

"Come on in," Jenny said.

"Shut the blinds, Earle, and make some cocoa, Earle," Jenny said. She had her hands on Tessie's and Annie's shoulders and gently pushed them down onto the sofa, then she sat right down with them while Earle closed the blinds and heated up some milk.

"Bring the cocoa here, Earle, and then sit with us a spell," Jenny kept her voice even and kind.

"How are you doing, girls?" Before either one could answer, Jenny said, "You got to be feeling poorly. You got to be feeling deserted. I am so sorry. Don't you girls worry about school. You going to come with me to The Bee Hive while Earle finds out what is going on with your daddy. Right, Earle?" Jenny held Tessie's hand. Then she reached for Annie's. "And you'll find out where Annie's gonna stay, too. Get some folks to go with you to see Fuddah,"

Earle nodded.

"Buddy Jones is pretending you are my aunt and uncle, but he knows better. He's been knowing Daddy his entire life. It's the only reason they didn't take me, too," Tessie's voice wavered and she dropped the cocoa cup. Tessie sobbed. "I'm so sorry about the mess, Miss Jenny," Tessie said.

"Don't you worry a'tall," and in the next breath, she said, "Earle, clean up that spill, will you?"

"Of course, darlin' heart," Earle said.

"You all right, Annie?" Jenny asked.

"Yes, I am okay. That Buddy Jones is more poisonous than a snakebite."

Earle finished cleaning up the mess, drank a cup of coffee, and then headed into the police station to find out what Ray was facing. Jenny sipped her coffee and went over in her head how she could persuade the department of social services that she was as close to family as anyone could get without having a bloodline.

"I'm gonna pour me another cup of coffee before I put on my work clothes," Jenny said to the girls. "Once I am dressed, we will head on over to the shop."

Tessie and Annie curled up like cats and fell asleep on the couch while Jenny was dressing. They woke up confused when they opened their eyes and found themselves on the aqua sofa in Miss Jenny's trailer with Miss Jenny sitting beside them.

"Morning again," she said, watching them closely. "You remember now, don't you? Your daddy's with the police." She directed her gaze at Tessie. "And your mama's still in the hospital." She switched her gaze to Annie.

"Yes, ma'am. When is my mother coming home?" Annie asked.

"Yes, ma'am. Where's Earle?" Tessie asked.

"He's gone in to check on your daddy, remember? Want some coffee with milk and sugar?" Jenny said. "Annie, I'm going to call the hospital and find out when Josie's to be released and Earle's going to see Fuddah after he leaves the jail."

The girls put on their clothes while Jenny mixed up two drinks of one third coffee, the rest milk and sugar.

"You ready, girls? I need to get to work," Jenny said.

"Yes, ma'am. What about school?" Tessie asked.

"I told you not to worry about that."

* * * * *

At The Bee Hive, Jenny unlocked the door, shooed the girls in ahead of herself, and sat each one of them down at one of the hair dryers. "Now listen to me good. You don't have a thing to be ashamed of. You aren't crazy and you didn't run any dope on a shrimp boat," she said to Tessie. "And you ain't a witch doctor or in the hospital," she said to Annie. "I'm gonna look out for you today and for as long as either of you need me."

The girls watched her as they listened.

"When folks come in here today, I want you to be proud. I want you to act with courage. Keep your head up. I need your help, too. I want you to take all phone calls, set up appointments and check people out." She pulled two hard plastic chairs over for them to sit at her little white desk with the ivy leaves stenciled on it. " I want you to say, 'Hello. This is Jenny's Bee Hive.' You got that Tessie?" Then she walked Annie over to the desk and showed her the appointment book and the change drawer. Jenny took out her zipper bag from the bank and set up the drawer with tens, fives, ones, quarters, nickels, and dimes. "You be in charge of the money, Annie, while Tessie handles the phone and the appointments. I'm gonna keep the two of you busy!" Jenny said.

* * * * *

Humidity held the air low to the ground by 4 p.m., right about the time the magenta Four O'clocks bloomed, and it kept the fumes from the paper mill close enough to the ground that rich and poor, white and black, male and female, young and old had burning eyes and itching skin.

Tessie and Annie sat in The Bee Hive and watched layers of grayness shroud the horizon. The papermill stench distorted the sweetness of gardenia and juniper, wisteria and roses. The acrid scent of pulp seeped into The Bee Hive merging with hair spray and the smell of bleach--too thick to breathe, too sour to swallow. Tessie answered the phone, set up appointments and fetched whatever Jenny needed. Annie collected the money and thanked each customer.

The girls watched Miss Jenny greet the customers, put each one in her seat, and fasten the pink smock with hundreds of little scissors on it around each client's neck. "Look closely at yourself for a minute or two in the mirror, Geraldine," Jenny said, "and remember who you are before you tell me what you want to have done." She listened and said, "I think we can do that for you." Then she did it. Tessie and Annie forgot their anxiety for minutes at a time during the day.

At quitting time, Jenny said, "Close up the curtains. We're going home."

Jenny pulled up to her trailer. "Let's see what Earle found out." she said. They got out of the car. "It's gonna be all right, because it's gonna have to be. Remember that."

Earle sat at the counter drinking a Blue Ribbon. His face was screwed into a pout and his ear lobes were bright red.

"Uh-oh, Earle. You are looking fit to be tied!" Jenny said.

"You want me to talk in front of the girls, or no?" Earle began.

"We want to hear the truth, Mr. Earle," Annie spoke for them both.

"Well, it ain't good news. They gonna keep Ray for a while—maybe up to five years," Earle said.

"Damnation and chicken feathers," Jenny said as she slammed her fist on the counter, knocking over Earle's beer.

"Don't worry," Earle said, "I got me a twelve pack in the cooler."

"What did they say about my mama?" Annie asked.

Earle got up for another beer, and drank three in a row while Tessie and Annie waited. Jenny lit a new cigarette off of the one she was smoking.

Earle handed each of them a beer.

"It ain't good about your mama, Annie," he said.

-16-
Return

Josie returned to her place on the 'Geechee Road on a rainy Savannah afternoon in September in an ambulance with the sirens turned off. Two men carried her in on the gurney and lifted her from it by the sheet that they worked like a net. Hungry Mother Mountain may as well have occurred on another planet, in a different lifetime. Josie couldn't remember the trip at all, couldn't recall the accident happening, but she could remember the fire and the smell of gasoline, could remember the flames licking her face and the men pulling her away from the fire. She mistook Annie, her beauty girl, for her mother, Ol' Dolly. She wondered who the white girl with the blue eyes was and what she was doing in her home. She'd never been with a white man, so she was sure that the girl wasn't her daughter. She remembered having a daughter of her own, but she figured that her baby must have died.

I am no Jesus, that's for sure, Josie thought. I've tried to be like him, but I can't raise myself up from this bed, let alone raise Lazarus from the dead, can't launch my old fishing boat, let alone walk on water. She remained quiet for almost an hour. Then she said, "Bring me water and my Bible. Hey, I said, someone bring me water and my Bible!" Then in a quiet voice, she said, "Please."

Tessie and Annie had scrubbed everything in the house and every part of the house. They washed all the linen, the towels and Josie's clothes, and made a roast chicken for dinner with turnip greens and cornbread.

"She doesn't know who we are, Tessie," Annie whispered as they gathered her Bible and fixed her a glass of cool water. "She knows her house, but she doesn't know her own blood or you, who are almost kin to her."

Tessie fixed Josie a plate and helped her by spooning small bites into her mouth. After Josie finished eating and drinking, Tessie brought the bedpan.

Later, Annie said, "I'll keep first watch, and I'll read to her from the Bible. The Word usually calms her down."

"It's time for her pills, Annie, 'fore you start reading. Says two white ones every four hours to control the pain." Tessie watched as Annie got another glass of water, shook two of the white pills in her hand, gave one pill to Josie, held the glass to Josie's mouth, waited for her to swallow, gave her another pill, held up the glass again, and watched her swallow the last one.

"Okay, Tessie. That's taken care of. You want to go on now and tend to yourself while I read to Mama." Annie picked up the Bible and Tessie left the house to sit on the porch.

"What you mean, 'Read to Mama?' Aren't you Dolly? Aren't you my mother?" Josie's confusion brought them both to tears.

"No, Mama. I'm your Annie. Dolly's long dead. Fuddah, your father, is still in this world, and lives by himself down in the 'Geechee Swamp. I want you to lie back, now, and let me read to you."

Josie stayed bolt upright in the bed.

"Please, Mama. You gonna have to trust me if you want to stay here and not go back to the hospital. We're gonna have to work together to mend your memory. Please, Mama. Lie back."

Tears spilled from Josie's eyes. She lay back down and Annie opened the Bible.

"I'm gonna read from Luke, Mama, remember what you told me? Luke was the physician. He wanted Jesus' words to heal the world."

Josie gave no sign that she had heard, no sign that she was listening.

"Jesus and John the Baptist," Annie began. "Now in the fifteenth year of the reign of Tiberius Caesar, Pontius Pilate being gov'nor of Judea, and Herod being tetrarch of Galilee, and his brother Philip tetrarch of Itureaea and of the region of...."

"Skip that part, whoever you are. Just skip all of that and get on with the story," Josie said.

"All right," Annie said. "All right, Mama. 'O generation of vipers, who hath warned you to flee from the wrath to come? Bring forth therefore fruits worthy of repentance, and begin not to say to yourselves, We have Abraham to our father: for I say unto you that God is able of these stories to raise up children unto Abraham. And now also the axe is laid unto the root of the trees: every tree therefore which bringeth not forth good fruit is hewn down, and cast into the fire.'

"Go to the end of this part, girl. Go to what John says."

"All right, I will.

"I indeed baptize you with water, but one mightier than I cometh, the latchet of whose shoes I am not worthy to unloose: he shall baptize you with the Holy Ghost and with fire: whose fan is in his hand, and he will thoroughly purge his floor, and will gather the wheat into his garner; but the chaff he will burn with fire unquenchable."

Annie stopped. "That's the part? Being baptized with the Holy Ghost and with fire?"

"That's the part, Annie girl. I'll wait for the Holy Ghost to baptize me. I've already been baptized by fire. When the Holy Ghost comes, I will be healed."

Annie's heart swelled when her mother recognized her.

"Amen," Annie said.

"Good night. I am going to be fine. Go on out on the porch with that white girl."

"That white girl is Tessie, Mama. She's white and 'Geechee."

Annie bent over and kissed Josie's face where it had been grafted together.

-17-
The Healing

Henry thought about how he had made love to Emily in the early years of their marriage as he drove her and Fred to Savannah. He remembered lighting the candle and getting the broom. He and Emily loved a clean house, but they agreed no one would sweep down the cobwebs except on the nights when one of them wanted to make love. Collecting cobwebs let them repair the hurt. If there weren't any cobwebs, one of them pretended there were.

Henry never stopped wanting Emily. She was his, his forever.

Henry remembered getting Ray's letter. He called him right away to see where the openings were at the mill, and was told "In the vat room. I'll put a word in for you. Come on back."

Henry moved back quickly, working all day and packing in the evenings. At last he could give his two weeks' notice. He called a realtor in Savannah and had him select a house out toward Armstrong State, as far from the paper mill as he could get: 449 Magnolia Lane. He and Emily met the realtor there, and Henry—who didn't trust banks—paid for the house outright with cash.

Henry's new job at Union Bag made him work swing shifts, but he didn't mind. "It makes me friends with every hour of the day," Henry said. And then he winked at whoever was extending him sympathy for not living by a 9-5 routine that many people around him clung to. He claimed the shifts didn't throw him off the way they did a lot of the men. At the mill, the joke was, "How can you get jet lag without traveling anywhere?" And the answer was, "Work at Union Bag."

Henry supervised the paper vats, checked temperatures, double-checked the timers, and kept the workers alert. He made foreman faster than anyone ever had, but had no ambition to rise higher than that, to be in charge of too many men.

He heard about Ray, Tessie, Josie and Annie's accident on Hungry Mother Mountain on a day when the vents couldn't cool the plant down enough to make it tolerable. He was distracted by the clanking machinery, the failed vents, the accident, and his nerves were taut. So were the nerves of the other workers on the 11-7 shift, and tension was high. That night, Ron Hibbard and Alfred Bodean got in a fistfight. Henry walked in on the cheering sideliners who, saturated from the night's heat, saw the fight as fun.

"Look 'a here, now. Listen here," he yelled. The men didn't hear him. "I said, 'Listen up,'" Henry yelled. He shoved his way into the crowd of men and kept pushing in order to separate them. As they suddenly parted, his momentum sent him flying into the pulp vat. His skin began to melt and by the time he was pulled out and rushed to Memorial, sixty per cent of his body had third-degree burns.

The doctors at Memorial told Emily and Fred that Henry would die. "Even with skin grafts and our best medical treatment, we can't save him. We will make him as comfortable as we can while he's here at the hospital, Mrs. Simmons."

Emily disregarded that and ignored the posted visiting hours. Enlisting Jenny Conroy to keep an eye on Fred, she moved into Henry's hospital room. The hospital refused to set up a cot in Henry's room, so Emily went to Newberry's and bought one. She brought her Bible and a small overnight bag.

Word on the 'Geechee Road was all about fire—Josie's burns from the car accident, Henry's from the pulp vat, Laura Jean's electro-shock treatments.

Emily prayed. She read from the scriptures, especially the passage about fire. She only slept when someone from the 'Geechee Road came to relieve her.

Henry lost three fingers on his left hand. Muscle from his legs was used to make graft upon graft. Dr. Star, who was Jewish, gained a new appreciation for the power of prayer and returned to Temple after years of absence.

* * * * *

One year after the accident, Emily took what was left of Henry home. He didn't talk except to say yes and no. The only person whose help he accepted was the hired male nurse. All the nerves in his body cried out. He had been to Hell and he was marked by fire.

Henry moved into the spare room and refused to sleep under Emily's serpent banner with the crawling snakes. Morphine had played a trick on Henry. He knew he had fallen into the pulp vat at work, but what he remembered was a thousand snakes chasing him toward a river of fire, and in the chase, he had no choice. If he turned away from the flame, he would die from snakebites. So he ran headlong into the slippery, licking flames that danced themselves bloody as they ate away at him.

"I got to learn all I can about snakes," Henry said to Fred. It was his first full sentence. "The more I know, the better I can protect myself from them. The next time, I can turn away from the fire. I can change the outcome. I can get whole." Henry planned on being prepared for when he had to choose between rocks and hard places—between serpents and flames.

"I'll get the books, Daddy." And true to his word, Fred went to the library and got book after book about snakes.

Henry learned that it was possible to catch a snake if he had a forked stick, two-pronged—the kind folks use for toasting marshmallows. Put the fork right behind the snake's head and press down fast and steady to prevent the snake from turning and striking.

Henry studied the constellation known as the Serpens—using his eyes to connect its sinuous shapes between Ursa Major and Ursa Minor—its slinky tail trailing off toward Gemini, its poisonous head aiming toward the pole star. The Serpens coiled around the North Pole—searching for stars to swallow, hoping the pronged shapes would not perforate its skin. And the sky serpent, beautiful and labyrinthine, remained safe to Henry in its cold distance.

Emily bought him a telescope so he could observe the stars. He became the memory he held of himself before the burn—strong, with his fluids contained except when he relieved himself or sweat hard or made love with Emily.

Henry's skin peeled off as it healed—like ten million sunburns—and while it continued, Henry had Fred, Emily and sometimes Tessie, read to him about snakes and how they shed their skin.

"The snake secretes an oil under the skin which loosens it. The snake pushes the loose skin back over the upper and lower jaw by rubbing among the rocks, catching the moist, tissue-like garment in the stubble. Next the snake crawls forth, turning the skin wrong-side-out the entire length of its body, taking as long as thirty minutes to undress," Tessie read aloud.

Henry saw his dying skin as a garment, as raiment made of lymph and glistening blood, the weave of which was lost. Tessie went back to Annie and Josie with her facts about snakes and fire, and shared them.

Henry asked for the part about shedding to be read over and over to him. He hoped for an oil to loosen his burned flesh, and during the day, he rocked in his sheets, working to shed skin, crawling an inch up and an inch down on sheets and sheepskin. Wrong-side-out, trying to undress.

-18-
Judgment

Tessie split her time between her trailer, Annie's, the Conroys' and Henry, Emily and Fred's. Henry was hospitalized the same year Ray was arrested and sent away, so Tessie helped out at The Bee Hive. In exchange, Jenny Conroy took care of any trailer expenses, feeling that that was the least she could do for Laura Jean and Ray's girl.

One night after Ray had been gone for about three months, Tessie was at the Conroys' for a supper of red eye gravy, grits and shrimp. About twenty bites into Tessie's meal, Miss Jenny broke the news. "I can't keep paying utilities and all at your trailer. God knows Earle and I love you as if you were our own," Jenny said.

"You know that, Tessie," Earle said with his mouth full of grits.

"I can stay over at Annie and Josie's; I know they can use my help," Tessie said.

"Well, I don't know, Tessie. You will have to ask Josie, but we'll need to keep it on the QT because of social services and all," Jenny looked uncomfortable. "Social services has been giving us a little money to help us out with you, really hardly enough to cover Earle's beer. Ain't it true, Earle?"

"Uh-huh. It's true, especially with Tessie helping me drink it now," Earle said and winked at Tessie who felt relieved to be leaving the Conroys' trailer—not because she didn't love them, but it was all a little too close.

"And Tessie, I can't let Josie have that little bit of cash because that's fraud, you know, and Earle and me could get in trouble with the gov'ment. So you'll have to let her know that, and all. We'll have to just let social services still think you're here. I don't know how they might be about, you know, the color thing, but I think they too busy to notice. OK, sugar?" Jenny said in one big gush of air.

Tessie nodded.

"Now finish your grits," Earle said. When Earle took his dishes to the sink, he stopped by Tessie and whispered in her ear, "You getting prettier by the minute, Miss Tessie."

Tessie felt a rattle at the base of her spine.

* * * * *

Josie continued to heal. Soon she was well enough to go back to taking in ironing, doing laundry, and tailoring clothes, and now she had Annie and Tessie to help. The three of them raised an all-year garden for vegetables. They canned and dried food, and Josie caught and skinned catfish.

Josie loved her old white frame house with its red tin roof out on the 'Geechee Road, away from drinkers and yellers, mill workers and bartenders. She wanted as few people around her as possible; she wanted to be near the swamp and the trees, the cottonmouths and the frogs, the fireflies and the river. Josie loved the land that had belonged to her family for as far back as blacks could own land. Very few whites or blacks wanted to be near the swamp. She lived far enough away from the river not to get flooded, but close enough to be able to fish and shrimp, close enough to walk down at night and run her hand in the water, stirring up the phosphorous, and watching the iridescent green shine in the moonlight.

Tessie loved Josie. Josie had the strength and presence of a river and a goddess. Annie cut the sleeves on Josie's store-bought blouses so the fabric would not rub her tender skin. Her cheekbones rose out from under her eyes like shelves, and the scars tissue from the burn continued to fade and heal.

"I swear your mama has a halo over her head, Annie," Tessie said. Josie overheard her. Tessie was hoeing the garden and Josie was making a foot high rock perimeter around the flower beds.

"The only thing holding my halo on, Tessie, are my short little horns hidden under my Afro," Josie spoke in a loud whisper before her face broke open in a laugh.

Josie was, after all, Ol' Dolly's daughter. She knew about laughter and loving and the magic of stones. Josie thanked God every day that she was also the daughter of Fuddah Osaha, 'Geechee witchdoctor and trader. When Fuddah was without clients and without raccoon furs, he had worked on Ray's boat. He showed Ray where the shrimp ran when everybody else's nets were coming up empty. Fuddah worked long enough to get the money he needed, and then he went back to his hut in the swamp. But there wasn't any more shrimping work for Fuddah, since Ray had been sent up. None of the other shrimpers wanted Fuddah on their boats; especially the Italians.

Tessie moved into Annie and Josie's house within a week of the conversation with Miss Jenny. She kept herself clean and silent at school. She seldom associated with Annie at their integrated junior high school. She didn't want either of them getting in to trouble with the white kids or the black ones, and she didn't want the department of social services realizing that she was no longer staying with her "aunt" and "uncle." The girls got off the bus together at the end of the day, they waited for the bus to pull out of sight, and then they shifted their books to their outside arms. They linked hands and skipped down the dirt road the way they had when they were little.

Annie knew enough about life to know she had to have had a father, but she didn't know who he was. The facts Josie gave Annie were sparse. "You got his nose, girl, 'coz you sure don't have mine!" Josie proclaimed.

Annie had a long narrow nose that looked nothing like Josie's flat one. "You must be someone else's child to have such straight teeth," Josie teased Annie. "Where'd you go to get them long legs, girl? T'other side of this town?" Josie would laugh and pat Annie on the arm. "I don't care what kind of nose you got, and I'd love you even if you had crooked teeth like mine. Hell! I might even love you more if you did."

Josie had lovers, but no one stayed overnight. She hung a wrought iron sign outside her door that read: "Dogs preferred to men." And if that wasn't enough to keep undesirables away, the fact that she was Ol' Dolly's and Fuddah's child, who kept a big brown bloodhound right inside her front door, did. The truth was almost everyone on Highway 17 was afraid of magic and swamps, snakes and each other.

It took the people from Family and Children's Services about three months to figure out that Tessie wasn't staying at the Conroys' anymore. Then it took them another month to organize a home visit to the Osaha household. A black woman and a white woman came to the door, and Charlie, the hound, sniffed them suspiciously. The black woman asked questions, while the white woman wrote pages and pages of notes. When the outcome of their report came back in the hands of a Chatham County Sheriff, it was fairly simple. The sheriff handed the envelope to Josie. Once she opened it and saw the state seal on it, she figured, rightly, that it was bad news for all of them, so she handed it back to the sheriff and asked him to read it aloud:

To Josephine Osaha
who resides on the east side of Swamps End Road,
November 17, 1969

Be it known that this residence is not acceptable for foster care. Code 70358 has been violated in the following ways: unvaccinated hound; unacceptable septic system; source of well water--unknown; no known source of income; head of household--single unwed female. Elizabeth Harnish, a fourteen-year-old white female, may no longer dwell at this designation, and will be removed forthwith by County of Chatham Family and Children Services on November 18, 1969 by five o'clock (5:00 p.m.), Eastern Standard Time.

I have set my seal invested with the power granted by the State of Georgia herewith.

                                                    Judge William Frank

It was silent for a moment, then the sheriff spoke again. "You'll need to sign where the X is, Miz Osaha. If you cain't write, just make your mark." Josie picked up his pen and in well-formed letters signed, "Josephine Aija Osaha." Then she threw the pen down.

"Great God Almighty! What is going on here? I don't give one good goddamn about the judge and the court," Josie yelled.

She snatched the court order back from the sheriff. She read it out loud again.

The sheriff looked stunned. "Why'd you have me read it if you could read?" he demanded.

"I wanted the bad news coming from the mouth of someone other than me," Josie said. Josie held the paper in readiness to tear it, but stopped herself. The Chatham County Sheriff had narrowed his eyes at Josie. He had taken out his notepad and pencil, and he looked like he was going to write down anything else she said.

She pulled herself together and said, "We thank you for bringing us the news, even though we don't like it, Sheriff. Good day."

After the sheriff left, Josie put her arms around Tessie and Annie and they cried together.

Josie spoke first. "I ain't gonna let them take you for very long, and I ain't gonna let them take you very far. You hear me, Tessie?" Tessie didn't hear her, instead she heard the sheriff's voice saying as he read "this residence is not acceptable for foster care," and she wanted to scream, "Why—too much love here, Sheriff?" She didn't register his departure any more than she registered Josie's words. Josie knew Tessie was in trouble because her deep blue eyes shifted around the room—unable to light on anything—just like Josie had seen Laura Jean's do the day they came to take her away, just like a bird who cannot find a place to land when it is caught in a house.

"Tessie. Tessie!" Tessie heard Annie's voice—off in a distance and went to look for her. She found Annie first and then Josie, and began to breathe again.

"Mama and I are right here. And we're going to figure something out, aren't we Mama?" Annie said.

"Yes, baby, we are. I'll figure something out, Tessie. I promise," Josie said, her guts churning. So it's going to be white, drunk and white, stupid and white winning over black and female, black and love, Josie thought.

Annie believed in her mother's strength and the power of her love for Elizabeth Harnish. Surely Family and Children Social Services couldn't be so blind as to think that Tessie had to be with a white family who didn't know her over a black family that loved her.

The next day Family and Children's Services sent a woman from the orphanage with the same police officer. No one pretended anything, which meant no one spoke. Tessie hugged Annie and Josie goodbye and then carried her old blue suitcase filled with the objects of her life out the door and down the three stairs. The officer loaded the suitcase in the trunk, loaded Tessie in the backseat behind the cage, and drove away. Tessie felt like Ray looked when they arrested him—mournful and mad.

In the backseat of the sheriff's car, Elizabeth Harnish looked about four and felt about ninety. She was trapped and ready to run. Her heart kept beating the questions, "Isn't being fourteen supposed to be about being protected, loved and free?"

Family and Children Services placed Tessie in a foster home with a white family on the other side of Route 17 where she had to go to a different junior high school. The first thing she did after she was shown to her room and left alone was to unpack her bag. She didn't let a single emotion show in front of the new people.

She took out the three cobalt blue jars her mother had given her on her ninth Christmas. She held them up to the dim bulb that hung from the ceiling and admired the deep, deep blue. Then she saw her face in the smoky mirror across the room.

"I am as blue as these jars, sad and blue," she thought. She set each blue jar on her dresser. Her eyes, almost the color of the glass, considered the puzzle of three empty jars from her mother, three cobalt blue jars bought empty, wrapped empty, and now sitting empty on her dresser in a foster home near the paper mill at the MacIntoshes. She had a small room in the basement, an old fold-out couch, a piece of gold shag carpeting that covered some of the floor.

The MacIntoshes made lists: clean the toilet, scrub the floors, wash the windows, tidy the kitchen, rake the yard and feed the horses—the job she loved.

Her foster parents had four horses and a small barn, and Tessie went there every day, every chance she could to be with Whitley, the blue roan.

"It's a horse of a different color," Tessie wrote to Annie. "I think it is my horse. I mean, I know it isn't, but...well, it's hard to explain. I asked Mr. MacIntosh about Whitley today. 'How come you call it a blue roan?' I said. He said, 'That horse started out with mostly black hair that got toned down with some white ones. When the coat grows in, it shines blues.' Then he took me over to Whitley and showed me how much black there was underneath all the white. 'You got to look close at her all year long, Tessie. You'll see that she doesn't change color like the grays do. They get lighter in the summer. Whitley don't. And look here at this scar, Tessie, see how it is all black? Well, that's how you know she's a roan, 'cause all the hair grew back black—not one white hair. The stud was a black roan, too, and the mare was a Paint.'" Tessie kept writing.

"I love the wildness in Whitley, Annie. She doesn't want any one else near her or riding her. So I am the one who broke her out and the MacIntoshes let me ride her as a reward for tending to her. I don't own her, but she's mine. Last week I took her for a ride along the river. I wish you had been there, too, Annie."

Tessie hated the watered-down orange juice and the stale bread she got from the MacIntoshes for breakfast, but she loved Whitley so much, she could put up with her foster family's stinginess when it came to food. She knew how much the state paid the people who kept her, and she knew that hardly any of that money got spent on her. She missed Josie's fried chicken and fried fish, hush puppies and red rice, and she missed Annie and Josie right down to her bones.

Stubborn and raw as Ray and Laura Jean had been sometimes, they had also been loving and prideful. Other foster children that Tessie knew, swore and spit, cried and hit, stole and hurt themselves and others. Tessie kept her chin up, kept her voice low, and remained kind and quiet. She hid her tears and stole from no one.

At the MacIntoshes' there were two other foster children, a 13 year-old girl and a 15 year-old boy. The boy caught her in the barn and tried to kiss her. Tessie ducked him and when he tried to kiss her again, she kicked him in the shin.

"Who do you think you are anyway, Tessie Harnish? Just cause your real name's Elizabeth, don't mean shit. You're plain ole Tessie to me," he said, and then he spat in the straw.

"I don't have anything to say to you. You try this again, I'm telling the MacIntoshes. Lizard boy, that's what you are—scaly old lizard boy!" Tessie hurled the words at him like rocks and ran away.

Tessie knew her daddy had named her Elizabeth after his mother, but the nickname "Tessie" had been her mother's invention from a book she'd read in high school by Thomas Hardy. Tessie decided it was time to read the book, so she went to a bookstore in Savannah and bought it. She read about the heath and heather, the damp and the dark, passion and desertion.

It wasn't only the foster kids who had attitude about Tessie. People on the 'Geechee Road thought she and Laura Jean and were uppity. Even Josie. But Josie didn't think uppity was bad and came to get Tessie from the MacIntoshes' place to bring her back to Swamp Road for good. Maybe it was pity or maybe it was divine intervention, but after less than two months, the Chatham County DDS had gotten the judge to reverse his decision and let Tessie leave foster care and live with Annie and Josie until either Ray or Laura Jean came home.

On the ride home, Tessie told Josie about the boy asking her who she thought she was. "Good God Almighty!" Josie yelled, and then she pulled her car to the side of the road. "White folks been telling me and my people that we are uppity for a long time. They beat some of us when we wouldn't step down. The white men used uppity as an excuse to rape our women and lynch our men folk for having minds of their own. I got to tell you, Tessie, that you got a mighty spirit, and most folks don't like that in someone else. It makes them afraid." Josie paused, not sure if she should go on with sharing the rest with Tessie.

"What is it, Miss Josie? I can tell there's more, you may as well go ahead on and tell me whatever is stirring around in your mind," Tessie said.

"Tessie, I don't want you to go crazy like your mama. Some of us think the reason your mama went off is because she read and thought too much. She wanted more. Your daddy'd give her a trailer, she'd want a house. He'd buy her a fancy gold wedding ring with three diamonds, she'd want a solitaire. He got her a nineteen-inch color TV, she wanted books. I remember him buying her a whole box of romance books from the drugstore for her birthday before you were born. She opened the box and started crying. 'What's the matter, darlin'?' he asked her. At first she didn't say anything. Then she said something she shouldn't never have said. 'You big dumb redneck. Those aren't books, those are trash, and so are you.' So if I was you, Tessie, I'd be careful how much you let yourself shine. Learn and do, but don't show it. You hear?" Josie said.

"You just go ahead on and be uppity, Tessie, but try to be careful, too," Josie said.

Then she got in her car and headed back on to the 'Geechee Road. "Be careful, too." The words rang in Tessie's mind, and she got scared again. Nothing was simple. Nothing.

-19-
Temperature

Back on the 'Geechee Road, Tessie tried to get some balance between being uppity and being careful, and she knew right off that she wasn't any good at finding the place where the scales didn't tip. At school, she tried to keep herself in check by sleeping in class. It was how she remained invisible.

Some of the high school teachers let Tessie sleep. Others woke her and humiliated her when she didn't know how to answer their questions.

In ninth grade science class, Tessie stayed awake for discussions of the digestive system,

Mr. Headington started class one lazy October day by asking, "Why can't humans swallow their food whole?" He paused. Then he called out, "Tessie?"

"I don't know. I do know how to help snakes swallow their food whole. You know they don't have teeth, don't you, Mr. H.?" The class laughed. They could tell Tessie was on a roll. Mr. Headington was one of the teachers who liked Tessie. In the teachers' lounge when the other teachers complained about her, Head, as the other teachers called him, argued that she had an inquisitive mind, and that one day she would be a beauty.

"How do you help the snakes, Tessie?" Mr. Headington asked.

"I rub their necks and their bellies until the frog or mouse or whatever begins to dissolve." The class snickered and John Henry who was taking ninth grade science for the third time called out, "You can rub my neck and belly, anytime, Tessie Harnish."

Tessie turned in her chair and hissed at him, "Shut up, boy. I ain't afraid of you anymore. That playground was a long time ago." Just hearing John Henry speak made Tessie's knee scars itch. "I hate you." John Henry smiled at her as if he were drugged or stupid or both. Tessie knew she had bewitched John Henry—he wanted her.

Mr. Headington pretended not to hear John Henry who was a lot bigger and meaner than Mr. H. wanted to deal with. "Thank you for sharing your knowledge with us, Tessie."

Later that day in World History, Mr. Smith discussed insanity in the royal houses of Europe. "Insanity is often a result of inbreeding," Mr. Smith declared

Tessie's hand flew up. "Why would someone go crazy if their parents hadn't been related?"

Mr. Smith, hoping not to appear foolish and not wanting to deal with the issue at hand, generalized. "Well, there are all kinds of things which cause insanity."

And Tessie, not to be silenced, said, "Like what?"

And Mr. Smith, to avoid answering, pulled down a map of the world and touched his pointer on St. Petersburg and began talking about the Tsars. When Mr. Smith avoided the question, Tessie put her head down and slept. He let her, glad to have her quiet.

The next day in science, Mr. Headington wouldn't let Tessie sleep and he wouldn't let her go off on tangents. He began the class by introducing the term poikilothermous. Tessie became so excited that many of her classmates thought she was having a seizure. (They had been studying epilepsy in health and saw themselves as experts. Justin Rhoades called for a pillow, and Freddie Willard yelled, "Don't let her swallow her tongue!").

Mr. Headington raised his voice and called out, "Now class, sit down," Mr. Headington said, "Yes, Tessie, what is it?"

On the lined paper in front of her, Tessie copied what Mr. Headington had put on the chalkboard:

poi-ki-lo-ther-mous (poi'kil'- -thûr'm s) adj. Also
poi-ki-lo-ther-mal (-mal). Zoology.
Having a body temperature that varies with the external environment; cold-blooded. Compare homoiothermous.

ho-moi-o-ther-mous (ho-moi'o-thûr'm s) adj. Also

149

> ho-moi-o-ther-mal (-mal), ho-me-o-ther-mous (ho′me-o-thûr′m s)
> *Maintaining a relatively constant and warm body temperature that is independent of environmental temperature; warm-blooded. Compare poikilothermous.*

"I'm both," Tessie said.

"You can't be both, Tessie. You are either one or the other. And we can tell by looking at you that you aren't a reptile or a fish," Mr. H. said, pleased with his humor.

"I know I am a mammal and that I ain't no fish or reptile, but I've been taught how to make my body temperature the same as the Earth's. And I can prove it, too," Tessie said.

The class wanted everyone to march outside while Tessie proved it because they didn't believe she could. Mr. H said, "I believe you, Tessie. You can show us another time."

At the end of class, he went to the office to find out where Elizabeth Harnish was eighth period. Then he left the note he had written her, in a sealed envelope, with her English teacher.

It read, "Take me somewhere private soon and show me how you are both, homoiothermic and poikilothermic."

Tessie felt sick to her stomach. Mr. H. wasn't any different than the boys on the bus. They wanted to get her alone then touch and kiss her.

Tessie tore the note into many small pieces and pushed the remains into her desk. The teacher rattled on about the function of appositive phrases and Tessie let her heart harden.

Annie would only leave Josie if Fuddah could come to sit with her. "You got to be there, Fuddah, or I can't go to school. I know she seems better, but I still worry. If I don't go to school, then social services gonna come around and take me and Tessie away and put Mama in some kind of assisted living. They don't want Mama to be back on her feet, back on her own."

Fuddah understood—he came Monday through Friday and sat with Josie, quiet as a stone. He helped Josie when she asked for help.

Annie had Mr. H. for science, too, but during a different period. Tessie didn't tell Annie about Mr. H.'s note or about the class, but Annie heard through the grapevine that Tessie had mentioned she could be like a snake by making her body the same temperature as the earth.

After the lesson on warm-blooded and cold-blooded animals, Tessie stopped talking in Mr. Headington's class, but she still listened. Several weeks passed like this. Then the day of the big test came with all the new terms they had been studying. Tessie didn't like tests, but being angry with Mr. H. made her want to do better in his class, so she studied hard. She looked up all the terms for the test, except for morrow. That one she figured she knew from the lecture he gave.

"The bone has morrow and from the morrow, new-blood comes." A statement about the future, Tessie thought, and she wondered what new blood she would have tomorrow, would it be strong enough to see her through? She heard Laura Jean's voice mixing with Mr. Headington's, "You come from good blood, Tessie, good blood will see you through."

The first time Tessie heard the word marrow in class, she confused it with morrow which was used in Shakespeare, "On the morrow, kind sir," rang in Tessie's ear.

On the morrow, the day of the test, Tessie set up her paper with her heading just like the school wanted it. Her name and the teacher's name in the upper left corner of the paper, the subject and the date in the upper right.

Tessie wrote her definitions with care and was surprised by Mr. Headington spelling morrow wrong—not catching his own mistake. So on her test, she crossed through the "a" and wrote an "o" neatly above it. When she got the test back, there was a long comment on it from Mr. Headington which read: *90%, Tessie. I'm surprised you decided to play a joke on number 10. It is clear that you looked all of the other terms up and that you memorized the definitions. Why would you sabotage yourself on the last one? You know marrow—it's the soft jelly you will find in the bone of a steak—sweet when it's still hot—fatty when it's cold. It is essential to the life of a body because it is in the marrow that red blood cells are made. See me if you have questions. Mr. H.*

After class Tessie approached Mr. H.'s desk. "Mr. Headington, I wasn't playing a joke on you or me. I really thought you said "morrow." I remember last week in class when you talked about the morrow being the place where new blood comes from. That's why I wrote morrow is the future of blood? And in a way, I'm right. Aren't I?" Tessie asked.

She watched as Mr. H. unscrewed the lid to his fountain pen, watched as he crossed out the 90% and made it a 95%, continued watching while he erased the score in the grade book and entered the new one.

"Next time you are a bit confused, Tessie, ask for help, please," he said.

Tessie felt her face turn hot and red, and she hated that she couldn't control the rapid rise of heat and color to her face. "Maybe I've been wrong about you, Mr. H."

And now it was time for Mr. H. to blush. "What do you mean, Tessie? Wrong about what?" he asked.

"Maybe you aren't like the others," Tessie said.

"What others, Tessie?" Mr. H. asked.

"Men," Tessie said, as if that summed it all up.

Maybe he does care if I learn things, Tessie thought as she walked out to catch her bus. Maybe he cares about my mind and not just my body.

* * * * *

Tessie and Annie were brave enough to sit together on the bus, and for some reason no one bugged them about that. Tessie plopped down by Annie.

"How come you didn't correct me on marrow, Annie?" Tessie said.

Annie bit her lip for a couple minutes before she confessed, "I wanted to get a higher score than you, Tessie."

Tessie hit Annie in the head with her science book, then Annie knocked her into the aisle. Tessie scratched Annie's face and drew a trickle of blood.

"You, girls! Stop it right now, or I'm a gonna write you up, 'hear?" The bus driver didn't move out of his seat, but he kept his eyes on them in his big mirror.

"Stop, Tessie, just stop. It's only five points different, besides Mr. H. has a crush on you. He'll give you an A no matter what," Annie said. "You're going to get us thrown off this bus."

"Go to hell, Annie," Tessie whispered so she wouldn't get written up for swearing. "Go to hell, with gasoline on your shoes!" Tessie said.

From that day forward, Tessie fought for the bone in the sirloin steak, and she got it. She wanted the marrow because she believed if she ate it, her family would heal from her strength, Josie's and Henry's burns would heal, and they would both rise from their beds and be whole again. She sucked out the marrow to get strong, to secure her future, and save two of the adults she loved.

-20-
The Unfriendly Nest

Tessie closed her eyes and prayed for a vision, but try as she might she could see no image that told her how to rid her mother of the craziness that kept her locked up. She and Jenny were making another pilgrimage to Milledgeville.

"You want to stay long enough for me to give your mama a hair cut, Tessie?" Jenny asked Tessie, interrupting her thoughts.

"Yes, ma'am, I sure do," Tessie said. The first words out of Tessie's mouth when the orderlies brought Laura Jean down for her visit were, "Mama, you want Miss Jenny to give you a hair cut?"

"I'd love that, Tessie. Will you, Jenny? Can I?" Laura Jean directed her gaze at Willie Mae, the orderly who knew her best and was always assigned to her.

"I don't see as how it can do any harm. Go ahead, but be sure to clean up your mess," Willie Mae said.

Jenny retrieved her scissors and comb from her purse, and went to work. She cut Laura Jean's hair into a stacked bob, and set it on the pink plastic rollers to give it more body. She showed Laura Jean the four colors of nail polish she had packed: Really Red, Oh So Pink, Aren't You Orange, and Cantaloupe.

"Which color, Laura Jean?" Jenny asked. No answer came from her, so Jenny picked Aren't You Orange, wishing that Laura Jean was any color but gray.

No one talked. Jenny was mad as a hornet at Laura Jean for giving up. She didn't believe in mental illness, she believed Laura Jean was choosing to hide out at Milledgeville, of all places. Tessie couldn't think about her mother without seeing clouds, heavy with rain. She knew enough about sorrow and the river to know that when the river meets the rain, the world floods.

When the makeover was finished, the effect was profound.

"You look great, Laura Jean," Willie Mae said, and smiled. Although Laura Jean's once black strands had faded in Milledgeville, the haircut worked wonders. Laura Jean's face no longer looked dull. Her hair was smooth and straight, the cut precise.

"Maybe this will help me untangle my memories," Laura Jean said. Then she smiled at the three women and most especially at Tessie. "I will try to come home soon, Tessie, I promise, and Willie Mae will help me, won't you, Willie Mae?"

"I sure will, Laura Jean. I will do my best so you can go home to your family," Willie Mae said with conviction.

Tessie hugged her mother's neck, and Laura Jean hugged her back. She hung onto her, but she didn't recite or pick at her.

Jenny walked out with Willie Mae who said, "You should get your Doc Maines involved in helping to get Laura Jean released. It's like getting a pass in high school, if you know what I mean."

Tessie smiled. She can get well, she thought; she can come home. It had been her plan to tell her mother about Josie and the accident, Ray and the drug bust, her time in foster care—all of it—but in that place her will failed her and she decided instead to send a letter.

* * * * *

Willie Mae tried to maintain Laura Jean's new haircut. She brushed out the tangled, unfriendly nest after the electro-shock treatments. She took her to the barber in the men's ward and talked to him about how to keep the lines and angles Jenny had cut into Laura Jean's hair. During each visit to the barbershop, Laura Jean sang "Shall We Gather at the River," and the more the barber cut, the louder Laura Jean sang. "Not so loud, Laura. Not so loud or we'll have to take you back to the Edison Ward." Willie Mae and the barber chuckled.

Laura Jean got quiet.

"Granny, how come you keep your hair like that?" Laura Jean addressed the image in the mirror.

"Like what, Laura Jean?" She answered herself with a question.

"In a stacked bob. You ought to put some color on it," Laura Jean told herself.

She wanted to see herself better so she thought for a few minutes to get the right words in the right order. "Hand me a mirror, please," she said.

"You got a whole wall a mirrors directly in front of you, Laura," the barber said.

"Please, sir."

The barber handed Laura Jean a hand mirror. She put it in front of her face, looked at her reflection directly, intently, silently, then put the mirror down flat on the counter in front of her. "That woman in the mirror is me, Willie Mae?"

"Yes, sugar, it's you. We all get old, Miss Laura," Willie Mae said. Laura Jean had turned as calm as pond water. So this is who I have become, Laura Jean thought, and stood up.

"I want to see the doctor, please."

"I'll let the floor nurse know as soon as we go up, Miss Laura. Come on, now," Willie Mae took Laura Jean's hand and led her back to the ward, then she told the floor nurse that Laura Jean had had some kind of breakthrough in the barber shop.

"Will you set up that appointment with the psychiatrist as soon as you can?" Willie Mae asked.

"Of course," the head nurse replied.

-21-
Into The Current

Tessie wrote the letter to Laura Jean who read it, but did not answer. Laura Jean asked for paper and pen, but once she had them in her possession, she found herself devoid of words. She had become a caged bird at Milledgeville.

The letter she received from Tessie read:

Hi Mama,

Josie, Daddy, Annie and I went up to Hungry Mother Mountain ten weeks ago to see the snakes—a great big hole had been dug out and filled with canebreak rattlers. Daddy got drunk, so Miss Josie made him ride in the truck bed on the way back. On the way home, a semi jack-knifed in our lane. Miss Josie's hurt bad. They just sent her home, and me and Annie are trying to take care of her. She can't work, so money's real tight, and Buddy Jones, down at the sheriff's office, hauled Daddy off to jail for running dope on his boat.

I saw a hummingbird there. It made me think of you and how you used to love birds and their feathers? Do you still?

I am staying between places—sometimes with Jenny and Earle and sometimes with Josie and Annie. It was good to see you. When are you coming home?

Love,
Tessie

Laura Jean cried when she read the letter. Then she balled it up and threw it into the trash. She put the pen and paper back on her nightstand. She couldn't write. Instead she watched the birds fly outside the window at the end of the ward until she felt she had become one of them. She loved them all: painted buntings, pileated woodpeckers, and ruby-chested humming birds. Her three-year stay at Milledgeville had earned her the best bed in the house, the one best for watching birds. She let other women watch with her.

At 9:30 a.m. every day, they sat anticipating the woodpecker's arrival to feed on suet that an orderly brought from the Piggly Wiggly.

Directly beside the suet, a blooming trumpet vine hung on an ancient live oak tree from mid-March until late October. The orange flowers brought the hummingbirds to suck nectar, hovering, hovering and beating their wings to stay aloft, burning the nectar as fast as they ate it.

Laura Jean loved painted buntings the most—they made her think of Tessie and the dream pillow she had made for her when she was a baby. Dressed in lime, red, purple, yellow and indigo feathers, the tropical birds flew outside her window. They were very rare this far north and Laura Jean was convinced that they came especially to see her, that they had been sent by Tessie to bring the tropical and exotic colors of the low country to the dry, pale landscape of middle Georgia.

In the darkness of a middle Georgia night, with the half-light of night lights, Laura Jean forgot about birds and forgot about her daughter. Her mind became a house full of shadows and closed doors. In the Institution for Mental Health, Laura Jean slept with a pillow between her legs to guard against the night orderlies raping her.

One hot dry summer day ran into another, one hot humid summer night ran right into day in Milledgeville, and every day, Laura Jean considered birds. She ordered books on interlibrary loan and read and re-read them. She learned everything about birds, and some of the facts stayed with her despite the electro-shock treatments. With the help of her trusted orderly, Willie Mae, Laura Jean chronicled facts about birds, writing them in spiral notebooks that Tessie sent her in monthly care packages. She did send a thank you card to Tessie for these, her messages kept simple: "Got your box. Love, Mama"

In her readings, she was reminded that birds are closely related to reptiles, that birds bathe in smoke because of its medicinal cleansing powers. While they bathe, they feast on bugs driven up by the heat. She wished she had transparent eyelids, too, to help her when she wanted to fly. She loved the idea of an eyelid she could see through and that also kept out the bugs and dirt.

She was surprised to learn that baby bird poop arrives in the world encased in mucus sacks. This keeps the nest clean. She learned that goldfinches eat thorns and thistles. She remembered from church that goldfinches tried to save Jesus by pulling out the nails that held him to the cross. She wished a bird would arrive during shock treatment and draw the volts out of her brain. Maybe the buntings could do that if she called to them.

Laura Jean imagined birds flying through dark caves, relying on their powers of echo-location. She identified with blinded birds that flew until they dropped from the sky—starving and thirsty—flew and flew until they were spent. She wanted to go outside and search for fallen feathers.

"Willie Mae, can we go out to collect the feathers?" Laura Jean asked.

"No, Miss Laura, we can't, but I will pick them up when I go out for a smoke," Willie Mae said.

She brought fallen feathers in and a hummingbird nest measuring one and one half inches wide.

"Here you go, Laura Jean," Willie Mae said and she handed the little nest over.

One tiny egg, Laura Jean thought.

If there had been two, Laura Jean could have fit both of them on top of a penny.

One unhatched egg. One unhatchable egg. A nest. An abandoned nest with an egg too old to hatch.

The egg made Laura Jean cry because it made her think of Tessie. And the tighter she held it in her hand, the more her heart cracked. She could hear it cracking. She could feel it breaking into tiny pieces. Her great cracking heart smelled rotten. Laura Jean heard a raw screeching sound filling the ward, like a crow that has been shot but is still alive.

Other wild sounds joined the crow—some strange noise that was part dinosaur and part fighter plane. She dropped the egg, brought her hands across her chest in an X, and then she began to move her arms like a bird in a straight jacket. Trying to take flight, but never leaving the ground.

Four orderlies arrived, grabbing at Laura Jean's flailing arms until they held her down. Two of the patients gathered up the tiny, broken, rotten egg. The orderlies put Laura Jean in a straight jacket and took her away. The maintenance man arrived with pine-scented cleansers for the floor, but the smell was too strong. One of the orderlies opened the windows, then stood like a sentinel while the patients flocked to the open air. No one could find the nest or what remained of the egg.

Days later when Laura Jean returned from solitary confinement, the bird nest appeared on her bedside table. She awoke in her bed, without restraints, and saw the little nest waiting for her with a blue cat's eye marble in it. Laura Jean smiled. She cleaned out her top drawer where she kept her extra nightgown. She laid the nest gently inside the drawer. Without the egg. The nest. Laura Jean's thoughts came to her in pieces. Am I the nest? She put the nest in the drawer. She thought of Tessie all those years ago in her dresser drawer. Feathers. My baby. Where's my girl? How? Can I fly? Home?

Each day became clearer. Laura Jean could see connections. She began thinking about her escape. As she became more lucid, she also became more jealous of her feathered friends' flight patterns and migrations. Their destiny was mapped for them. The feather-edge of reality made her a tentative woman, feather-brained and feather-headed. Because of the shock treatments, Laura Jean could not concentrate on T.V. or read, but she could embroider—French knots, cross stitch, and feather stitch. For hours on end, Laura Jean embroidered napkins with her favorite birds—and she embroidered painted buntings two to one over other birds. As she sewed, she noticed the feather veined pattern of her skin and felt as if she was part bird.

Laura Jean, flooded with memories, thought about how much she had loved forming letters in third grade. She liked the sense of control she had when she was counting things. In fourth grade, she memorized all the prepositions and the multiplication tables up to 12. She learned to dip the tip of her fountain pen in the dark blue ink that was housed in the circular hole at her desk's upper-right corner. With her pen, she practiced her name over and over again using the Palmer method. Her teachers praised her for her eye to detail and her ability to memorize.

While Laura Jean watched the hummingbirds hover above the lilies outside the ward window, the painted bunting appeared again at the live oak tree. The woodpecker drilled its supper from the dying pine bark, and so she considered the list of small words she learned long ago; over under around and through, off down out up in at to from, among with on against within without by of. She was missing some; maybe they'd return like the birds, like her mind, if she could concentrate and be patient, if she could learn the anatomy of flight, of wings, of feathers, of beaks searching.

In her arm. In her bed. Wrapped in the ice pack. With an ice pick. Out of luck. Out of money, almost out of time. For love. For money. For nothing. For everything. For Tessie. Overdue, overworked, overwrought. You're overwrought, Mrs. Harnish. You keep working yourself up like this and we won't have any choice but to send you down for shock. Down and out. From where? From whom? For what? To overcome your fear. In her heart. In her chest. In her mind. Where fear and hope fought against each other—such natural enemies. Out of nowhere. In a heartbeat. Like white on rice. Without mercy. Within minutes. Without hope. Full of fear.

The prepositions positioned themselves to overtake sentences, feeding Laura Jean pieces of language, parts of thoughts, frames of a film, notes from a song. Bird seed. Language as birdseed. Bit by bit. Piece by piece. How to get full? Entering her mind to nourish her. Could she live by eating her own words one letter at a time?

And what about numbers? What if she counted every action she took, each action she observed, counted them one at a time? Would she be able to tell the difference between the ones she observed and the ones she participated in? Were observing and participating the same thing? Not when it was her daughter's life. Could she multiply her swallows by blinks, divide them by tears, subtract the past from the future and somehow arrive in the present? Add all her mistakes and failures to her successes and joys and get what? Her life back? Or would she retrieve a long list of numbers on paper, impossible to decipher, hopeless in their digital precision of a life?

*****

"Electro-shock is our best hope for curing you, Mrs. Harnish. We wouldn't use it if it weren't helping you, now would we?" the doctor's grainy voice prattled on.

"One, two, three, four, five, six," Laura Jean counted the seconds as soon as they strapped her to the table. Then she lost consciousness. The first sign that she was returning after the treatment was when she could begin counting the birds in her mind—one, two, three, four, five, six, seven, eight. The numbers, old friends, following each other neatly in a row. The way she thought life would be. Measurable. Safe—in a sequence. But she knew love was passion and not order, and children were messy and not neat, and she didn't know how to proceed when her bones were so tired she could barely rise, and when she did rise, she saw the little worms.

Willie Mae brought a bouquet of flowers from her garden and a caterpillar came in on the flowers. Laura Jean picked up the bouquet and a caterpillar fell on her leg. Laura Jean's first response was to scream and then to never move again, but she was able to prevent the scream from coming out of her mouth and she was able to take her hand and brush the caterpillar on to the floor.

Willie Mae gasped. It was the first sign of hope.

Laura Jean had decided. She was going to get well and she was going home to Tessie. She didn't know what she thought about Ray, sitting somewhere in a North Georgia prison. Each day she said one sentence over and over again. Get home to Tessie. It was her first thought and her last one. It was her dream and her hope. Get home to Tessie, before it's too late. And it replaced her preoccupation with worms and lint, prepositions and pain.

-22-
Painted Buntings

Jenny Conroy added a dab of half and half to her coffee thermos and then put the lid on before she gave it a shake. She took the two extra sandwiches she had made while she had packed Earl's lunch, threw them into her cooler, grabbed her Chesterfields, her cup and her keys, and hurried to her car before she could drop anything or be interrupted by a phone call or a visitor. She hadn't told anyone, leastwise Tessie, that she was driving to Milledgeville to see Laura Jean. She wanted to see her old friend. It was time for them to talk again.

She put her favorite Charlie Pride eight-track in and began the drive, her coffee on the dashboard, a cigarette in her hand, and a soulful Charlie singing about lost love. Jenny remembered Laura Jean's moving-in at Little Bit and the first time the two of them went out without Ray and Earl. Men's eyes followed Jenny and her slender hips and big breasts. And then the men's eyes landed on Laura Jean and her subtle features, her winsome smile and the waspish delivery of her hello. The women were flowers, the men bees.

Jenny's thoughts ran through her head like a movie: Ray and Laura Jean moved in during a brilliant Georgia spring. They planted magenta, crimson, pink, white and orange azaleas. Indigo buntings visited to suck nectar. Jenny drank coffee at Laura Jean's counter and talked and talked and talked, so glad to have her friend close by.

Jenny stopped once at a Denny's to get more coffee and check the air pressure in her tires. Then she hopped back in her new Chrysler Cordoba and drove fast until she pulled into the state mental hospital parking lot. She parked her car by the fire hydrant and marched into the reception area. She signed herself in and left her driver's license with the person at the desk. Then she went directly to the common room where she found Laura Jean watching birds.

Jenny didn't bother with hello or a hug. Instead, she started right in. "You've swallowed your own tail. You've let the rainbow serpent in; that's what you've done, Laura Jean. God knows you need to get the hell out of this place where you got yourself surrounded by crazy people," Jenny said as she stubbed out her cigarette. "You didn't even have the pleasure of breaking any laws to get in here!"

Laura Jean ignored her.

"Laura Jean Harnish! I am talking to you," Jenny yelled.

"I hear you, Jenny Conroy and so does everyone else. Now lower your voice, and let's start this visit all over again," Laura Jean said.

Willie Mae walked over. "Is there a problem here?" She eyed Jenny up and down.

"No, ma'am," Jenny said. "I'll tone it down. I've come to talk some sense into this woman, right now."

Willie Mae placed herself firmly between Laura Jean and Jenny. "I don't want you to frighten her, 'hear? She hasn't had a rough spell or a shock treatment for a good while, and I want to keep her calm so she can come home soon."

Willie Mae turned to Laura Jean. "Do you want to talk to this friend of yours, Laura Jean, or do you want me to send her on her way? She's driven a good way to see you, but that doesn't mean you have to visit with her."

"She can stay, Willie Mae. Thanks for asking," Laura Jean said.

Willie Mae went back over to the other patient, who was working on a counted cross-stitch, and sat down.

"Well, if that woman isn't crazy already, she will be soon doing counted cross-stitch. Good Lord!" Jenny said. Laura Jean and she laughed.

"Sit down, Jenny. Why didn't you bring Tessie?" Laura Jean said.

"I needed to be able to talk with you without her here. You see, I don't think you are crazy, Laura Jean," Jenny said. " Stubborn? Yes. Sad? Yes. Afraid of your own husband, sure and with good reason. In love with your daughter so bad you're afraid you'll ruin her life, so you leave her. Scared to death, blind to hope, lost. Yes, yes. Oh Lord, yes! Life has convinced you that you are crazy, but I don't think you are any crazier than most of the rest of us, just a lot more scared." Jenny talked and talked. "Everyone's crazy, Laura Jean. I know I am. I see and hear things when Earl's working nights."

Jenny took a breath, and started back in. "That's why I got me a bunch of lovers. I can't abide being alone in the dark. And God bless me, Earle puts up with it!" Jenny stopped and waited for Laura Jean to speak.

"Well, Jenny, you put up with Earle," Laura Jean said.

Jenny laughed.

Laura Jean waited.

"You think you're crazy, Laura Jean because you see bugs when there aren't any there. Laura Jean, are you listening to me? Are you still seeing them?"

"I don't see the bugs anymore, and I am listening, Jenny Conroy, but so is the whole common room. You could learn something about being quiet and calm. It would improve you," Laura Jean said.

Jenny paused to light another cigarette. Here was her friend, talking back at her. Praise God.

"What if when you got tired of Ray, you had taken you and Tessie away, or kicked his sorry drunk self out your door and gone to work? Plenty of other women have done it before you," Jenny said, talking softer now.

"It's easy for you to say, Jenny. You say you scared of sounds and the dark, but what really scares you, Jenny Conroy?" Laura Jean demanded.

"I'm scared of plenty, Laura Jean, I already told you, but I deal with my demons, best I can, and I keep a man with me that I love and a few others that I like all right to help me forget what frightens me. I stand up for what I care about. When you gonna start doing that for yourself?" Jenny's voice had gotten so soft that she was whispering.

"I'm doing it right now with you, and I am learning how to do it with the people in this place. I'm changing, Jenny, and I've set me a date to get out of here. Willie Mae's helping me, too. She's a good and smart woman," Laura Jean said.

"You're stuck here and your daughter's living between places. Family and Children has taken her away from Josie and from me," Jenny said.

"What do you mean?" Laura Jean kept her eyes right on Jenny's eyes.

Jenny couldn't hold the gaze. "Well, me and Earle needed a little private time…"

"You mean you needed time for when Earle isn't home to be with your boyfriends?" Laura Jean said, shaking her head.

"Pretty soon, some man's going to come along and take Tessie off with him and hole her up in another trailer somewhere. And how's her life going to go then? Like yours? Like mine?" Jenny asked. "She's got herself a little boyfriend now, Fred Simmons, Henry's boy. He's still staying at home with his folks, but he won't be for long. What's he? A couple years older than Tessie? He's got himself a rock and roll band."

"Henry's boy? You mean his stepson with Emily? They moved back to Little Bit?" Laura Jean asked.

"No, they moved back, but to the south side of town, off of Abercorn Extension. Henry got himself a good job at the mill, and then he had the accident. Do you remember the accident?"

Laura Jean sat still and thought about it. "If you so smart," she said, "how about helping me get out of here? Look over yonder at that pretty woman with the red hair and the straight jacket. She sees animals around her all the time—lions and tigers and bears, oh my." Both women laughed. "She says that phrase over and over as if she is in The Wizard of Oz. Is it bad that she is seeing things that no one else sees, or is that vision? The young man wandering around the room with the baseball hat can't have his glasses. If he holds anything sharp, he hurts himself, cuts lines across his stomach." She paused. "Is being crazy losing the ability to talk--or is that silence? Is leaving a place that's breaking your heart better or worse than staying? Which one is cowardice? Which one is bravery? And who's to say? You, Jenny Conroy? Are you the authority? Because I don't see anyone offering you a job here, do you?"

Jenny grabbed Laura Jean by the shoulders and hugged her hard. "I am so glad to hear you again, Laura Jean, glad to see you get riled up about something. This is the fight you gonna need, woman, to get back on your feet." Willie Mae stole glances across the room at Laura Jean and smiled as she watched her stand up to Jenny.

"If you can get strong enough to get out of here, I'll help you when you come home, Laura Jean." The only sound in the room was Jenny's loud breathing—taking a hit from her cigarette, holding the smoke in, and then exhaling the smoke in loopy rings. "Think on it, Laura Jean. Tessie's gonna be sixteen on her next birthday."

Laura Jean's face brightened. She tried to laugh, but all that came out was a raspy sound; it had been so long. She took in a big breath and let it out, took in another breath and held it. The air intoxicated her.

Before Jenny Conroy left, she asked Laura Jean straight out, "When are you coming home?"

"As soon as I can," Laura Jean said.

Two days later when Laura Jean met with her psychiatrist, she asked him, "Can you help me get off the meds now that I don't have to have the shock treatments anymore, and get me out of here?"

"This is a change. Am I talking to the same Mrs. Harnish?" the doctor's voice patronized Laura Jean, but she ignored the tone.

She smiled at him tentatively. "Yes, sir, you are. It's time for me to go home. My daughter needs me."

"Oh, yes, I can help you get better now that you want to get well. I need to know a few things first, though, so I am going to need your cooperation at all times. Can you give me that?" Dr. Banes asked. While he awaited Laura Jean's response, he took out his silver fine-toothed comb to up-sweep the sides of his hair. Then he patted the comb on the handkerchief he removed from his left jacket pocket. "Well? Can you?"

Laura Jean disliked him. She nodded.

"Good. Well, let's see, do you still see fairies?" Laura Jean shook her head no. "You are going to have to use your words, Mrs. Harnish."

"No, sir, I don't."

"Do you hear voices from God?"

"No, sir, I don't."

"Do you want to live or die?"

"I want to live so I can be with my daughter."

She knew the right answers because they came from her healing heart. The truth was she still saw fairies on the backs of birds and she heard voices, too, but none of it scared her anymore.

Dr. Banes nodded after each response. Laura Jean nodded back.

At the next session, which occurred a week later, Dr. Banes had a different line of questioning. "Do you think you will freeze up with your husband, Mrs. Harnish? Says here on the chart, 'Husband denied access to his wife. Frigid woman.'"

"Can't hardly freeze up in coastal Georgia, Doctor Banes, and besides, my husband is in jail for running dope," Laura Jean said, grateful that Tessie had written her.

"Please be serious, Mrs. Harnish. We don't have enough time here to be wasting it on jokes. One of his concerns was your lack of sexual response," the doctor said.

"I think I am fine, sir. 'Sides, as I said, Ray isn't home these days." Laura Jean kept her voice neutral and controlled.

"Are you having visitors, Mrs. Harnish?"

"My daughter, Tessie, and my friend, Jenny Conroy, have been to see me," Laura Jean said. "Tessie sent me a letter telling me she couldn't come anymore, said it broke her heart to hear me say the same things over and over again, said she hated to see me picking the lint. And our family friend, Josie Osaha's been in a bad accident, so Tessie's helping out there, and she's got herself a sweet boy, named Fred. Fred's daddy is an old friend of the family."

"Are you having other visitors, Mrs. Harnish? Are you hearing voices?"

"No, sir." But thank God she was. She could still translate the various birdsongs to help give her life meaning. And she had written a song that she sang at the beginning of each day, a song that made her heart into several birds. She sang songs to thank the birds for being her friends, for living within her, even in this closed-off place.

* * * * *

After Laura Jean left the doctor's office, she saw painted buntings flying around her while she walked; their lime, yellow, crimson, turquoise and indigo feathers carrying her through her days.

Willie Mae greeted her. "Are you having a vision, Miss Laura? Is it the buntings?"

"Yes. The buntings are with me, they were sent north and west from Savannah by my girl," Laura Jean said. "When Tessie was just a little bitty baby, her shoulder blades sat on her back like wings. I dressed her in bright colors and kept her pretty as a bird."

Willie Mae nodded. "I love those pretty birds, too. My mother used to gather their feathers to decorate hats for the women at church. The white ladies across town had plumes and fancy hats, and my mama said, there ain't no reason why black ladies can't have them, too."

* * * * *

Laura Jean sang songs each weekday she worked in the kitchen wiping down the stainless steel appliances. She sang little ditties she made up, "Pretty little bunting, no one's gonna hunt you, preen and pick your feathers, and do the birdy waltz." The hospital called the work Laura Jean did 'kitchen privileges.' In the outside world people called them chores or a job. Inside, here, it was a privilege to be allowed off the ward, to be with people from the outside, people who went home at the end of their shift or stopped on their way home to shop for groceries. Some went to the bar. They were all more or less responsible for their lives, but to whatever degree they were failing, they were succeeding enough to be outside Milledgeville. She stopped rubbing the stainless steel and laughed at herself. At the end of kitchen chores, the employees left the building, but she returned to her ward. They got paid; she didn't.

The next morning when Willie Mae came on the ward, Laura Jean went up to her. "You know, sometimes I hate you, sometimes I love you and other times I envy you. You get to make your own decisions and do it well enough that no one calls you crazy and locks you away."

"Anymore," Willie Mae reminded her. She looked Laura Jean up and down, and then she ran a work worn hand over her own brow. "You may not believe this, but sometimes I feel those same things about you. My skin is its own kind of jail, and I wish I had someone who took care of me or had me some pretty feathers to protect me from racists and bigots."

Laura Jean paused. She hadn't ever thought of things from Willie Mae's point of view. That's how she knew she was getting better; she had become interested in other people again. She no longer needed to hide in Milledgeville, no longer feared Ray. She figured she made decisions as well as most of the folks who worked in the kitchen with her. She envied them going home to their children. Almost four years of not seeing Tessie, except when Jenny brought Tessie to see her. Four long, lonely years for Tessie and for Laura Jean. Tessie had turned from a girl into a young woman without her mother. Thinking about her absence in her daughter's life made Laura Jean more determined to be released. She could decide when she wanted fried chicken or gelatin. She knew if she wanted a bath or a shower, and she knew if she wanted to live or die. She ate gelatin first. She took baths in the winter and showers in the summer. And for the past five months, when the therapist asked, "Mrs. Harnish, if you could choose between dying and living, which would you choose?" Laura Jean said, "Living."

Dr. Banes noted improvement on her chart, "Catatonic behavior gone. No incidents in the past five months." For five months, no shock treatments. She was allowed to go outside once a week, one on one—accompanied by a nurse, an aid, or an orderly. Laura Jean always asked for Willie Mae, her friend. She took a sketchbook with her and she taught Willie Mae what she knew about drawing. She began painting birds. She was tired of embroidering them. Her birds had human faces and their hearts were on the outside of their bodies. The director paid her ten dollars a wall for four murals in the main entrance.

Next she did a series of more buntings for the corridor leading to the cafeteria—indigo and painted ones, one in flight, one stopped mid-air, one feeding, one hatching from an egg, one dead on the ground. The director and the psychologist thought they had been painted in this order: hatching, flying, feeding, stopped mid-air, and finally, lying dead on the ground. But they were wrong, Laura Jean painted the dead one first, then the one stopped mid-air, then feeding, then flying, and last hatching. But she didn't argue with them or try to explain her order. Sly Laura Jean had learned that the order of her world was different, that the logic of her world was unique, and that knowing her world would never change these people in power over her, no more than their world made sense to her. She had to learn theirs, but they didn't have to know or understand hers.

She learned the right answers, over time, to most of their questions. She learned to read their faces, eyes, eyebrows, and mouths. She learned the response, "Just kidding!" for when she picked the answer that made sense to her, but clearly was not what they wanted to hear.

She was learning survival as clearly as she had learned it in the house of her parents, and better than she had learned it in the trailer with Ray. This time though she knew she was doing it and she knew why: she wanted to be outside making choices—no better and no worse than Sam's, the cook, or Rita's, the nurse, or Dr. Banes', the psychiatrist, or Willie Mae's, the orderly and her friend.

On her last scheduled session with Dr. Banes, he asked her, "What is the biggest lesson you've learned here?

She confessed. "The biggest lesson I've learned in Milledgeville? I'm not any crazier than most of the rest of the people in the world." She remembered the day Jenny Conroy had spoken to her about swallowing her tail. Her problem had been thinking she had no choices, that she couldn't stand up to someone like Ray, that someone else could raise her daughter better than she could. She had believed more in other people's power than in her own.

-23-
The Jars

Looking at the three cobalt blue jars made Tessie calmer. She carried them with her between Jenny and Earle's place and Josie and Annie's place. She heard her mother's voice when she sat, alone, in front of them. She heard her mother sing her own version of "Mockingbird":

> *Hush little darlin', don't say a word.*
> *Mama's gonna kill you a mockingbird.*
> *When that mockingbird don't sing,*
> *Mama's gonna buy you a diamond ring.*
> *And when that diamond ring don't shine,*
> *Mama's gonna pay God's dying fine.*

So many things about Mama are just flat out sad, Tessie thought. She put the jars in the bottom dresser drawer that Annie kept empty for her. As she put on her black tank top and her tightest jeans, she remembered Fred's kisses and wondered if he'd give her a promise ring at Christmas. She'd seen what she'd like at K-Mart, a tiny diamond set in the middle of a very small heart in 10K yellow or white gold. She lacquered her lashes with blue mascara and put bright blue eye shadow under the wing of each brow. I can't wait to get to Teen Town, she went on dreamily. I can't believe Fred named the new band The Swamp Rats—silly and true to the nature of those boys. Imagine them, putting coon tails on their cowboy hats as if coons and rats had anything to do with one another!

Annie called from the other room, "What are you laughing about, Tessie?"

"Fred... and his band's new name...The Swamp Rats! Did I tell you they put coon tails on their hats—as if that has something to do with rats!" Tessie said.

"Damn, Tessie. What do you see in that white boy? He's going to turn out just like your worthless daddy," Annie said.

"Hey, at least I know who mine is!" Tessie shouted back.

Within a flash, Annie was in the room, "I'd rather not know who my daddy is if he's anything like yours! 'Sides, you're going to end up like your crazy mama. No one can say a bad word about mine—except that she's hurt and that isn't her fault. If your stupid father hadn't got drunk at Hungry Mother Mountain, there wouldn't have been an accident—we wouldn't have left when we did, the truck would not have been in the line of that jack-knifing semi, and..."

"Take it easy, Annie. Take it easy," Tessie said. "Calm down. Josie's gonna hear us and then she'll know that we are mad at each other again. Calm down."

Annie stared at Tessie. If Annie had been a cartoon, smoke would have been coming out of her ears.

"Jenny's gonna pick me up soon and drop me at Teen Town. Josie said you could drive her car to bring me home," Tessie said.

"Why doesn't Jenny just pick you up, too?" Annie waited. "Oh, I see," Annie said, "she's taking you so she can get back to her bed."

"Shut up, Annie. Just because you don't have someone, don't give you the right to be hard on those of us who do," Tessie whispered.

Tessie paid her $2.00 at the door of Teen Town and walked in just as Fred Simmons began playing the chords to "Wild Thing." Fred sang his heart out, the way Laura Jean had when she sang her crazy lullabies. He closed his eyes, got as close to the microphone as he could, and sang as if he was kissing it.

Tessie stood by herself against the wall and watched the dancers. She didn't want to dance; she wanted to be at the same microphone with Fred, their mouths close to each other, close to the mike, and their voices blending.

Fred's band went on break after 30 minutes of hard rocking, and Tessie met him in the parking lot. They greeted each other with hard kisses, and the hard kisses made them forget everything. Their hands reached for each other and they grabbed for the other one's back and butt and everything in between.

"Fred? Fred? Hey, boy! Where in the hell are you?" A man's voice came at them from the doorway to the rec center.

"I got to go back in now, Tessie. I'll be singing each song for you, baby," Fred kissed her one more time, deep and hard.

Tessie straightened out her hair, tucked in her tank top, and went back in to the dance.

Annie was standing by Fred's guitar.

"Where have you been, Tessie? Don't answer. All I got to do is look at your lips and I can tell what you been doing. It don't matter a never mind to me where you been doing it, and God knows, we can all guess why. You so hot for that boy. It's funny if it wasn't sad. Mama sent me to get you early. She doesn't want any harm coming your way," Annie said.

Tessie didn't speak on the car ride home. She went straight to the chest of drawers when she got in the house, pulled out the cobalt jars, and removed the lids—hoping they'd catch her nightmares. She set them on the dresser top, put on her nightshirt, and got into bed.

The next morning, Tessie rose from her bed and went to the dresser to get her hairbrush and toothbrush. Her hand stopped midway. One cobalt blue jar sat apart from the cluster of three. It was full of river water with red clay sediment, an inch thick at the bottom. The sediment looked purple through the blue glass.

Instead of picking up her brushes, Tessie picked up the cobalt blue jar and dipped her index finger in the tepid water. Next she touched it to her temple, and then she dipped her finger again. This time she touched the corner of her eye with the water. Then she watched herself in the mirror. And the mirror, which had previously reflected Tessie's image back to her—with pimples, with eye make-up, with sad eyes, with glowing ones, instead returned a series of pictures: Laura Jean in Milledgeville being disconnected from the electric shock machine, and Ray sitting on a narrow cot behind bars. The jar had caught a dream for her, whether she wanted it or not.

The images alternated back and forth—shifting from Laura Jean to Ray and back again.

"Annie, Annie!" Tessie yelled. When Annie didn't answer, Tessie ran to Josie's bed and told her what had happened.

"Mmmmm, hmmm, mmmm," Josie muttered. "Well, girl, something's fixing to change. We will have to pay mind to the dream you have tonight," Josie said. "Now go on to school."

* * * * *

At school, Tessie didn't hear anything: not the teachers' voices, not the PA system, not the wind outside the window. She skipped her afternoon classes and sneaked off to the river to think. She knew if Laura Jean or Ray, or maybe both of them were coming home, she would have to live with them. They were family. They were her blood.

At Josie's, Tessie didn't eat her dinner, didn't talk to Annie or Josie, didn't watch TV. She went to bed as soon as she could. That night she had to pay attention to her dreams. She had to know what was coming.

While Tessie slept, she saw her father coming home, she saw herself living with him in a house like Fred Simmons' family. In that house, there was no drunken father, no mother in pieces. In that house, Ray shaved and bathed daily, didn't swear or sulk, went to work and liked his job, and came home to Laura Jean. Laura Jean didn't suck on one Pall Mall after another just to remember to breathe. She sang the real lyrics to songs instead of her made-up ones. She baked cookies for her daughter and kept the house clean enough that Tessie could have friends over without being ashamed.

In this house, her parents understood why dolls talked and how cobalt blue jars carried dreams. In this house, her parents shared her belief that discarded things could re-form into new life. They understood when a young girl needed to be held, what a family was, where the river met the rain, and who Tessie's spirit was under the flesh and under the river, where it reformed into glory beneath the Georgia clay. They understood how much a good friend mattered, regardless of skin color, and they loved their daughter and themselves.

Tessie woke up. She tiptoed to Josie's bed. "Are you awake, Miss Josie?"

"Now I am, child. What is it? What was the dream?" Josie propped herself up so she could better see Tessie's face and she listened. When Tessie was finished, Josie said, "I think both of them are coming home soon. It will be a good thing, Tessie. I just don't know what that means. But time will show us. Time will tell."

-24-
Spark

"Fred started playing piano on a cardboard keyboard made by his mother, Emily. When he hit the note, she sang it. As soon as they got some money, she bought an old upright, so Fred could learn to play on a real piano for Sunday school." Tessie was talking to the two men sitting at the bar. It was her first day working the evening shift at the Flamingo, the day after she turned 16. Her work papers had been signed by Jenny Conroy. Tessie couldn't understand how everyone on the 'Geechee Road loved Fred and his music, except Annie. Annie's just flat out jealous, Tessie thought. Annie turned 16 the same year as Tessie, but in February, not October.

According to the Chinese calendar, both girls were born in the year of the snake. As a result of studying the placemats at Mei-Lee's Chinese Restaurant, Annie decided to collect shed snakeskins and preserve them under the glass of her vanity to honor the changes in her and Tessie's lives—the good ones and the hard ones. Annie gathered the snakeskins one at a time in her thin long hands and carried them home. After she had ten of them, she phoned Tessie on her first day of work at The Flamingo and told her, "Come over here as soon as you can."

Tessie asked one of the men who had been talking with her about Fred, to watch the register. "I'll be back in a half-hour," she said as she hurried out of the bar room

When Tessie arrived at Annie's house, Annie was waiting for her on the porch. Annie held her hands out in supplication and lying across them was the freshly shed skin of a canebrake rattler.

"For you, Tessie. To bring you luck. Sleep with it under your pillow. It will make your dreams clearer."

Tessie stood with her hands on her hips. She flushed. "You telling me you called me away from my job to look at a snakeskin? I left the bar and rushed over here for you to show me a snakeskin? Have you lost your goddamn mind?"

Tessie turned on her heel and marched to the truck.

Annie dropped the snakeskin and ran after her. "Wait, Tessie, don't leave. Don't leave mad. I wanted to give you some magic."

"The hell you say," Tessie's mouth spit fire. "What makes you think you got more magic than me?"

"Look at you, Tessie. You look like every other white girl on the 'Geechee Road. Thought you were going to be different. What happened to your dreams?"

"It's none of your business, Annie. I'm gone."

Tessie hopped into the truck she had borrowed from one of the men at the bar and sped back to The Flamingo.

Annie stood in her driveway feeling like a fool. She turned on her heel, went back into the house, opened up the suitcase she kept under her bed, and added the new snakeskin in with the other eight.

Savannah State College offered Upward Bound for poor people of any race, but no whites went. Folks like Ray might let their children play with black children in the neighborhood, but they were generally suspicious of the need for education past eighth grade, suspicious of college in general, and completely suspicious of a black college. Tessie qualified for Upward Bound, and so did Annie. But Tessie didn't go and Annie did.

Tessie accepted being a bartender. Every day she worked on getting rid of her desire for magic and stopped believing she was going to get a clearer vision from what were clearly just cheap blue jars from Newberry's.

On Saturdays and in the summer, Annie went to Savannah State in the Upward Bound Program so she could go to college at Spelman. Tessie knew that when Annie went to college in Atlanta, she'd have to give up the ocean, the swamp, and painted buntings. Tessie planned to keep all of those things in her life. She decided she wasn't ever leaving Savannah.

Once Tessie got back to The Flamingo, she wrote a list of wishes on the back of her inventory tablet:

1. I wish I could wake up with the person who I love and who loves me.
2. I wish Laura Jean were either alive or dead, but not this somewhere in between place.
3. I wish Ray was out of prison.
4. I wish I had a baby.
5. I wish I was in Fred's band and touring the country singing with him.

That night, Fred called her to the stage to sit in. She removed her apron and threw it behind the bar. She took one quick look in her compact mirror. She pushed her hair way up in the back, spit on her fingers and formed her sideburns into pixie points. She walked on the stage, took the microphone in her hand, smiled at the crowd, looked deep into Fred's eyes, and said, "'Satin Sheets,' boys." Fred winked and blew her a kiss.

The noisy crowd got quiet as soon as the familiar chord met the air. Tessie sang out the words as if she had written them, as if they were part of her body. *Satin sheets to lie on, satin pillows to cry on, still I'm not happy, don't you see? Big long Cadillac, tailored-mades upon my back, still I want you to set me free.* The steel guitar player created wounds with the sounds he made, and when Tessie looked out at the crowd, she saw trickles of blood running down people's faces from their foreheads.

During the bridge, she reached for Fred's bourbon and took a big swallow to wash away what she saw. Oh, God, am I turning into a crazy woman like my mother? Oh my God. The band continued to play behind her, waiting for her to come back in. She returned to herself on the third time through the solo. *I found another man, who loves me more than you can, tho' you've given me everything money can buy. But your money can't hold me tight, like he does, on a long lonely night, you didn't keep me satisfied.*

The song ended. "We're going to take a break, ladies and gentlemen. See you in fifteen."

"What happened, Tessie? You look like a ghost. Hey, girl, you're shaking. What's going on?" Fred had unstrapped his telecaster, leaned it against his amp, and had his arms around Tessie.

"I think I am going crazy, Fred. Just like Mama. I'm getting me another bourbon. Can you meet me outside?"

Tessie knew for certain she'd kill herself if she was turning crazy like Laura Jean. She'd die if they put her in Milledgeville, so she didn't share what she saw. She went outside with Fred. She handed him her bourbon, and he passed her his joint.

Being with Fred made Tessie feel safe. She forgot the hardship, and didn't worry about the future. She wanted to be able to spend the night with him after they made love, she liked walking with him, holding hands, and kissing.

"Do you love me, Fred?"

Fred took a while to answer. Tessie couldn't tell if it was because she was stoned, or he was, or both, or if it was something else—like maybe he didn't love her.

"I do, Tessie." But when he said it, he said it with his eyes sliding to the left, the way he played up to the women in the bar. When the break ended, she poured herself another double and drank it fast to drive away the cold space in her chest.

*****

Tessie and Fred sneaked into her parents' trailer and made love. They had cleaned her old room up and they ignored the rest of the mess. Afterward, Fred said, "I want my own band and a touring bus—just like Waylon Jennings or Willie Nelson. Can't you see it, Tessie?" And then as an afterthought, "You could come along with me, Tessie."

Tessie ignored the pain she felt at being left out. "Dream big, Fred," Tessie said. "Think of those old guys as being the opening act for you instead of you being the opening act for them."

Fred tickled her feet while he told her stories about his life along the Ogeechee River where he had hunted snakes and alligators. "I know all about that life, Fred. You know that. I've been living it, too."

At least she believed as long as she didn't tell anyone about the bleeding dancers she saw when she sang sad songs, or about the cobalt jars and how she made decisions, she was safe. If anyone knew her secrets, anyone but Annie and Josie, she believed they'd lock her up, and as much as she wanted to be with her mother, she didn't want to be in a place for crazies.

Annie didn't doubt Tessie's vision ever—Annie saw things, too—ghosts and God and shape shifters. But Annie didn't tell anyone except Tessie and Fuddah about what she saw. She kept quiet in school, did all her work, and listened to her Talent Search Counselor about where she could go and what she could be if she stayed in school, didn't get pregnant, and was willing to leave Savannah.

And Annie's answers were yes, she'd stay in school; yes, she wouldn't get pregnant; and yes, oh yes, she'd leave Savannah--leave it in a heartbeat for Spelman and Atlanta. Annie got her power from planning to leave and Tessie got her power from planning to stay. Annie got her wisdom from books and Tessie got hers from melting Fred, taking him in his hard heat and melting him right down to nothing.

-25-
Shedding

The sound of loud clanking machines woke Henry. In his dream he was working the floor in the pulp section of the mill. Once awake he could not keep from thinking of Fred coming home drunk and stoned. *What has happened to that boy? When did things go wrong? What happened while Fred lived with Emily's mother?* Fred had good grades until tenth grade, but for the past two years, he was barely getting by. *I wonder if he's gonna get into Georgia. Emily's about to lose her mind with that boy's drinking and doping.* Henry shook his head.

Tessie remembered the day Mr. Henry went to hell the first time. She was cleaning house on June 17th; another humid summer day was breaking. She heard the siren go wailing past the bar, heading to Pooler and the mill. She did what she always did when she heard a siren. She prayed. "Please, God, bless that person and bless their family. Amen." Then she went back to washing dishes and scrubbing floors.

That's when Jenny Conroy arrived and began pounding on the door. "Let me in, Tessie. It's Jenny. I got to talk with you right now!"

Tessie unlocked the door. "What on Earth, Jenny!?"

"It's Henry Simmons, Tessie. They don't think he's going to make it."

"What do you mean?" Tessie's voice broke and she dropped a beer glass, splintering it into fragments.

"The air conditioning in the mill failed during the 11-7 shift. The humidity and the heat had everyone nervy and taut. Folks say Henry was upset when he arrived, you know, worried about Fred and his drinking. Ron LaDieu kept his lunch on the second shelf of the refrigerator in the break room. Alfred Bodean kept his on the third. Ron picked up Alfred's and ate it, and then he was still hungry, so he ate his own. Lazarus Smith watched the whole thing, but he didn't know Ron was eating someone else's lunch. Ron left the break room before Alfred arrived.

"Lazarus was finishing his apple and his ice tea when Alfred opened the 'frigerator door and found that his lunch was gone. 'Lazarus, you taken my lunch?'

"'No, sir, Alfred. I got my own food here. Why'd I want yourn?'

"Alfred eyed Lazarus closely. No doubt, Lazarus was telling the truth."

Tessie interrupted. "What happened? Was that ambulance that roared by here for Mr. Henry?"

"Yes," Jenny said. "Turns out Lazarus told Alfred that he seen Ron eating two lunches."

"Story goes that Alfred was out the door and down the ladder to the bottom floor where Ron worked. Alfred walked up behind Ron and grabbed him by the throat. People were yelling and egging them on. All of them crazy from the endless heat!

"Turns out Lazarus went looking for Henry right away to tell him about the stolen lunch. Guess he could feel the momentum coming for a fight. Henry ran to the pulp vat station and flung himself through the throng, his own momentum sending him airborne into the vat. He screamed so loud people heard it above the clanking machines. Thank God the beaters weren't on or the burns would have been the least of his problems. Lazarus Smith and two other men pulled Henry out of the vat, but sixty per cent of his body had already melted away."

* * * * *

Dr. Star took Fred aside at the hospital. "He's probably not going to make it, son. We won't be able to save him, even with skin grafts and the best medical treatments available. We'll try to make him as comfortable as we can while he's still alive. That's the best we an do."

Fred looked the three doctors straight in their eyes and said to them all, "You are wrong. You are wrong. You are wrong. His life isn't yours to save. He belongs to God. So you do what you can and what you will, but God will save him. Make no mistake!"

For weeks, Henry was a silent, wrapped figure; then for months, a moaning, wrapped figure. But he did not die. The doctors saw his living as a miracle. Dr. Star, the primary authority on burns, had two doctors working with him who were Baptists. The Baptists told about the healing of Henry Simmons at Bible study class. Dr. Grant always included the part about Lazarus Smith being one of the men to pull Henry out. "It's a sign," he'd say. "We should have known we'd be wrong about Henry dying with a wife like his and a co-worker named Lazarus!" He laughed at his own cleverness, but he also grew more humble, which pleased his wife and a lot of his patients.

* * * * *

Henry dreamed of using Emily as a pillow, wanted to rest his head directly over her heart, wanted to use her as a mattress, lay his whole body down on her, wanted her to be a field that he could till. But all touch hurt.

Henry dreamed of dying, but when he saw his soul, it was a giant serpent in the heavens, except Henry's soul could not fly. He dreamed of the 'Geechee River as a slithering snake on fire. He became a water serpent, holding his tail in his mouth, becoming both beginning and end. Other times, he was a strong serpent, able to carry the globe on his back. He was life and death and resurrection when he woke to sloughed-off skin, he imagined his spirit as a kundalini serpent. He thought of it as the double image of the doctor's caduceus.

Fred watched his father, trapped in burned skin—rivers of clear mucus erupting as old skin peeled off. Sloughing off pieces of himself. Fred loved Henry—heart and soul. Fred hated the smell of medicine and sickness. He wanted to do anything he could to ease Henry's pain.

One evening after Tessie and Fred had made love, Fred said, "I'll do anything to help my daddy, Tessie, anything." Tessie was putting her jeans, a pink sweatshirt, and yellow swamp boots back on, and she stopped, her eyes meeting Fred's.

"A course you will, Fred. That's what families do," Tessie said.

"I want you to do me a favor, Tessie. I want you to go to Fuddah for help. I'll do anything for Daddy, if I have to, but I ain't no good with swamps and snakes. And you a natural at that," Fred said.

"All right, Fred. For you and Henry. I'll go find Fuddah. I'll be back before dawn. You wait for me on the porch. Fuddah will know what to do for your daddy. If he doesn't know something, then there isn't anything to do." She lit a cigarette and left Fred.

Out into the night and into the swamp and mud, that's where Tessie went. That's what felt like home to her. Tessie knew the way to Fuddah's best if Annie were leading her, but she had gone often enough that she knew the marks—the broken bridge under a pit. She aligned herself with the stars. And to keep her spirit brave, she hummed a G note, softly, in accordance with peepers, in accordance with owls, in accordance with herself. She had been hiking for almost an hour when she reached Long Way—the point of land upon which Fuddah lived. In the almost-full moon, she could see that the door to his shack was open, and as she drew closer she could discern his battered face.

"Hello, Fuddah."

"Hello, Tessie."

"I need your help, Fuddah."

"I figured as much, nice though it is in the swamp at night," Fuddah said and chuckled.

"It's about Mr. Henry."

"I know what it's about, Tessie. I knowed you were coming before Fred asked you to."

"A course you did, Fuddah."

"I want you to set yourself down here and listen careful to me. I got a story I need to tell you and you need to hear."

Fuddah offered Tessie a hand-hewn chair, made from a stump. Then he left, went inside his shack, and returned with a blanket for himself and a bottle of water with two tin cups.

"You comfortable?" he asked Tessie.

"Yes, sir. Are you?"

He didn't answer her.

Tessie waited for the story to begin. She stopped listening to marsh hens and peepers, cicadas and alligators. Instead, she listened for the deep voice of Fuddah and the story of how to heal Mr. Henry. And she knew the story would be told in code and she would have to cipher it—turn herself into a hypodermic needle and inject herself into his story—draw out the blood from the vein, draw out the marrow from the bone. Knew she'd go home almost too tired to walk through the swamp, almost too tired to speak the cure.

Fuddah began talking.

"When you look up at the moon, depending upon the time of month and the time of year, you be greeted by a different face. And each face show you a different side of moon.

"When you look at yourself in a mirror day-to-day and year-to-year over a lifetime, you're seeing a different you. Sometime you'll like what you see with the moon and sometime you won't. And sometime moon will be all the way gone, so tired so shamed or sad, she don't want no one looking on her. And sometime you be the same, too. Too weary, too sorry for what you done or left undone to let anyone see you—you won't look at yourself in the mirror, you won't come near Fuddah or your blue jars, you won't even let my sweet Annie see you, Tessie.

"So Mr. Henry going into that room alone and not letting anyone from outside see him, well, that makes sense—'cause he so worn an' weary, so shamed he don't want no one to see how much of him be gone. Wonder of it is, he don't just drop down into his own waters and die.

"Powerful 'mount of love keeping him here, and it be coming from Miss Emily and Fred, you and Annie. Mr. Henry be a mighty man when I knew him in the boat of Mr. Ray's.

"Now look close to me, Tessie. Look at Fuddah's face. It don't change the way the moon do. And it don't age the way yourn do. It just one scar after another, sewn together with age. When I brought this face up from the street, stone was in it. Some lines are cleaner 'cause they cut in with a razor—some lines are not lines at all 'cause they were put there by shoe and pavement—my face in-between.

"So you thinking, 'What's this got to do with Fred helping Mr. Henry heal?' Everything and nothing, Tessie. Can you figure on this and tell that boy of his and yourn what to do?"

Tessie didn't know yet what all this meant, but she knew she could dream on it with a snakeskin under her pillow, and she knew Annie would give her one. She knew she would make sense of it—before long. Fuddah handed Tessie a small jar filled with a white waxy cream.

"Take this back with you. Three different people need to rub it on Mr. Henry's burns—once in the morning, once at dinner, and once at midnight. There's enough here to last until this time next month. It's the same cream I sent to help Josie heal. Send his boy to get it next time. You can bring him as far as the pit. Then he's got to come the rest of the way alone. Time for him to become a man. Making love don't make you a man, you know? Tessie? Becoming a man means doing the things you don't want to do, the things you don't like to do, the things that scared even Jesus. This swamp gonna be Fred's wilderness."

"Thank you, Fuddah." From inside her shirt, Tessie drew out a pack of cigarettes, two packs of gum, and a pearl."

"Thank you, Tessie."

Tessie knew she had to reach home before dawn or she wouldn't be able to figure out the meaning of Fuddah's story, that the sun would come up and the stories about the moon and scars and healing would lose their power. She hurried through mud, past the pit, over the broken branches, back to the porch where Fred waited for her. She left her swamp boots on the steps and stumbled toward her bed.

Fred kissed her feet for carrying her to Fuddah and back, then he kissed her knees, her thighs, her nipples, and her mouth. A long, wet thank you. "Here's salve. Fuddah said that it must go on Mr. Henry's worst wounds three times a day and must be put on by three different people—in the morning, at dinner, and then again at midnight. It's the same cream we used on Josie to help her heal. It worked, Fred. And there's more, but because Fuddah gave it to me as a story and I have to dream on it. Then I can tell you more."

"Thank you, Tessie."

"Go on now, Fred, before your mama finds you gone from home."

Tessie slept but no dreams came. So the next day she went to Annie's room, dragged out the suitcase and took the snakeskin home. She put it under her pillow. She put it there every night before bed, then knelt and recited almost word for word what Fuddah had told her before he gave her the salve. And then she had three dreams.

She bought a watermelon at the roadside market knowing it wasn't quite ripe, but knowing that within a few days it would be. She put it on the counter to ripen. Ray cut it open before it was ready, and she had to throw it away. She puzzled over the fact that fruit cut open won't ripen while whole fruit left on counters will.

She saw Laura Jean at a beach, filling her sand bucket with snow. Tessie yelled to her to look up, but Laura Jean couldn't hear her over the sound of the wave that carried her out to sea. Tessie sat on a large rock which felt sacred to her, and wept, crying so hard she did not hear the returning wave. When she looked up, she saw Laura Jean seated upon the foam, covered in starfish, singing.

Tessie picked up a small square mirror, which only let her look at two inches of her face a time. Then she opened a compact mirror that distorted her eyes to look like a squid. And finally she walked into a room of mirrors, but by then she had no face.

When she woke, she wrote down each one of the dreams and, at the end of a week, she walked back to Fuddah's to read them to him. She traveled in daylight and arrived with her fishing pole, two sandwiches, and a thermos of sweet tea. Fuddah smiled when he saw her, grabbed his pole, and they headed out together in his aluminum boat.

Fuddah sipped his tea and listened.

"Well, well; well, well; well, well; well, well. Humph!"

"I think you were telling me that there isn't anything can hurry a cure—that's the watermelon, right?" Tessie asked.

Fuddah nodded.

"And that a disaster may be a freeing? In disguise—if we just keep listening. And who am I to try to see more than I can see when I don't yet know my own face, when I haven't yet seen enough pain to recognize joy?" Tessie concluded.

Fuddah chewed on his sandwich, keeping one eye on Tessie and the other one on his pole.

"Makes some sense to me," Fuddah said.

A school of croaker came by, and pretty soon the two were hauling in fish so fast they had to stop talking about dreams and stories. The gold-scaled fish filled the boat's bottom with a sound that had given them their name.

"And Fuddah?" Tessie said as they moved back to shore, "You want me to tell Fred to tell Mr. Henry that he's going to all right once he starts loving again?"

"That's right, Tessie. And you tell Fred to tell Mr. Henry that Fuddah said so."

But Henry didn't believe the vision of Fuddah's story and how it fed Tessie's dreams. He couldn't love back. He needed to know more. He needed to see the future.

"Fred, will you ask that swamp beauty of yours to come back here and talk with me?" Henry asked.

"Yes, Daddy," but Fred was worried. What was his father going to do with Tessie? What else did they have to talk about? Him?

Fred asked Tessie to go to his father, despite his fear. His love was greater. "Can I stay while you all talk, Daddy?"

"No, son. You go on now. Tessie will be safe with me here, won't you, Tessie?"

"Yes, sir. I will be fine Fred, now go on," Tessie said with more conviction than she felt.

Fred left.

"So Tessie I heard rumors about Fuddah being able to read the future by shaking and throwing a dead person's hands. You know anything about that?"

"Well, yes, sir, I do. I'm not supposed to talk about things like that, but I will ask Fred to ask Fuddah what he can do, then we'll come back and tell you."

"You do that, darlin'," Henry said.

That's how Tessie and Annie got appointed to go grave digging for a pair of hand bones.

* * * * *

Fuddah sent Tessie and Annie to the graveyard to bring back a set of hands. Old hands from an old grave. "Put the grave back the way you found it when you're done," he said. "I'll be back in six hours. You got your watch, Annie?"

"Yes, Grandpa."

Fuddah knew how terrified Annie was if she was calling him Grandpa. And Tessie didn't speak—looking bloodless and dead. He and Annie were trying to help her and Henry, the boy, and Emily. The hands were for Mr. Henry to see what his life was going to be now that he had lived through the first year of the burning.

Fuddah gave each girl a bloodstone to keep in her pocket to prevent either one of them from getting contaminated. Annie knew the stone from school—heliotrope. The dark-green chalcedony flecked with red jasper burned in the girls' pockets as they walked to the old part of the cemetery.

Tessie had a flashlight with her. She had spent the week before searching for the right grave—John Hillman Clark—a nineteenth century composer and pianist. She was certain his hands had been full of magic—that his hands, stripped of their flesh, still were. His hand bones would speak to Mr. Henry and help him heal, letting him look into the light and dark of the future—past his own pain, letting him look at hope.

Tessie dug first. Then Annie. They alternated who watched the time, too. Then clouds floated over the salmon-colored moon. Marsh hens cackled and mourning doves cooed. The young women worked quickly—digging—the sound of loose dirt landing on hard ground. Annie and Tessie put bandannas over their noses and mouths before Tessie pried the casket open.

They put on gloves before they touched the bones. Annie gathered them up and passed them to Tessie to put in the red satin bag. They were running out of time. They weren't going to be able to put things back the way they found them. Fuddah wouldn't like this.

"We'll come back, Tessie. Stop worrying, please," Annie said.

"We can't, Annie. What if between now and tomorrow night someone sees that the grave has been tampered with? We'll get caught."

"Well, you're right. We'll come back tonight, if Fuddah will let us," Annie conceded.

So they ran to Fuddah's truck, gave him the satin sack with the bones of John Hillman Clark's hands. "We got to go back, Fuddah, to put the grave right. We need one more hour."

"You got it, but you best be done before the sun comes up over the Wilmingon River."

They hurried, shoveling the dirt back, laying the turf on, then kneeling to thank John Hillman Clark for his hands.

When the girls told Emily what they'd done, she didn't like any of it. She didn't like looking into the future, didn't want a dead person's hand bones brought into her house, and wasn't comfortable around 'Geechee Fuddah. And she didn't like Henry lying in his bed bloodless and bone dry in spirit, seeping and sore in his body. So for his sake she reluctantly agreed to the hand bones being thrown and read. But then they would be kept forever in the red satin bag on the same shelf as her Bible. She knew God took many forms: in a live oak, in the fangs of the serpent, perhaps in the magic of 'Geechee Fuddah.

Fuddah came—hand bones in hand—and he came alone into the house. Annie and Tessie waited on the screened-in porch. Henry looked closely at the scar that made up Fuddah's face, and Fuddah looked just as closely at the scar that made up Henry's body. The two men found themselves filling up the room with laughter born of pain and recognition.

Next Fuddah gave the hand bones to Henry to hold. "You got to think on them," Fuddah said. "Hold them close as you can to each part of you—head to toe. When you think those hands know you as well as God himself, give them back to me. Then it will be time for them to speak."

Henry held the bones in his bandaged hands, moving them up and down his body. Fuddah was silent and watchful.

He handed the bones back.

"Thank you, Mr. Henry."

Fuddah received the hand bones as if they were the host—reverently, silently, so as not to disturb their work; but within minutes he began shaking—from his hands up to his head, his hands down to his feet, his whole body vibrating as if he would soon erupt. The hand bones flew out of his Fuddah's own and landed at the foot of Henry's bed in a mound—one over the other, as in a person waiting.

Fuddah collapsed, unable to hold onto anything, even his consciousness. And now Henry waited, watching Fuddah and the hand bones, more alive than he had been since before the accident.

When Fuddah came to, he was a different person, transported by the energy of the hand bones to the place of prophecy. "I see. Uh-huh. Yes, indeed. I do see it."

Fuddah laughed and cried, sat up and lay down and sat up again. Without either of the men moving the hand bones, without either of the men touching them, the hand bones opened out into the gesture of giving, at which point both men fainted.

By the time Fuddah left Henry Simmons' house, the sun was setting. Tessie and Annie had kept silent vigil on the porch for the entire day, lending the power of their spirits to Henry and Fuddah's endeavor. Neither man revealed what Henry's future was to be, but each retold the events of the morning and afternoon when the hand-bones moved on their own. And Henry began to really heal—and he often laughed and cried—in Emily's arms.

-26-
Resurrecting Bones

"What do you mean you went to Bonaventure Cemetery and dug up a grave, Tessie? You and Annie? And Fuddah drove you?" Josie's voice was nearly inaudible, which was always a bad sign.

"Annie? Annie! Get in here right now! Now, I said," Josie's voice grew like a hurricane wind.

"What is it, Mama?" Annie called back.

"Now!"

Annie came around the corner and saw Tessie's face. "What happened? What's the matter?"

"I told her where we were last night and this morning, Annie. I know you said not to, but I think we ought to get the hand bones from Mr. Henry and have Josie try them, too. I think Fuddah could help her see the future with her in it," Tessie said

"You think? You think? I don't believe that you think at all, Tessie," Annie wailed at her.

"You know better, Annie. You know better than to go digging in a graveyard with your grandfather. I'm all het up and jealous, too. I want to be healed, I want to see the future, I want to be loved and held again by one of my men. I expect you to go the swamp, Tessie—"

"But, Mama, I ought to go, he's my ...."

"Oh yes, he's your grandfather all right. But you be staying here with me, and Tessie be the one who is going to be petitioning him. You tell him, Tessie, that his own flesh and blood wants the same help he's giving Henry Simmons. Annie will be staying right here with me, where I can keep an eye on her. You best get going, Tessie, because Annie's not going away from me until you and Fuddah come back here to help me," Josie sighed deep and leaned back. Her energy was all used up.

"Can't you learn to keep your mouth shut, Tessie? For God's sake! You best be going to Fuddah and hurry along. You bring him back with you, 'hear?" Annie didn't look at Tessie when she spoke.

Tessie practically flew through the swamp.

*****

Fuddah wasn't looking at any particular thing in the shack. He sat perfectly still and stared forward at a clapboard wall. Then Tessie noticed his hands, which moved as if he were repairing a net. Tessie imagined him holding a large crochet needle in one hand and heavy cording for a shrimp net in the other. There was enough moonlight for Tessie to cast a shadow, but Tessie felt as if he had not seen hers, so she greeted him in a quiet, unhurried way, despite the fact that everything in her felt urgency about Josie, and with that sense of urgency her blood surged in a loud rush like waves breaking against the dunes of Tybee Island.

"Fuddah, sir. It's me again. I've come to you with a petition from Josie, sir."

"My daughter doesn't send petitions, Tessie. We both know that. She sends demands." Fuddah's hands stopped moving, but he kept staring forward. "What gives her the right to send you to my place when she's the one with the need?" Fuddah's voice thundered at her.

"Remember she can't walk well or far, Fuddah? Remember the wreck?" Tessie said gently.

She set her teeth and ground them back and forth to stop her chattering jaw. For the first time ever, she was afraid of Fuddah, afraid of the swamp, afraid that he didn't remember that Josie was bedridden from the accident and the burns. Each of them having 'Geechee blood did not reassure her. At last sentences formed in her mind, the truth, and she spoke in a voice that was pinched and weary.

"Josie needs your help, and she's feeling hurt that you went to Mr. Henry first, instead of going to her. She's mad at Annie and me for going to the cemetery to get the hand bones, and Annie's mad at me for telling Josie we did and you did and …" Tessie began to whimper.

A wind came up and the live oak trees rattled against each other.

Fuddah turned and faced her. "All she had to do was ask," he said. Tessie's breath came in fast. At that moment she didn't recognize him at all and later, no matter how often she called the image to mind, she could never describe how he looked. She drew back into herself.

"I meant no disrespect coming to you, Fuddah, sir. I meant no disrepect by not coming first thing when Miss Josie got hurt. I mean no disrespect now. I will do what you need me to do. If you need me to leave, I will be gone. If you can help me by helping Josie, we will all be thankful." Tessie took a long breath. She was winded and her throat had gone dry.

Fuddah looked her up and down. He rubbed his eyes, and then he rubbed his hands together. "Sure is hard work mending nets. My hands cramp up on me something bad. What you got to say to me about that, Tessie? Ain't you going to ask what nets?"

Tessie paused at the questions. Was there a trick? Outside the shack cicadas chirped. "I know you were repairing nets when I got here, Fuddah, sir, invisible nets. What do you use those for?"

"I use those nets to catch the truth for my dreams. I use those nets to sort out stories. I want you to set yourself down here and tell me a story that you think can heal Josie."

Fuddah saw the conflicted look on Tessie's face—an odd combination of fear and trust. "Yes, Tessie, I'm gonna let you stay, because right before you got here, I caught a dream story and you need to hear it. But you keep in mind that any time you come here again, you got to ask my permission first. You leave me a note in one of those cobalt jars you carry about, and put the jar by the oak tree at the pit.

"You understand what I'm saying? I want you to think hard about the last dream you had that came out of one of those jars." There was a silver gleam in Fuddah's eye, as if a piece of the moon were lodged there. Or perhaps it was scar tissue in his eye, where he had been stabbed with a piece of bone. Tessie remembered some story Annie had told her about Fuddah and street fighting. He read her mind.

"It wasn't a bone, Tessie—it was a metal sliver that went in my eye—lucky I can see out that eye at all. Now quit thinking about how I look and go back in your mind. We are going to sit outside for the story." Fuddah rose and moved past Tessie who followed him away from the shack.

A warm rain began to fall. Tessie closed her eyes. She could not remember a dream. The more she tried to force it, the emptier her mind became.

Fuddah watched her eyes and he knew she had fallen asleep. He continued to crochet his imaginary nets as he watched. He had all night to wait. She would dream and then she would wake. She would tell him how to help Josie. He was counting on Tessie and her magic.

Tessie reached for the cobalt jar. When she touched it, it turned to water and rained down on her the way a cloud bursts. And then a phone rang, or was it two phones? One was the correction officer calling for her father, and the other was Willie Mae, the orderly calling from Milledgeville. They talked loud and over each other. Your father, your mother, your father, your mother, your father, your mother....What? Tessie yelled out. *He's coming home. She's coming home. I've got a ticket, Tessie. I've got a ticket, Tessie. The water rushed at her and in the center of the stream was Josie, riding in a boat, eating turnip greens, calling for help the way you do if you are kidding. Fred was holding the red satin bag with the hand bones, opening it by the strings and pouring it into a blender. Laura Jean moaned and then lifted one of the jars and used it as a megaphone. She called, 'Baby? Baby?' and Tessie called out, 'I'm here,' but before Tessie could reach her mother, the ancient Siamese cat ran in front of her and made her fall. Annie yelled, 'Pick her up!'* Tessie *grabbed for the cat. 'Not the cat! Pick Josie up. Don't let her burn!'*

Tessie saw her mother and her mouth opened but no words came out. Laura Jean stood in the kitchen and smells came flying at her: cigarette smoke, fat back and greens, mildew and musk. She was young and beautiful. 'You escaped, Mama?' 'Yes, I did, darlin'.' Laura Jean grabbed hold of Tessie so hard that Tessie could barely breathe. And then Miss Emily fell to her knees and began testifying while a canebrake rattler slithered around her neck.

"Wake up, Tessie. Wake up. It's almost dawn and you been tossing and turning, yelling and grinding your teeth. Tell me," he ordered, "what you dreamed and what you think it means for Josie."

"So much of the dream was about Ray and Mama coming home and crazy things, like Fred putting John Tillman Clark's hand bones in a blender, and Mama's old Siamese cat tripping me, and so much rain. Onliest thing about Josie was her riding in a boat, eating Mama's turnip greens and being whole. She wasn't hurt even though Annie thought she was."

Fuddah nodded.

"Oh, wait, I understand something. Josie doesn't need hand bones to get well, she doesn't need us digging around in a cemetery for her to heal. She's already healing in her own way and in her own time…."

Fuddah nodded again.

"You best go back now, Tessie, and don't go walking through the swamp. Take my boat. It's just like your daddy's old 16 foot Mitchell. You remember how to drive it?" Fuddah asked.

"I do, Fuddah. Thank you. What am I to tell Annie and Josie? They'll be expecting me to bring you back," Tessie said.

"Tell them what you told me. That's what they need to know. I am sending another salve home with you for Josie. You tell her that she's gonna be back on her feet before you girls graduate high school. Tell her to be patient and to rest."

Tessie steered the boat away from one side of the swamp, across the river, and back to the other side. Her dreams had reminded her of the deep loneliness she felt for her parents and what she thought her life was going to be. *Annie knows loneliness, too, she knows it like it is her sister, like it is me. We are each other's mirrors.*

"You go on down to the riverbank and wait for her. I am sure Fuddah sent her home in the Mitchell. Don't you tell her anything till the two of you get back to me, 'hear?" Josie said.

"Yes, Mama. I hear you, and you don't need to worry. I don't want to be the one to tell her," Annie said. Then she kissed Josie and went to wait for her friend.

-27-
Return

"What do you mean y'all got calls from Daddy and Mama? They called Josie in the middle of the night? That don't make any sense!" Tessie stared at Annie. "If you think this is some kind of joke, Annie, you'd be wrong!"

Tessie tried to push past Annie on the riverbank, but the rain had made the ground so muddy, that Tessie lost her footing and fell onto her knees and elbows.

"Slow down and listen to me, Tessie. Mama made me promise not to tell you, but I wanted you to know first off, and I wanted to be the one to tell you. And no, they didn't phone in the middle of the night. You've been gone for two nights and a day. They called while you were with Fuddah, trying to help Mama and me," Annie said in a rush.

"First off, the orderly called, that lady you have talked with me about, Willie Mae, right? She called to make sure your mama had the right number, and once Mama told her, yes, yes this is the right place, then Willie Mae handed the phone to your mama."

Tessie stared at her. "Go on. What else?"

"Well, first, please get up off your knees and sit beside me on the log. Don't be mad, Tessie. I think this is good news. I am just not sure what it means yet."

Annie took a breath. "Your mama said that the state voted to close Milledgeville and two other mental institutions. So Mama sent me off to get a paper, and sure enough, there was an article on the front page about it. We can read it when we get back home. We no more than got off the phone, and Ray called. He didn't want to talk with me at all. He wanted Mama. I could tell from the things she said that he was asking her all about her health. Then she got real quiet. For a good while. Finally, she said, 'Well, I'll be damned.' Then she paused again for a bit before she said, 'When?'"

"I am not surprised, really, Annie. I saw it all in a dream when I was with Fuddah. I heard them talking over each other the way they did when they used to fight, that they were coming home," Tessie said.

"Well, you have to act surprised when Mama tells you, else she'll give me a whipping. You know how she gets!" Tessie and Annie rolled their eyes and started laughing.

"She can't give you a whipping right yet," Tessie said. "She can't even get out of bed but for a little while each day. I think you are safe for now."

The girls became solemn when they remembered how Josie used to be and how she had become.

Upon their return to Josie's, Tessie managed to register surprise when Josie announced that Ray and Laura Jean were coming home. She also gave Josie the new salve and retold the part of her dream that reassured Josie she was healing. " I want you to hear what they put in the paper, too, Tessie," Josie said, and she began reading, "The Georgia State Legislature voted today 215 to 184 to close three state mental facilities and to greatly reduce residential care facilities. Most notably, the state under recommendations from a panel of prominent psychiatrists, has decided to release two hundred and seven residents from the Milledgeville facility alone, citing the first amendment and skyrocketing costs. Halfway houses will take in residents who do not have family to provide shelter. All other residents who are not violent and who can function, at least minimally, will be returned to the care of their next of kin."

Tessie listened.

"I have to go to bed now, Miss Josie. I am flat worn out," Tessie said.

"I bet you are, Tessie, I bet you are. So am I. I'm no spring chicken anymore," Josie said. "Let's all try to get some rest. Who knows who will call next or who will arrive at the door?"

* * * * *

Willie Mae helped Laura Jean pack. "What are we going to do about the way you look, Laura Jean? We want you to look your best when you arrive home to your girl," she said.

"Hand me a mirror, Willie Mae. Please," Laura Jean said.

In the mirror, Laura Jean saw a sad, old woman with hope in her eyes. She saw a woman who had fallen into a world of medication, shock treatments and depression. She looked as gray as the linoleum floors, as flat as the cement walls. "I'm trying to think. Tessie gonna be 17 this coming October."

"You know you have yourself a young woman waiting for you, Laura Jean. Now about this hair of yours—I think we best wash it, and put some curlers in it so it doesn't hang all limp around your face. You best practice smiling more, too. It will help you look younger, I promise."

"I am going to miss you, Willie Mae. I don't know how I would have made it in here without you," Laura Jean said while Willie Mae washed and set her hair.

"I'm gonna miss you, too, but I know you are going to a better place. Now you sit here until your hair sets. I have to go help some of the others get ready, but I will be back before the van comes to take you to the Greyhound Station. I'll get your hair combed out and give you one last hug," Willie Mae reassured Laura Jean.

When Willie Mae returned, Laura Jean had done her own hair and had one of her 3 foot by 5 foot pictures of a painted bunting rolled up with ribbon around it. "This is for you, Willie Mae. And if you ever get down Savannah way, please look me up. I will be living somewhere on the 'Geechee Road, probably at Little Bit of Paradise Trailer Park."

Once outside, Laura Jean was shocked by car horns, loud radio music, crickets rubbing their hind legs together, silver jets rumbling over head, leaves sighing around her like the tired women on the ward at night.

At the Greyhound Station, Laura Jean purchased a one-way ticket to Savannah with the money the state had given her. She tucked the remaining forty dollars she had earned painting the bunting murals inside her bra. She boarded the bus, made sure she got the front seat behind the driver and directly beside the window where she watched light reflect off metal roofs painted silver, off waxy magnolia leaves, off tarred road surfaces, and off the rocks in creek beds where water ran to the sea. And she saw herself as water and rock, fluid and hard, blood and bone, returning with the birds, returning to the coast, returning to herself, returning to her daughter.

Laura Jean phoned Jenny from the station. Word had spread on the 'Geechee Road, so Jenny was expecting the call. "Great God Almighty!" Jenny screeched when she picked Laura Jean up at the bus station. She hugged Laura Jean so hard that Laura Jean lost her breath. "Get in the car, get in the car. I'm taking you to my place first. I made you mustard greens, lady peas, rice and ice tea. Once you've had something to eat, I'll take you over to Josie's where your girl is."

"I'm not really hungry, " Laura Jean began.

"Oh hush, Laura Jean, you got to eat something before you do another thing!"

Earle heard them drive up and opened the door for them. He lifted Laura Jean, swung her around and said, "Let me take a good look at you, sweetheart." He sized her up. "You looking pretty good considering where you been spending your time. Give Jenny a week or so, and she'll have you looking great in no time."

"You never were a good liar, whatever that is, Earle Conroy. Now put me down. Jenny said I have to eat before she takes me to Tessie. So let's eat!"

-28-
Seventeen

Annie stood at her locker exchanging her textbooks for the afternoon class, when Vera Jones sauntered up to her.

"What you doing helping out a honky? Tomming it? What are you doing having her to your house? She's such trash, Annie, and she smells bad, too, like all white folk. You aren't going to have her over to your house anymore, are you?" Vera James had cornered Annie at her locker. At first Annie didn't answer, and then she pushed Vera away.

"Get the hell out of my face, Vera. Get gone and stay gone."

Vera tripped over her feet and fell. She hadn't expected to be pushed, certainly not by Annie Osaha on the topic of trailer park trash. She got up, dusted her clothes, and walked away. Annie kept her eyes on her locker, as if she had lost something but just might find it again if she looked hard enough.

Four more weeks until graduation, Annie thought. Keep your sights set on Spelman. She could hear Ms. Baylor's voice in her head. You want to write the truth of the world for a newspaper, help chronicle history and have it be from your point of view? Well, then, you can't let yourself get in fights with anyone at school. You got to keep it clean, keep it clear. Annie hoped that Vera didn't go to the office and report being pushed. Four more weeks. Annie took a great deep breath and went to her next class.

Tessie only wanted to finish, get her diploma, and be done. Once she graduated, she had another goal: marry Fred. But for now, she had to "keep her eye on the prize'—that's what Ray kept saying to her.

Fred came to The Flamingo during her shift. "Can you take a break, Tessie? I got news!" Fred said.

"Look around here, Fred, there isn't anyone here but me!" she laughed. "Shift isn't over at Union Bag, so of course, I can take a break."

"I want you to be the first to know. I haven't even told my folks." Fred radiated light.

"Well, go ahead then. Tell me." Tessie stood back and folded her arms. He isn't breaking up with me. That's not it, she told her beating heart. But she kept her arms across her chest anyway, making her own kind of shield.

"I want us to be together. You know that I love being near you, and looking into your blue, blue eyes. I love being inside you. In fact, I wish I was inside you right now."

"You didn't drive out here to tell me that, Fred," Tessie said. "Go on, now. What's so important that you are telling me first and that you come to tell me whatever it is at work?"

Tessie was thinking record deal, record deal, record deal. So when Fred said, "I got into University of Georgia!" Tessie felt relief then disappointment; relief because he would be nearby, disappointment that he was going away from her to what may as well be another world: a campus with new girls. "It was my audition that got me in, Tessie. You and me both know it wasn't my grades. It was my guitar playing and the original songs on the tape I sent in with the application." Fred waited. "Well, say something, Tessie."

"Congratulations to you, Fred Simmons," Tessie said, but even to her own ears her voice sounded flat and insincere. Fred going to UGA and Annie going to Spelman, and her staying right here on the 'Geechee Road, wiping down the bar, sweeping up the peanut shells off the floor. Her on the 'Geechee Road with her mother just back from Milledgeville and her father returning today from the North Georgia prison.

"You don't sound like you mean it. Don't you want me to be happy, Tessie?"

"'Course I do," Tessie said. Then the bar phone rang. Tessie ran to it, picked it up and said. "Hello?" There was a long pause. Fred, wrapped up in himself, was taken by surprise when he looked to see that Tessie was crying.

"Daddy?" she said.

On the other end, Ray said, "Well, I have had a hell of a time tracking you down, girl. The state owes me a one-way ticket to my destination, so I am picking 'home.' Where in the hell else would I go!" Tessie listened to him coughing at the other end. "I mean to collect on anything they owe me. Wished I lived clear the hell out in California so I could milk 'em for a more expensive ticket."

"When are you coming?" Tessie asked.

"Tomorrow on the 6:37 p.m., Greyhound Station at West Broad. I'll see you then. I suppose you look the same, just taller, right?"

"Right. Taller and my hair is long enough to sit on, and the same jet black. Some folks say I look like you and some folks say I look like Mama. I think I look like you both a little bit, but mostly I look like myself." She waited for him to comment. "Daddy?"

"Well, I reckon I'll know my own flesh and blood when I see it, I mean, when I see you tomorrow evening," Ray said.

Tessie could not imagine what Ray would look like, how he'd smell, or what he'd say to her first thing. She had forgotten about Fred who was standing about three feet from her, staring. "That was my father, and he's coming home."

"Yeah, I heard. I guess it's best I go on home and tell my folks about my acceptance. Leastwise they might care." Fred turned on his heal and walked out the door.

Whatever, Tessie thought. She picked up the phone and called Josie's. "He's coming home, yep, yep, uh-huh. I know, well. I think he'll stay at the Conroy's till he can get the trailer cleaned up." There was a long pause. "I know, Josie. Who'd have ever thought they would come home within a couple of weeks of each other. Gotta go now." There was another pause. "Yes, I'm calling Jenny right now. I'm going to stay over with them tonight." Pause. "Yes, you are right. I don't want to be around Mama right now. Talk to you later." Tessie hung up.

Tessie felt guilty and then not guilty. She left me alone often enough, she thought.

Tessie dialed The Bee Hive and Jenny answered.

"You aren't gonna believe this, Miss Jenny. Daddy's just called and he's coming home tomorrow by bus at 6:30."

"Do you want me to go with you to pick him up?" Jenny offered.

"No, ma'am, but I do have a favor," she paused. "I need you to go sit with Miss Josie and Mama when you leave work, and I want to stay at your place. I don't want to be around Mama. I need some time to sort things through."

"All right, Tessie, I will do that for you. Earle won't be home tonight. He's working the 11-7. That okay with you?" Jenny asked.

"Yes, Miss Jenny. That's the best," Tessie said. "Thank you."

Tessie got to spend the night at the Conroy's. She spent the day laying about their trailer and walking in a long slow pace from the trailer park to the swamp.

Around 4:30, she couldn't wait anymore. She knew she was going to get to the Greyhound Station early, but she couldn't walk back and forth from the swamp one more time. Jenny Conroy had kept offering to go with her, right up till she called the taxi, but she really didn't want anyone, even Jenny, with her, when she saw Ray for the first time. She wanted it to be her eyes meeting his eyes, and his eyes meeting hers.

So she hired a taxicab to drive her and the driver took the only route to get her there: Highway 17, The 'Geechee Road, past the bars and strip joints, past the road she used to walk with Annie, and directly in front of the sugar cane experimental station.

All the way to the bus station she worked on her memories of her father. She could remember how he smelled of shrimp and fish and beer. She thought of his face, all clean shaved and shiny, and remembered the roughness of the stubble when he'd been out on the boat for days. She remembered how she liked to sit in the crook of his arm while they watched bass fishing shows. And she remembered him taking her camping with Annie.

As she waited for Ray's bus to arrive, she sipped on an RC Cola and munched on moon pies. She finished her snack before she took her spiral notebook from her red leather purse. She could not think of anything to write, so she drew pictures of dogs and horses and birds while she waited.

She had another hour before Ray's bus was scheduled to arrive. She got another pop, lit a Marlboro, and picked at her nail polish. She paced. Then she gave up, sat back down, and reopened the notebook.

She wrote:

My mother used to tell me, "Tessie, don't you wear your heart on your sleeve! Boy'll see it there and think it's meant for him to pick off--just like it was a red ripe strawberry." As soon as my mother spoke it, I saw a satin heart sewn on my sleeve, saw a strawberry cut in half laying on the white cotton of my blouse, the juice bleeding into the fabric. I saw my own heart, barely connected to my chest, drooping over my arm. I thought about ways to make this vision disappear. I drew a red heart on a piece of paper, cut it out, and put it in one of the cobalt blue jars from my mother.

When I see magicians perform at the county fair, I don't expect cards to come out their sleeves. I expect to see them pull out their hearts. I am wearing my heart for Fred—I want him to pick me.

Tessie sat for a while trying to think of what to write next. While she sat waiting for inspiration, Ray's bus pulled in, and Tessie put her pen and notebook away quickly. Tessie watched as an old woman with a worn straw hat and a dry, wrinkled face like a drooping sunflower got off. A thin, white man with silver hair trailed after her. He wore a pair of faded navy pants and a tan shirt. Two boys in army fatigues came next. A black man with a box suitcase stepped down. The scar on his forehead made her think of Fuddah. Then no one else came. Tessie waited. Then she realized the man with the gray hair had to be Ray. He had walked over to where the taxis waited, and he kept looking around. Tessie waved at him. "Daddy?" Her voice sounded like a little girl's voice—wafer thin and high.

"That you, Tessie?" Ray said.

"Daddy?"

"Yes, girl, it's me. Well, look a here. You've grown a lot in a couple of years," Ray said.

By then he had reached her. He put his hand on her shoulder and said, "Tessie, Tessie. You one beautiful girl. You don't look like me or your mama. You look better than the whole damn family."

"Well, let me hug your neck, Daddy." On her way to wrapping her arm around his neck, they looked into each other's eyes. It felt the same as if Tessie had seen a star fall right there at twilight--a bright fast motion, then gone, as if it had never been.

In the taxi on the way back to Little Bit, Ray held on to Tessie's left hand, humming a tune in a minor key. Three long years without the good and the bad of Ray, she thought. Three long years with neither of them and even longer without Laura Jean. Tessie held the tears in, she held the anger back, and she felt old, she felt like his parent and Laura Jean's, not the other way around.

Earle had been busy. He had scrubbed every inch of Ray's old place, opened the windows, and got the utilities running again. He put milk, eggs and bread in the refrigerator. The porch light didn't work, so he brought a candle over and set it in the dinette window. When the taxi drove up, Tessie gasped. The trailer looked alive. "Must be Mr. Earle, Daddy. Jenny's with Josie and Mama, and he's the only one I told that you were coming home."

* * * * *

Ray came home changed. Where he had been loud, he was quiet. Where he had been restless, he was still. Where he had been mean, he was kind. He built cabinets from cherry and oak and pine in the kitchens of the rich, the middle class and the poor.

He collected snakeheads, going into the swamp at dusk before the snakes began to hunt. He took his forked stick along to plunge over their heads and pin them down while he hacked their heads off.

He froze the heads in an ice-cube tray for twenty-four hours. He knew that a snake could still bite, even without its body attached, up to three hours after it was officially dead, so he took no chances. Then he dried the heads on the porch railing where the Georgia sun bleached them white before adding them to a chain. Soon he had wrapped them all around the sides and back of the trailer. Each appeared to be grabbing the severed neck of the one in front of it. He kept the steps clear, though, and stored the spares in his nightstand drawer along with his favorite fishing lures.

Ray also cut the Four O'clock blossoms when they were in full bloom. He carried the bouquets into the trailer and set them about. The sweet smell filled the trailer, countering the paper mill's stench.

"Why are you killing the snakes, Daddy? They not hurting you,"

Tessie said.

"I don't like 'em, Tessie, 'sides they dangerous," Ray said.

"Not if you leave them in the swamp where they belong. Leave them alone, Ray." It was the first time Tessie had called her father by his given name. He flinched when she did it. That's what she had wanted—to get at him, to remind him that he could be cut off, too.

"You cut Mama and me off. You cut her off mid-sentence when she tried to tell you things. You, all bottled up in your drinking!" Her anger came out of her like venom.

"I am sorry, Tessie. And I don't drink no more," Ray said.

"Well, that's the truth, but you best leave the snakes alone. Killing them like you do is going to come back on you. Mark my words."

Ray quit killing the snakes. While Tessie was at school, he cleaned off the rails. He put the snakeheads back in the swamp. That day he didn't go to the cabinet shop. Instead he waited for Tessie to come home.

As soon as she caught sight of the trailer, he could hear her laugh. She started yelling thank you as she ran toward him and their place.

Ray remembered why he had cut Laura Jean off mid-sentence: he loved and hated her all at the same time. And in the small place where he listened to her pain about being trapped, he had seen himself trapped, too, bottled-up, contained. And there wasn't any way for him to get loose except on the river, and he had even messed that up, hauling pot instead of shrimp. And he couldn't see any way out for Laura Jean who had turned white and then green on the river, throwing up all she ate, writhing in the bow of the boat that was named after her.

-29-
Swamp Angels

"I should've kept my grades up at school," Tessie spat at her reflection in the bathroom mirror. "If I had, I'd have more choices—date Fred or dump him; go home to my place and study; forgive my mother for falling apart and love her. I can't pretend she never left, but I can let it go."

She hated the tightly packed corridors of Savannah High, the girls watching her like chickens, the boys eyeing her like hawks. She shut her eyes tight then looked back at herself again.

She imitated Jenny's voice to calm herself down, and when that didn't work, she used Josie's. "It isn't your fault that you got those two for parents, Tessie. And they were doing the best they could. You have to be realistic, now. Finish school and save your money. You got choices. If Annie's got choices, you've got choices."

Tessie tiptoed from the bathroom to her father's bedroom door. "Ray? Ray, you hear me?"

He was sleeping. She went to her room to get her things. It was past time she did what Josie had asked her to do three weeks ago. "You best come and greet your mother, Tessie. She's the one you wanted home all these years, and there you are staying with Ray and acting like Laura Jean still in Milledgeville. You best come greet her and learn how to forgive." Tessie knew Josie was right.

She entered her room and began to whistle. She packed her bag and thought, Ain't life weird? This trailer is home and that man living here with me is my daddy. Things could be better and things could be worse. Tessie started laughing. Then she started to cry. And that woman over at Josie's is my mother, she told herself, and I haven't even been over to say hello to her.

"Tessie?" Ray was calling to her from the living room now.

"Yes, Ray?" Tessie picked up her bag.

"I wish you would call me 'Daddy.' Where you been, girl?" Ray said.

"You can wish all you want, Ray. I can't call you 'Daddy' until I feel like you are my dad. I been at The Flamingo working, and me and Fred got in a fight. It's late, I know. But I decided I'm going to Annie and Josie's, and I'm going to be there when Mama wakes up, and I'm going to stay there for a while. Try to get to know her. Try to get over being mad at her. Try to forgive her, I guess. So, you take care, Ray. Daddy. You take care. I'll be back. It just won't be soon." Tessie said the words in a rush.

Tessie held her shoulder bag like a baby. She didn't move toward Ray until he clicked his tongue the way some folks do to call their cats.

She walked to the couch and sat down beside him. It was the first time she had sat close to him since he had come back. She spoke before she had time to change her mind.

"What is it you want, Tessie?"

Tessie held still beside him like a piece of sculpture.

"Don't do me this way, Tessie. Speak," Ray said.

In her mind, Tessie passed down a corridor of closed doors trying to find the words to tell Ray what was in her heart.

"I want to stay with Josie and Annie and Mama, for now. I don't know much before or after that. I keep thinking I should've taken school more seriously. Last week I thought I'd marry Fred Simmons, but that ain't what I want anymore."

"Why not, Tessie? What's happened?" Ray asked.

Tessie got very quiet. "He's done me wrong, Daddy. All those girls throwing themselves at him, well, women, too. At the bars. At Teen Town. He lost his will power to say no."

"I never two-timed your mama," Ray said.

"But you used to yell at her and call her names, say she'd been with guys from the mill. I remember you doing that, Ray."

"It was the whiskey talking, Tessie, and my jealousy," Ray said.

"Have you gone to see her yet, Ray?"

"No, Tessie, I haven't. I don't know when I am going to be able to do that." Ray shrugged his shoulders and slumped forward.

Tessie waited until Ray went back to his room, then went to Annie's.

Tessie made her way on the well-worn path through the swamp. She didn't carry a flashlight. She didn't need one. She and Annie had bragged as little girls that they knew the swamp like the back of their hands, and they were telling the truth.

Tessie arrived at Annie's a little out of breath. She knocked on Annie's bedroom window, using the signal knock of three hards, three softs, and three more hards. Annie raised the window.

"What time is it? Never mind. Come to the back door, and try not to wake Mama."

Annie didn't ask questions after she let Tessie in. She filled a glass with milk, gave her a handful of Oreo cookies, and took her to her room. She waited until Tessie had eaten her snack. "You want to sleep or you want to talk?"

"Sleep, Annie. I am so tired."

So Annie began rubbing Tessie's back and singing, very softly. "Mary and Martha on the riverside, Hallelujah. Mary and Martha on the other side, walking to Jerusalem."

Tessie interrupted Annie's singing to say, "Josie's right. I need to see Laura Jean, Mama, and try to work things out with her."

Tessie reached her arms around Annie and pulled her close so they could sing together. "Mary and Martha on the riverside, Hallelujah. Mary and Martha on the other side, walking to Jerusalem."

When they finished singing, they lay wrapped around each other the way their voices had mixed in the air, two girl-women fending off the starkness of an old southern city, two girl-women who by the rules weren't supposed to be friends, but who were.

"Fred and I have broken up. I can't put up with him having girls on the side. I told Ray I am staying here with y'all for a while. I brought my bag, but I left the blue jars at the trailer. And I am going to try to do better at school, well, what's left of it," Tessie said. "Are you sweet on anyone, Annie?"

"No, I haven't seen anyone who seems very inviting. I know how to take care of myself, Tessie, the white boys who look at me like they own me, and all my fine young black boys trying to be Stagger Lees." Tessie had fallen asleep in the middle of Annie's answer.

Outside the night sky and the morning sky were moving against each other. Inside Tessie and Annie drifted off into dreams. Annie's fingers moved up Tessie's backbone, lightly—showing mercy to her friend. The rain began to fall at about sunrise and Annie heard it. She rose from her bed quietly and tucked Tessie in.

Here we are in the final months of our senior year, Annie thought. Soon I will be at Spellman and who knows where Tessie will be.

The next morning, Annie thought she must have dreamed it, but when she rolled over there was Tessie, sleeping in her country singer and bartender outfit: mascara circled her eyes, tight jeans encased her. Annie raised herself up on one arm and watched Tessie while she slept.

Josie limped in and went directly to Annie's bedroom to check on her. She saw her daughter before her daughter saw her. Then she saw Tessie. "What's Tessie doing here? Is she all right? Are you?"

Annie shushed her mother and waved her away, but Tessie was awake. "Hey, Josie. How you been? Come on over here and let me hug your neck."

"You come over here and hug mine, young'un!"

"Oh, please, Miss Josie, don't make me get up yet."

Josie, Annie and Tessie went to the kitchen together. Laura Jean was already up, too, and sat at the kitchen table drinking her coffee and staring at the bird feeder out the back window of Josie's kitchen.

She turned in the direction of the women's voices. "Tessie? That you?" Laura Jean stood and then sat, then stood and then sat.

"It's me, Mama. Is it you? " Tessie said.

"Both of you stop this nonsense now. Of course it's Tessie. Of course it's your mama. Now both of you give each other a hug, and let's have some breakfast," Josie reached for each of them and brought them together.

"I don't think I can eat anything, Miss Josie," Tessie said in a little girl's voice.

"Sure you can. Go sit on your Mama's lap. Go on. And Laura Jean, you sit down so she's got a lap to sit on." They did as Josie said.

"We have a lot of catching up to do, honey," Laura Jean said.

"We do, Mama. I brought my bag and I told Ray I was staying here until you and I know each other some, and that I thought you two needed to see each other, too. This broken family needs to figure out how to glue ourselves back together."

"Amen," all four women said in unison.

Josie directed Annie from her chair at the window. She still tired easily from the accident. "Two over easy for each one of us. Bring the toaster and the bread over here, and the butter, too. I'll be in charge of the toast. No meat this morning, Annie, but make us a batch of quick grits, too."

Tessie sat on her mother's lap—17 years old and being held like a child felt right to her.

"I can clean up," she offered after breakfast.

"No, child," Laura Jean said. "You go back to bed and sleep. We'll talk when you wake up. You look worn out from seeing me, I think. Go on, now." Laura Jean pointed Tessie to Annie's room, and Annie helped her get there.

Tessie slept late into the afternoon and woke to steamy, heavy air. She went to the screened-in porch and from there, walked out to the gardens where Laura Jean was moving bed to bed pinching wilted gardenias and pulling weeds from the vegetable patch. Tessie walked past a grove of bald cypress to a live oak covered with trumpet vine. She let her nose enter the persimmon trumpets, sniffing the citrus smell and then inhaling until her pulse drummed in her head and made her dizzy.

"Come sit with me, Tessie. You can help me shell the lady peas and limas," Laura Jean said. They sat together under the tree shelling the peas and beans, dumping them into the big red bowl and chucking the pods into the compost bucket.

-30-
Tooth And Nail

Tooth and nail. How Tessie and Fred became. Tooth and nail, cold stares and the silent treatment.

Tessie sang in the band some nights, but most of the time she stayed sober, went to school, worked at the bar, and tried to forgive Laura Jean for leaving her, for losing her mind. She wanted to celebrate her mother's return.

Tessie told Laura Jean about the taunts at school, about the bar, the music and Fred, about Ray's departure, and Ray's return, the details of Mr. Henry being burned alive and living, about stealing the hand bones from the cemetery with Annie.

Laura Jean listened. "What about Ray? How did he help you while I was gone and he was still here?" Laura Jean asked.

"I don't think that's a fair question, Mama. I mean, for one thing, when he was here, he was running dope. Just about everyone with a boat ran dope if they could. Just that Ray got caught, and yeah, it pissed me off good, but he was doing what he could to make money. He's changed some since he's home—still has those nasty tattoos he got in prison, with the snakes crawling up his neck and twisting down around his body, but he doesn't collect snakeheads anymore. He doesn't drink—drink was poison to him. Other night he came to hear me sing at The Flamingo, sipped his ginger ale and told me how I done good and I made him proud."

Tessie paused.

"That's good to hear, honey. I still haven't spoken to him," Laura Jean said.

"I think Fuddah helped Ray, because Fuddah knows what it's like to be lost and what it's like to think alcohol's gonna save you. Fuddah understood why Ray cut things off, because he was cut off from everything that mattered to him. The day Ray returned from prison, Fuddah bought him a very sharp knife, then taught him a prayer to make killing the snakes sacred. He put a limit on how many snakes Ray could kill, and told him only one snake between full moons. And he had to save the snake body for Fuddah, for healing. So Ray collected the poison, the skin and the body. He took the knife and the penny that came with it and honored Fuddah's rules. Within a few months, he stopped killing snakes, altogether. Well, because I made him."

Laura Jean nodded her head and said "Uh-huh" about every other sentence. Then she asked, "And Annie? How's Fuddah helping Annie?"

Fuddah was waiting for Annie at the pit, near the big live oak. Annie knew he would be waiting for her there. It was where she had been meeting him for years, ever since he had gotten sober and moved to the swamp. Annie was accustomed to his scarred face, his ability to shape shift, and his great deep hurts. She didn't know if he'd greet her in his man form or be there waiting as an egret, or a snake.

"There you are, Fuddah," Annie said and then laughed. He was there as himself.

"I got food waiting for you back at my place, Annie. Step it up!"

"What is it, Fuddah?"

"I made you a mean arrowroot stew, cooked up some mudfish and bullhead, boiled up some mudhen hearts. This food gonna keep you safe when you're away in Atlanta, gonna keep your blood strong." He smiled a crooked smile. "I've been missing you, girl. I'm glad you came alone to see me. I know we've got work to do."

Annie ducked her chin to her chest so Fuddah couldn't see her quivering lip.

"I kept away from your kudzu and scuppernong snares. Didn't want to end up hanging from a limb or upside down in one of your mudpits! Tessie and Laura Jean are watching Mama and the house while I am here. Mama said, 'Tell Fuddah his daughter is healing.' She's gonna be strong soon, Fuddah, because of the tonics and the magic you work. I can stay here with you as long as I need to—until I can see."

"That's good, Annie. I don't know how long your journey will take because I do not know your questions," Fuddah said. Then he reached for Annie's hand and walked with her to the new space he had prepared for her.

"I have prepared the way," Fuddah said. "I will teach you anything I know to help you on this journey."

Annie looked at the sweat lodge made from animal skins, dried by her grandfather. The South Georgia heat made her rebel at the thought of going inside the tent to more heat.

"You will need to use the sacred name I gave to you when you were twelve, the name that sounds like a leaf brushing against another leaf--Shihra. Do not use 'Annie' on you journey. Ever. Have you brought me anything?"

"Yes, Fuddah." She reached into her backpack for her notebook. "I'll read it to you. It's from a book called "The Spirit and The Flesh" by Walter L. Williams. A long time ago, he found a journal of Pedro de Magalhaes de Gandavo's. de Gandavo wrote an account of women warriors he encountered in Brazil in 1576."

"I will listen," Fuddah said.

Shihra, the leaf whisperer began, *"There are some Indian women who determine to remain chaste: These women have no commerce with men in any manner, nor would they consent to it even if refusal meant death. They give up all the duties of women and imitate men, and follow men's pursuits as if they were not women. They wear their hair cut in the same way as the men, and go to war with bows and arrows and pursue game, always in company with men; each has a woman to serve her, to whom she says she is married, and they treat each other and speak with each other as man and wife."*

"I don't want this, Fuddah. I am not sure who I am, but if I am part man and part woman and I want a woman for my wife, I don't want it to be the same as if I were a woman with a man. I don't want to have to follow somebody else's rules."

Fuddah nodded. "Read it again, so when you begin your vision journey you are sure what you are not looking for."

Annie read it again. When she finished, she said, "Is this who I am, Fuddah? Do I have to be this way? Or that way?"

"Only you can answer that question. While you work on the answer, Fuddah will be your guardian. I will protect you during your journey. I will protect you with my life."

So Annie entered the sweat lodge and she stayed there, on and off, for five days. A cottonmouth curled up at the entrance and only moved away when it heard the shihra of Annie's movement. An osprey circled above. Annie had glimpses of the snake which she was sure was Fuddah, and of the Osprey who she believed was Tessie.

Annie dreamed of a city of serpents where the spider mother of life and death wove a web made of day and night. The spider used black and white thread. Multitudes of snakes rested their heads on pillows filled with water. The male snakes fertilized the females by putting their heads in the females' mouths, dying as they mated. Annie walked in her sleep, and she chanted shihra, shihra when she walked. She walked onto the land where she could feel the great serpent, Snake-man, who sleeps inside the earth.

As Annie walked beside the 'Geechee, she heard the names spoken by the trees: *Kadi, Kali, Kore*—names that were new to her. She memorized the names so she could look them up when she returned. Time was clicked off by the singing cicadas. Fuddah's voice came to her. "Keep listening, Shihra." On the fifth day, Annie emerged from the sweat lodge and said in a voice barely audible, "I know who I am."

Tessie was having her own visions and dreams at Josie's house. Josie, who seemed just like a regular person during the day while Tessie attended to her, transformed in Tessie's dreams. Josie visited her dressed in green and carrying a black cat's bone in one hand and a chicken's wishbone in the other. She handed Tessie a little pill bottle, and when Tessie looked at it closely, she realized it held her baby teeth instead of pills. She woke screaming. Padding to the kitchen, she turned on the light and drank a glass of milk before she had the courage enough to return to bed.

Before falling back to sleep, she said aloud, "Can't you leave me be, Miss Josie. I just want to sleep."

No answer came until she was sleeping, and then Josie's voice said, "No, child, I can't leave you be. You got to heal and to do that you must do as I say. Go find a snake bone and shake it to keep your fear away. Grind up the long bones from a deer or a dog. Put the bone meal in a burlap sack. Keep it with you to protect your heart. Go to a graveyard and dig up a body."

Tessie interrupted in the dream, "Annie and I already did that."

"Don't interrupt! Take the hands. Make them your own. Throw them. Look at how they land. Sweep up the dust they make, and keep it in one of your blue jars."

Tessie heard crying and woke. It was Josie. She needed pain medicine. Tessie walked to her bed, held Josie's head up until she swallowed her pills. She wanted to talk to her about the dream, but she didn't want to upset her or make her feel blamed, so she said nothing.

-31-
'Geechee

Annie and Tessie walked to the big rock along the banks of the 'Geechee. The hot September sun beat down on them.

"Everybody around here calls us 'Geechee, Tessie," Annie began, "but Fuddah told me that isn't the real name of the tribe whose blood runs in our veins."

"It isn't? What is it then?" Tessie asked. "Yuchi? Long time ago, Josie told us that."

"Yes, Fuddah says we both got Yuchi blood in our veins. He says it'll keep us rooted to life when other things fail us. He says we have a bond, and whether folks call us Yuchi or 'Geechee, it doesn't matter, because that blood keeps us whole. The Yuchi sprung from this land and this land owns us, owns anyone with Yuchi blood, 'Geechee blood. The Yuchi didn't get dragged here against their will like the Africans, or sent here to a penal colony like some of the Europeans."

"That's what you learned, Annie, while you were on that spirit quest?"

Annie waited for a minute. She threw some stones in the river. She pulled a cigarette out of her pack and lit it.

"No, that isn't all. He told me the Yuchi were held as slaves for a time by the Creek, and he wanted me and you to remember that in the old times no one chose to be a slave, but now and then people could make themselves slaves out of their own weaknesses even if they were free."

"Holy shit, Annie. Why does Fuddah always have to be so heavy?"

You know why is what Annie's look said back to Tessie.

"There's more, too. Not what Fuddah told me, but what I felt and saw and dreamed. But I don't know what to do with that yet, Tessie, and I for sure am not ready to talk about it." Annie stubbed the cigarette out in the mud.

"I would have finished that for you, Annie. You wasteful." Tessie rolled her eyes at Annie.

Fuddah was relieved that he was able to be present for Annie's quest, his beloved Shihra.

After Annie left, he cut back all the brush in front of his shack, and he marked off a square like his father and his grandfather had done before him. He used rocks to delineate the boundaries of the square. He pounded them into the black dirt until they were flat. That way neither he nor his enemies would trip. In the middle of the square, he placed a bowl, the one piece of pottery he had that his grandmother had made. She had incised the rim with the three-toed mark of a gull claw.

The opening to his shack faced east. Each morning he saluted the sun. "Sun God, it's Fuddah. I'm thanking you this day and every day of my life. Amen." Then Fuddah walked down to the river and scooped up a handful of water. "This magic water going to keep me moving, going to keep me pure." Then he put his head into the water and made himself reborn.

Fuddah's new dog, Yancy, went with him to the river. Fuddah rubbed Yancy's ears with 'Geechee water. "I'm gonna make us four wishes," he whispered to Yancy. "Four is the magic number: it takes four days before a couple lets their newborn sleep in a hammock alone. It takes four months before a woman can be with her man again after the baby's birth. The year has four seasons. We have four souls. And you're magic, Yancy, because you have four feet."

Fuddah knew-- he had been told by his father, who had been told by his father--that each human being had three souls on Earth and a fourth to carry him to the next life. The fourth soul would give him the strength to get around any obstacle at the entrance to the sky. Fuddah knew already what his obstacle would be—the spirit of the man he killed.

He had a plan for judgment day: lie down before the man's spirit waiting there for Fuddah and kiss his feet. The man's spirit could kick him or spit on him and Fuddah would accept whatever the man's spirit needed to do. Whatever the dead man's spirit had to do would eventually stop and then the man's spirit would lie down beside Fuddah, one a lion and one a lamb, and Fuddah knew he was to be the lamb. Fuddah would get down on his knees and lift the man up, carry both of them into Heaven, the place above the sky and beyond the sun.

Both men would let their last drop of blood fall from the sky to bring strength again to the Yuchi, the 'Geechee, the land below.

Fuddah picked up a sharp rock shaped like a heart and pierced his forearm so one drop of blood was let loose upon the muddy black land.

-32-
Thunder, Lightning

Tessie couldn't translate what the 'Geechee River was saying to her. All her prayers, all her visions, all her dreams had gone into the 'Geechee all the days of her life—sometimes in dribs and drabs, drops and spurts, trickles and great gushing streams. She had prayed at its banks, her knees slipping in the mud beneath her. She had slept curled with the snakes along its banks and waited for visions and counted on her dreams. She had prayed for mercy for her father, for release for her mother, for life for Josie. She had pleaded for safety for herself. What else can I want or expect from you, Old River? she asked silently. You've given me hope when I couldn't find it anywhere else. I've asked you to sew the burned parchment of Henry's skin together and let him regain control of his fluids. I asked you to bring my parents home, to heal Josie and to set me free.

From where she sat on the bank, she stared into the low-slung tree branches watching for snakes. She looked across at the muddy bank expecting an alligator. She squinted at the sky, hoping to catch sight of the lime, lemon, crimson and purple blur that signified a bunting in flight. What you got to say to me, she wondered. What's left for you to show me? First she thought the question, and then she shouted it. She put her hands up to her mouth in a large O and hurled the words at the river, the mud, the empty blue sky. "What you got to say to me? What's left for you to show me, your 'Geechee girl?"

Her fury met silence. From the corner of her eye, she saw the syncopated slither of a cottonmouth woken and annoyed by her cry in the wilderness. She waited expecting more—a burning bush, Fuddah's appearance as if from nowhere, a marsh hen--too far upland from the salt water.

"Fine," she spoke in her calm, reasonable voice. "Fine, then. I'm going to work. I'll be back. We're not through with each other yet,

River. Not yet. Maybe you're waiting on hearing more from me. Maybe you're done giving me visions and dreams, tired of listening to my pleas and prayers." Tessie paused and listened to herself. She had heard something new and it came from within. She began laughing. The more she tried to collect herself, the harder she laughed. She laughed until she cried, bent over, holding her stomach the way she did when she drank too much. She laughed until the sun began to set and she laughed until she made herself late to work. She laughed herself into knowing what she was going to do.

Tessie drove to The Flamingo, pulled up and found the manager's pick up truck in her space. There was a long line of pick ups in place from the shift letting out. She parked in the first open spot, jumped out of her car, and pranced into the bar.

JM gave her an evil look. "Where the hell have you been, Miss Tessie? I can tell you where I've been—right here doing your job, tending bar for some mighty thirsty men!"

"Sorry, JM."

"You don't sound sorry, Tessie. You looking pretty happy, not sorry."

"I was down at the 'Geechee and I lost sense of time. I must have fell asleep. Come on now," she gave him a sweet smile, "I haven't been late once since you hired me. You can forgive a girl once, can't you?" She could hear her voice echoing Laura Jean's when her mother used to plead with Ray after she had been drinking.

The men at the bar responded for JM. "Sure he can. We forgive you, Tessie. We just glad you gonna be taking care of us. Your butt's a lot cuter than JM's old flat ass!" They laughed into their beer.

"Go on, JM. Leave the girl be. Tessie, set us up for another round."

Later that night, Tessie danced with one of the cowboys to Fred's band playing "Blue Eyes Crying in the Rain." When he pulled her tight against his hard-on, she pulled back until she got free. She didn't slap him, but she wanted to. Instead she went back behind the bar. The cowboy went up to the bandstand and waited until the song ended. He gestured to Fred to give him the mike. "Nice snake you got there, coun'ry boy!" Then he tipped his hat at Tessie and brought the mike up to his mouth. Fred tried to get it from him, but standing on the stage gave him the wrong angle. "Hold on, hold on. I ain't mad no more. I just want my tip back. I gave you that hundred dollar bill for your music and also because I wanted to get my hands on that pussy cat of yours. I didn't reckon you had yourself a snake."

"You can have your hundred dollars back, mister. No one said giving me a tip gave you the right to go after my girl!"

The next day, Tessie went out on the river in her sixteen-foot aluminum boat. She didn't worry about packing any food. She had learned to cast for shrimp, and after she popped off their heads, she ate them raw—shell and all. Their recent aliveness made her understand why snakes were sleepy after digesting mice. Tessie dropped anchor and rested, listening to marsh hens in the sea grass and watching turtles bob for food.

The brackish water smelled different than either the salt or the fresh. It gave off a richer smell of decay, marsh mud, and salt. Tessie carried a bucket and a bag of old chicken necks so she could crab. She had tried eating the crabs raw, too, but their flavor left her gagging over the side of the boat.

Ray had taught her to run an outboard and how to tinker with one when it was stubborn or flooded or cold. He wanted Tessie to be free, and Ray felt the freest on water. "It's the river rat in me. You like it too, don't ya?" The only time Tessie saw Ray at peace was when he was out on the 'Geechee in his boat. His hair blew wildly in the wind. He whistled and sang and laughed.

She appreciated what he had taught her because he was right, she was part river rat, too. She escaped people's watchful, critical eyes. Sharks and lightning scared her, but not like mean people. The small hammerhead sharks left her alone. The lightning announced itself with thunder and gave Tessie time to find shelter.

* * * * *

Fred Simmons bothered Ray, but he cared about the boy because he was Henry's stepson and Tessie's sweetheart. Every time Ray thought about Henry, he shuddered. Fred treated Tessie in some of the many wrong ways Ray had treated Laura Jean early on. Fred smelled like garlic and stale sweat, cigarettes, pot and beer. Ray didn't like the way his pants hung off his hips or his blonde Afro. He had to admit that the boy had changed since Henry got burned.

Ray paced back and forth in the kitchen, poured more coffee in his already full cup, spilled a little bit on the counter, set the coffee down and spilled more, looked for the dishtowel and couldn't find it, and then he stopped. His shoulders drooped forward for a minute then he stood up straight.

"It's be hard for me to go to The Flamingo, not so much because it's a bar, Tessie, but because it is where I went when I was mad and unhappy, it's where I went after fights with your mama," he practiced. "But I want to hear you sing again, girl, so I'm going to come."

Fred checked the PA and tuned his guitar and the electric piano. Although he played the piano best, he liked the guitar more, liked to play standing up and walking around, liked to slide his left hand up and down the long neck while he picked away at its belly. He played the guitar using different strokes and styles to please the slightly drunk early crowd, and played harder and meaner to please the later rowdy one.

Tessie wore a silver cowgirl shirt with fringe, brand new Wrangler jeans, and a silver and turquoise belt buckle. And, of course, she had on her now heavily worn turquoise cowgirl boots. Ray came in behind Tessie. People who hadn't seen him in years greeted him with handshakes. He sat at one of the booths with Jenny and Earle. When Tessie went to put her apron on, JM stopped her. "Not tonight, Tessie. You are our guest of honor." He could see her face light up and then fade.

"Thank you, JM, that's sweet of you, but I have counted on tonight's work and the money I'll be making, so I am going to have to respectfully decline," Tessie argued.

"Well, it'd be the first time you respectfully did anything with me, Tessie." They both laughed. "I know you were counting on the pay, and that's already taken care of, so you just be the guest of honor. Go sit with your daddy, Jenny and Earle until Fred calls you up. Go on now, girl."

She felt sad and happy while she waited for Fred to announce her, which he did at the end of playing *Green Onions*. "We have a special guest with us tonight, ladies and gentleman. Miss Elizabeth Harnish is here for the last time at The Flamingo. Tessie, come on up."

Ray reached across and squeezed Tessie's hand. "Knock us over, girl!"

"I plan to, Daddy." Tessie squeezed his hand back.

Tessie took the fifteen steps to the stage and unleashed the mike from its stand. "Good evening, everybody. Thank you for coming out tonight. I have a little surprise for y'all. You've been asking and asking for the new Tanya Tucker song, and well, here it is."

The band started and Tessie sang, *"When I die, I may not go to Heaven, I don't know if they let cowgirls in, but if they don't, just let me go to Texas, 'cause Texas is as close as I've been."* People pushed their way to the dance floor and kicked up their heels. When Tessie looked over at the booth, her father looked back at her and gave her a thumbs-up. Just as the song ended, Annie walked in with Josie. They joined Jenny and Earle and Ray.

"Y'all just missed my new song," Tessie said into the mike.

Fred grabbed the mike from her and said, "No they didn't. Let's do it again boys." The crowd applauded and Fred struck the first chord.

At the next break, JM took the mike from Fred. "Ladies and gentlemen, I think there are enough people here that qualify for those names that I can safely use them." He laughed at his own joke. "As you know, tonight is Tessie's last night here at The Flamingo, and it's the boys in the band's last night too. We're gonna miss all of y'all. To celebrate, we've taken up a collection for Tessie, we've got a cake in the back for anyone who needs a little sugar, and we want to say thank you to Tessie and the band, but mostly thanks to Tessie."

Fred waited for JM to finish. Then he took the mike from JM. "As you know, Tessie's my best girl, and although this is our last night here at The Flamingo, and I want to thank y'all for coming out to hear us tonight and all the nights over the past four years, this is not goodbye for me and Tessie. Yes, I am going off to Athens, but she's my girl and I'm her man, and miles aren't going to keep us from loving each other. The boys and I have something for you, too, Tessie. Eddie, bring the box up here."

The crowd stayed quiet while Eddie, the bass player, brought the box forward. "All the way from Texas, or heaven, sweetie."

Tessie opened the box and pulled out new boots—beautiful turquoise ones from Texas with red leather hearts topstitched up the outside leg. Tessie set the boots down gently on the stage, reached for Fred and kissed him. "Thank you, everyone, for being like family to me." She took her old boots off and put the new ones on to start the next set where she sang back up to Merle Haggard songs, pretending she was Miss Bonnie.

Fred didn't invite Tessie home, and she didn't offer to have him to her place. It had been a great evening, but they were both tired and Fred had a five-hour drive ahead of him the next day. And he still wasn't packed.

"I'll call you when I get there, Tessie." He gave her a hug. Then he turned to Ray, "Thank you for coming out tonight, Mr. Ray. I know it meant a lot to Tessie, but it meant a lot to me, too." He extended his hand, but Ray withheld his.

When he'd finished packing, Fred went to the shelf where the hand bones were kept. He was tired and low, fretting about the future. More than anything at that moment, Fred wanted to know what his life was going to be, and he wanted to know it right then and there. He wanted his own set of hand bones. Tessie and Fuddah refused to get them for him when he had asked earlier, and when he told Tessie he'd just use his daddy's, she turned on him. "Don't you even say that, Fred. Those hand bones aren't something to play with. They aren't yours. You know what will happen if you mess with them?"

"No, I don't, but I imagine you're fixin' to tell me." He practically spat the words at her.

"Fuddah says that once the magic of something belongs to a person, anyone else messing with that magic can die. That's how powerful the magic is, that's how powerful the ownership is." So Fred listened to her that day. But at 4 a.m. on the night before he was leaving everything he had ever known, his desire to know about his future was greater than any fear he had about hand bones and their magic.

So he broke a rule of Fuddah's and threw the bones that belonged to his daddy to see his future. He tossed John Hillman Clark's hands in the air and watched as the hand bones hit the floor where they disintegrated upon impact. "No big deal," Fred thought. He went to the kitchen to get the broom and dustpan to sweep up the mess. Fred swept up all the dust he could find, carried it to the kitchen, and opened the lid of the trashcan to throw the dust away. Then he had a second thought. He got out the blender, dropped the dust in, added some orange juice, blended it, poured it out into a glass, and drank down the orange juice with John Hillman Clark's hand-bone dust in it. Nothing happened. "So much for magic," Fred thought, and he went to bed. The next morning he got up early, kissed his mother and father goodbye, and headed north to Athens and his new life as a college student.

Henry found the empty bag several days later. "Emily, what's happened here?' The high pitch of his voice startled Emily.

"What is it, Hen? What's the matter?"

"The hand bones are gone. The bag's empty. Did you do something with the hand bones?" He eyed her suspiciously. He knew she didn't approve of Fuddah and magic.

"I swain, Henry. I did nothing with the bag or the bones. I never touch it. It's your business and I leave it alone."

"Only person who could have done anything with the hand bones was Fred, or maybe Tessie." Henry called Tessie at work.

"Tessie, I picked up the red bag today and it is empty. Did you do something with the hand bones? Did you take them back to Fuddah?"

"No, sir, I did not." Tessie paused. "Oh my God, it must be Fred, he must have taken them with him to Athens."

Henry wept as Emily took the phone from him. "You best come over here now, Tessie. Henry is mightily upset. I'll call Fred and see what he knows," Emily said.

"I didn't do anything with them, Mama," he lied. "I swear."

"You're lying to me, Fred. What did you do with the hand bones? Say. Say now."

Her demand was met with silence, more silence, and more. Then Fred, who could never outlast his mother, said, "I threw them the night before I left to come to Athens. When I threw them, they turned into dust. So I swept up the dust."

"Then what, Fred? Then what did you do, boy? Don't lie to me. There still may be a way to save you," Emily said.

Salvation was always his mother's theme. Fred wanted her to call on her God and any other powers who could help him, because the truth was that things were beginning to go both horribly right and wrong with Fred.

He was playing in a new group in Athens, writing songs that were complex and brilliant. No one could keep up with him on piano or guitar. An agent had been in to hear his band and wanted to do a demo of the group for Atlantic Records. He was surprised that someone Fred's age was playing with a bunch of boys, and said so.

"How old are you?" he asked.

"Twenty," Fred answered.

The agent laughed. "You albino or something?"

Fred's blonde hair had turned white. His skin was wrinkled and spotted and he wore sunglasses all day long. He was turning the color of dried bone. Fred hadn't turned 19 yet and he was dying.

-33-
Isle of Hope

Christmas came and went without Fred coming home. Henry couldn't sit long enough to drive to Athens, and Emily didn't drive, but Tessie still thought about going to see him. She remained angry with him for disregarding her and Fuddah's warnings, and she feared what the outcome of a visit was likely to be. She preferred to remember him as young, blonde and alive rather than see him die before her eyes.

Fuddah told her to imagine her heartstring attached to Fred's heart, and then imagine a very sharp knife, and cut the string. She said, "If love is a river, then I am building a dam. More likely love is a vein, so I have cut it and cauterized it. Goodbye, Fred."

Fred came home on a bus on January 19th, thin, bent, bald and looking 80 years old. Tessie went to meet him, and she barely recognized him. "Hello, Fred," was all she could manage.

"Hello, Tessie." His voice cracked.

"I best get your bag and put it in the car," she said, thinking, I got to look busy so he can't see how scared I am. She stood by the bus waiting for the driver to open the side trunks, then wiggled her way through the cluster of passengers to Fred's purple duffel. I am afraid he's gonna break. Or I will. She stepped back over to where he was, leaning against the phone booth, took him by the elbow and helped him walk to the car. The ride to his parents' house was silent.

Henry met the car. "I got him, Tessie. Set his bag in the drive, and then you best be on your way."

"Yes, sir," Tessie said.

Emily didn't wave to her from where she sat on the porch, pale as a magnolia.

Rumors grow in the South like kudzu, and the rumor this time was that Emily had called the deacons together to do a healing for

Fred at the 'Geechee River. "She say she gonna resurrect him, she gonna undo his aging, she gonna make her boy young again with the power of the lamb and the flow of the water," Josie told Tessie when she walked into the house.

"She gonna walk him into the water like he's a little boy, again, Josie?" Tessie asked.

"Someone gonna have to," Josie said. "Someone's got to wash the dust from those hand bones right out of his spirit and his blood, and bring him back to his golden haired self."

The day of the resurrection of Fred Simmons began with silence up and down the 'Geechee Road. People at Little Bit stood as if for a solemn procession when the black El Dorado went by. They could see the profile of the Simmons' family: Fred in the passenger seat, his mother behind him and Henry behind the driver.

Earl Conroy gasped. "That's Fuddah at the wheel, wearing a chauffeur's hat! I'll be damned."

Behind the El Dorado, a blue van followed with three deacons, two white and one black. Once they passed, the watchers went back into their trailers to shower, drink their coffee, their sweet tea, or just wait for the time when they had to go to work.

Fifteen minutes went by, forty-five, an hour. Then they heard one long whistle streak through the air—an alert that the tiny Simmons caravan was returning. Everyone heard it, or heard about it, up and down the 'Geechee Road.

Josie said, "Folks say Emily moaned and spoke in tongues, and her language merged with the water and healed Fred. Henry bound to be changed too. Maybe he back to sleeping with Emily, since she done took that crazy snake-chasing sampler down from the wall and give it away. That's what folks say."

Tessie said, "It would be the first time he's held Emily in his arms since the fire."

"Well, well, well," Josie said, "sometimes only fear and sorrow can heal fear and sorrow."

Henry came back to life because Fred didn't die. Strong, healthy, golden-haired Fred came back from the dust. The 'Geechee River saved him. The churned-up bone dust that Fred had drunk, the remains of John Hillman Clark's hand, got washed away. Henry came back to life and Emily thanked her God by starting a whole new cross-stitch. She drew herself a pattern of willow trees on a riverbank with water and the words from Ecclesiastes:

> *The root of wisdom is to fear the Lord,*
> *And the branches thereof are long life.*

Tessie understood how one thing is given and one thing is taken away and how the dust in her spirit made her thirsty. Her thirst drew her to the river. She boarded the fishing boat without a word to anybody and headed slowly out beyond the river, beyond the tidal water toward Isle of Hope.

As she floated with the direction of the water, she considered the distance she'd come and what she'd learned. I've seen light emerge from darkness, and darkness emerge from light, she reckoned. I've seen miracles from snake skins and hand bones. I've found sweetness inside the paper mill's sour, belching smoke. And even people who hurt me have carried me toward light, just like this boat. Mama deserted me, and she healed herself and came home, just like this river rolls out to the sea.

She inhaled the scent of the brackish water, and then looked down, deep into the black Ogeechee River. When she looked again, the sky seemed to open up for her, like the face of a large, soundless angel. Then down in the river she saw crystals reflecting light. She put her hand in and drew out a cluster of tiny starfish. Salt fell off them and ran through her fingers like sand.

Next she reached into the water and cradled a handful of floating baby sand dollars. I've got vision and abundance, both, she thought.

She was in the Sound now, so she turned the outboard motor off.

Sword-like voices sliced through the opened sky.

"Hurt nothing, not the Earth nor sea. Nothing, and no one." She put her hands over her ears. She knew the words and believed them. For a moment she thought she might be bewitched.

It was then she heard the clear and solid beating of her own heart: one, two, three, four.... She saw Isle of Hope in the distance surrounded by green-blue water and light-blue sky. She saw herself, safe in the middle of everything.

A heron flew overhead. She started the motor and turned the boat back toward the mainland.

About the Author

Lisa Ann Harris lives and writes in the Finger Lakes region of Central New York. Visit her at: www.LisaHarriswriter.com